**Carolyn Morwood** lives ~~in~~ Melbourne, Australia. Her poetry and short stories have been published in the UK and Australia. She is presently working on her second crime novel set in Melbourne.

Carolyn Morwood

# The
# Blessing
# File

First published by The Women's Press Ltd, 1998
A member of the Namara Group
34 Great Sutton Street, London EC1V 0DX

Copyright © Carolyn Morwood 1998

British Library Cataloguing-in-Publication Data
A catalogue record for this book is available from the British Library.

ISBN 0 7043 4586 2

Typeset in Bembo 11/13pt by FSH Ltd, London
Printed and bound in Great Britain by Cox & Wyman Ltd, Reading, Berkshire

To Phil, Dad and Dave P for help during,
and to Celia for finishing off.


And as always to Dave, Ali and Rob.

# Chapter One

*Yes! Melbourne Town's a lady,*
*And the breath of her is wine;*
                    *'The Old Love', Marie E. J. Pitt*

Melbourne, August 1992

You know how it is. You notice someone, a stranger, in a crowd. Something about them stands out, strikes a chord, and then you see them again and again. The woman is like this. I notice her because she reminds me of Adele.

When we get close though, I see that she is a dull version, the vibrancy missing. A mousy blonde against Adele's shining paleness. Her skin too is sallow, but the dark eyes in a small, square face, are almost exact copies. She is caught up in the swirl of passengers exiting from platform nine at Flinders Street station. A face in a crowd, gone but not forgotten. A few days later she comes into the shop.

It is one-fifteen. I take note of the time because I am waiting on a delivery promised for the morning and Jordie has just left. Now I can see the woman properly, I realise that she is shorter than Adele, her walk less fluid. She doesn't stop to browse or even glance at the displays, but walks directly,

1

purposefully, to the shelves of classics. She doesn't see me because I'm in the office, watching her through one-way glass.

The classics are at the back of the shop, at right angles to the office. If it weren't for the glass, I could reach out and touch her. She takes a book from one of the top shelves, flicks through the pages, fumbles momentarily and restores it to the shelf. Quick, precise movements. She leaves the shop without a backward glance.

I am curious about the book. That particular shelf holds editions of Dumas, Eliot, Fielding. None is rare, none terribly expensive. I examine the books but she has left no clue to tell me which one took her interest.

Back in the office there is a message that I hadn't noticed before in Jordie's neat, precise writing. *Lyn. Message from Alex Smith. Can you go round for a drink after work? Jordie A.* Yes, of course I can. My time is free and invitations from Smithy are more frequent now. He has guessed how things are. The door bell clangs, the first of a small rush of customers. A busy afternoon.

At closing time I use the back exit through to Flinders Lane. The names of the shopkeepers and businesses have changed during the many years our family have owned the shop, but Smithy still remains. Not the original Smith, George Smith, Grandad's mate, but his son, Alex.

The name Smith and the family tailoring business have long gone from the ornate directory in the foyer of the Bellview building. The business wound down years ago, tailoring increasingly unprofitable and the mainstay of the clientele preferring George to Alex. Alex earned his living in other ways. The list of his diverse occupations seemed romantic to Adele and me as children, and he would tell stories of his stints as rigger, gardener, journalist, ranger. No job lasting for more than a few years. Smithy has retired now, an early retirement, he is careful to stress, in which he has found his niche. He paints and sells well. Bold Melbourne landscapes are in demand.

After the demise of the tailoring business, the premises were unwanted and unsaleable. Smithy moved in, flaunting the city's strict fire regulations, and converted the office into a well-appointed flat, the old cutting room into an airy, spacious studio. For privacy's sake he closed off the main entrance, blocking it with a heavy table. The only way in now is through an alley — a single, unmarked door in the corner of a loading bay.

Sometimes when I stay at work overnight, I think of Smithy sleeping in the old offices and I believe we are the only residents in this whole vast city. Suburbia snarls all around us, but is kept at bay by some undefined barrier: the river, the railway tracks, perhaps the buildings themselves. The city of Melbourne lying dormant, waking with the morning's first trains and trams. In the middle of the night it can feel strange and lonely. I think of Smithy close by and am glad of his company.

The alleys into Flinders Lane are old, convoluted as a maze. As kids, when Grandad owned the shop, Adele and I used to play there. We learned the intricacies of the alleys, the labyrinth of subways, corridors and loading bays. From time to time, developers come out with plans to modernise, replace the existing buildings with a shopping plaza, full of light and air. So far the alleys remain.

Smithy opens the door promptly to my knock as though he has been waiting for me. A tall, bony-faced man with rounded shoulders. This is the second time I have come here in the past ten days and I feel slightly guilty because I am just filling in time, putting off the moment of solitude, when thoughts come crowding in, unbidden and unwelcome. Smithy is unquestioning, but I wonder how much he sees behind his deep, brown eyes.

'Lyn! Come in.'

He stoops down and kisses me on the cheek, leads me to the couch. The flat is relaxing, the colours subdued and tasteful, complemented by a vase of apricot roses. The walls are hung with his most recent works, the ones ready for exhibition. From my chair, the outside view is of the loading-bay wall, scored with the dark haphazard lines of drainpipes. The only clutter in the room is some mailing in progress. Post-office cylinders with Japanese addresses: Osaka, Tokyo, Kyoto. Smithy passes me a drink and removes the cylinders, placing them out of sight, somewhere in the studio beyond.

'Selling to Japan now?' I ask.

'Hoping to.' He flourishes the glass, bends mockingly towards me like an old-fashioned waiter. 'Let me introduce my new drink. I've called it "Melbourne Sweet".'

'As opposed to Melbourne Bitter?'

He raises his glass. 'Good luck.'

A long glass of amber liquid that looks like beer but tastes completely different, lingers on the tongue, sweet and mellow, and is, I suspect, immensely potent.

He sits next to me on the couch, extending his long legs with a sigh of pleasure. In profile, the boniness of his face is even more pronounced, a large nose, a jutting forehead. We sip our drinks, looking out at the view. The high, dark wall of the loading bay is brimmed with the city's hazy light, glowing like an early dawn.

'Have you heard, Lyn? They're opening up the city. After all these years we'll have company.'

I nod. I have heard the latest Melbourne City Council proposals. The imminent launch of Postcode 3000. The Address: Melbourne.

'The fire regulations are being eased. I will no longer be an illegal resident. It seems strange after all these years.'

'It doesn't really affect me, Smithy. For me the city is just a temporary refuge. I don't intend to stay. I'm going home again soon for a touch of country air. Not to live of course, but to visit.'

He looks at me and nods slowly. 'I envy you that place, Lyn. Such peace.'

'And what about you?' I ask. 'Will you stay?'

'I haven't decided. They're offering incentives to developers to convert the old buildings. It'll be like a tide. Unstoppable.'

I take a sip of my drink, enjoy its lingering sweetness. 'Sounds like there's money to be made somewhere. You could cash in on it, Smithy.'

'Not me. I've enjoyed these years of privacy, of being on my own. Tavistock House has already gone. That's just down the road. Cream rendering, Brunswick green trims. All prettied up. God knows how many more are on the drawing board.'

'I understand how you feel, but I quite like the idea. The city needs livening up.'

'Yes, well. Most people seem to think so. It's hardly a fate worse than death, I suppose. I've had a good enough run while it lasted.' He looks at me and smiles, shakes the mood off. 'Anyway, Lyn, drink up. Let's enjoy it while we can.'

He shows me his latest painting. A huge landscape hanging on the studio wall. It is Melbourne again, but a strange Melbourne, its icons displaced. The Shrine, the Arts Centre, Princes Bridge, the Exhibition Buildings are all muddled in together, looming up boldly from the Yarra bank, lit by a grey moon. The painting shows minute details: a broken window, a rag of curtain, a face looking out, a bird in flight. It reminds me of a children's picture book, where the task is to find certain things: people, keys, dogs. It doesn't feel like a children's book, though. It feels bleak and grey, almost disturbing.

'Is this the latest?'

'It's called *Melbourne Moonrise*. Do you like it?'

'Mm. It seems, well . . . a bit grim.'

He laughs. 'Matched my mood perhaps.'

'What will you do with it?'

'Hand it over to my agent. He'll place it soon enough.'

'Lucky Smithy.'

He looks round in surprise at my tone, his brown eyes watchful.

'No I mean it,' I say. 'You are lucky.'

'Yes. I suppose I am.'

I stare at the painting and the dense layers of colour blur into blocks of lilac and grey.

'I like the colours.'

He grins. 'Not like you to be untruthful Lyn, even for the sake of politeness.'

'No.' I laugh. 'I do. They're subtle. A lot hidden in a few different shades.'

'The art of concealment.' And this time there is something in his tone that makes me look up. His face, though, is bland.

'Another drink?'

'No thanks Smithy. It's getting late. I have to go.'

I don't, but now I have company I am oddly restless, in need of solitude. I collect my bag from the table and Smithy walks with me back along the deserted alleys to Flinders Street. Friday night, the city is still quiet, the period of lull; city workers gone, night life not yet begun.

I turn in at the back entrance to the shop and Smithy makes no comment.

'Thanks Smithy.'

'What for?'

'For seeing me home. For the drink. For not asking questions.'

The streetlight is behind him and his face is in darkness. I can't quite make him out. He seems remote somehow, as though in darkness he is a stranger. His voice, though, is the same, a deep voice, instantly familiar.

'Friday night, Lyn. The night just beginning and you are off to bed.'

'Well, not quite bed yet. Some accounts. Things to do. You know.'

'Why not come out? Have dinner with me somewhere.'

'Thanks, Smithy, but not tonight. Some other time. When I'm better company.'

'Lyn, your company is always special. You just don't know it.'

There is a small silence between us.

'Lyn, if I can help . . . You could stay at my place for a while.'

'Thanks. But I'm okay. Really. The shop's fine for the time being. I have everything I need.'

He reaches for my hand as though to shake it. Instead he holds it firmly in his own and looks down at me. 'Don't forget and don't be too proud. I'd like to help.' He turns abruptly away, moves back into the alley and out of sight.

Inside the shop, I check the blinds to Flinders Street, make sure there are no gaps to show chinks of unexpected light and switch on the lamps. Small lamps that cast soft patches of light on nearby cabinets, on the collections of rare poetry. It always pleases me this, the pale light gleaming on leather bindings, the richness of gold tooling.

I walk slowly through the shop. Everything is clean and tidy, nothing out of place. In the office the rapid blink of the answering machine signals three messages.

'Hello, Lyn. This is Vanessa. Listen darling, we're having a party at my house. Tomorrow week, the 29th? Eight o'clock. Please come if you can. Everyone will be there. Ring me.'

Second message. 'Lyn, this is Ruth Stone from Melbourne University. Can you ring me please at a convenient time.'

Third and last message, Barry. 'Lyn love. Ring me back. Please.' On tape his voice seems disembodied, unfamiliar, tinged with pleading. I don't ring.

# Chapter Two

On Sunday, I wake early. The office is cold and dismal. The light coming in through the high windows is dull and grey, does little to dispel the gloom. The room is large, almost spacious, but now part of it has been taken over with the requirements of living: a mattress, bedding, clothing, the basics for food preparation. All necessary given the circumstances, but today it seems dreary and dispiriting, endlessly depressing. Sunday is my day off, a day I usually look forward to, but today it stretches before me, long and unplanned.

The only thing that seems of interest is a collection of poetry I began last year, courtesy of Matthew Blessing. Matthew was my grandfather and founder of the shop, and like me a bookseller and author. In his time he was at the forefront of Melbourne literary circles. A methodical man, and, like other members of our family, he kept a diary. One volume for each year of his adult life.

His diaries are studded with information on different authors and poets of his time. One name stands out from all the others. Furnley Maurice, a pen-name for Frank Wilmot, Matthew's friend, fellow author and Melbourne bookseller. Last week in the storage cupboard in the office, I read through Matthew's private collection of magazines and came across some more of Maurice's work; obscure poems I hadn't read before, poems that haven't been anthologised yet. I wonder how they will fit in with the collection I have started. This seems to be the only inclination I have. The only way to spend the day. The problem is, the poetry collection is still at the flat.

I think about ringing Barry, imagine him answering. His guilt. His eagerness. When I do ring there is no answer and I am relieved. I walk to the corner and catch a number 16 tram to St Kilda.

St Kilda Road. An avenue of trees, the winter bareness of elm and oak. The Arts Centre, the Gardens, the Shrine. Miles of office buildings. An elegant mix of styles set behind established gardens. The sun glints on a million panes of glass. The turn into Fitzroy Street, the familiar sweep around the coast. This morning, even the colour of the sea is uncertain, a heavy green but washed with blues and greys and pale flickers of sun. I get off the tram in Acland Street and thread my way through the quiet, narrow roads into Spenser Street. The flat, Barry's flat now, is behind the main block. One unit in a double block, surrounded by lawns and native trees. A pleasant, private place to live.

Both flats, Barry's and next door's, are closed up, curtains drawn. I cannot tell whether he is in or not. I have only been gone three weeks, but already it seems longer, as if this part of my life were set back further in the past, with no relevance to the present. The curtains twitch next door. I am being watched.

I knock briskly on Barry's door and wait. No answer. I turn the key in the lock and he is there before I open the door.

'Lyn! Come in.' His face is eager as a spaniel's ready for a treat. He is just out of the shower and has a towel around his waist, another draped around his neck. 'I was hoping you'd come.'

'I left some papers here that I need. In the small case. I did ring but you didn't answer.' And spaniel-like, he is crestfallen. It seems hard to imagine that I ever loved this man. I cannot remember now why I did. What qualities he had. What need in me he fulfilled. He closes his eyes in exasperation. Heavy-lidded eyes, like the eyes of a fish.

'Can't we talk?' He stands in the hallway, blocking my way.

'Let me pass, please, Barry.'

'Lyn, don't be like this. Christ! I've said I'm sorry. What more can I do?'

His hands reach for mine. I look at them coming, almost as though in slow motion. Clean hands, the fingernails cut short and blunt. Treacherous hands.

'It's over with her. She was never important. Believe me Lyn, it didn't mean anything.' Fluent hands that stop at chest height, upturned for my inspection. An eloquent gesture. Would I lie to you? See there's nothing in my hands, nothing up my sleeve.

'Let me pass Barry, or I'll leave.'

He moves back, exaggerates the movement, stands hard up against the passage wall despite its ample width.

'Can I go through?' I ask.

He shrugs a reluctant assent. Already he is sulking. I ignore him. When I pass, he is so close I can smell the clean scent of soap on bare skin. He does not follow.

The case is in the bedroom, a large room partitioned off with a screen, and behind this, Barry's collection of gym equipment: an exercise bike, a workbench, a set of weights. He comes here in the mornings, a half-hour's training session before work. He brags he has never missed a day.

The bedroom is already tidy, surfaces clean, bed made, no sign of another occupant. The colour scheme is striking. Doona and pillow slips a rich blue, edged with a pale turquoise to match the curtains. I remind myself that we chose all this together. It should be like biting on a sore tooth, but nothing stirs, nothing hurts. The case is on the wardrobe floor. I take it out and my side of the wardrobe is now completely empty. His clothes still hang rigidly in one half of the robe, pressed hard against each other. I leave my key on the bedside table and let myself out. Barry is nowhere to be seen.

I walk on the Esplanade, delaying the moment of return to the office. The sun is out, but there is a cold wind off the sea, a smell of sea air. The street is busy with market stalls, market-goers. I browse as I used to with Barry, on our pleasant Sunday morning strolls, aware that this lingering is part of the goodbye, part of the process of moving on.

'Lyn. Hey. Where's your fellah today? Let you out on your own, did he? A lovely lady like you.'

Marcus is full of Sunday morning conviviality. The owner of the stall where Barry and I bought each other photos of the area: mine, a view of the pier; his, sailing ships on the bay.

'Clarissa, where you hiding? Come and say hello to Lyn.'

Clarissa is his partner, a tall woman with long chestnut hair, dark, close-set eyes and a clear complexion. From a distance she is stunning, but when you get closer you are not so sure. There is something evasive about her eyes. She is normally friendly, but today she seems stand-offish and stays firmly in the background. Marcus puts his arm around her, hugs her into his body. A woman next to me indicates an interest in a photo of Luna Park. I drift off.

I cross the road and walk on the pier, past people fishing, the few tourists braving the cold. In the café, I buy a cappuccino and sit at a window table, looking over the ruffled waters of the bay. Despite winter, the view is almost tropical. Yachts bob in the sheltered water between the pier and the sea wall. Palm trees fringe the coast and behind them blocks of flats, a glimpse of Luna Park.

I sip the froth on my coffee. Through glass, the sun is warm and I sit contentedly, idly, gazing thoughtlessly at the thin parade of people on the pier. A couple walk towards me, entwined in each other's arms, heads close. At first it is the

11

woman who catches my attention; the long stride, the flowing chestnut hair. They stop a moment to look at something out to sea and for the first time I see the man's face full on. Barry. Barry with his head bent against Clarissa's. An unexpected, jolting combination.

They walk towards me, unaware of my presence. I should get up. I should make my presence known. I should confront Barry with his own easy lies, watch the play of emotion on his face. Guilt. Regret. Defiance at being caught out. The romance not over, as stated in pleading terms just half an hour ago, and, judging from the body language, in full, lusty swing. Instead I sit there, strangely calm as though watching a film. As though those two clinging figures have little to do with me.

Barry stops to admire someone's catch but Clarissa looks pointedly at her watch, her face flickering with impatience that she doesn't trouble to conceal. Her allotted break from the stall must be over. She tugs at his arm and they walk briskly away, back down the long pier and out of sight. I sip my cooling coffee and that brief moment of unreality lifts and the emotions spin in. Anger. Outrage at the ease of Barry's lies. But mixed in with all this are faint stirrings of amusement at the farce-like quality of the scene.

It is early afternoon when I get back to the shop. I clear a space at the table and go through the files in the small case. But Maurice seem less interesting than I thought, his work less significant, of uncertain literary value. The task I have set myself seems both monumental and worthless. I pour myself some wine and lie on the mattress in the office with a book I have already read, comforting as an old friend. Three glasses of wine later I fall asleep.

The phone rings and I jump, waking edgily, dry-mouthed and heavy from the unaccustomed wine.

'Lyn, I'm in need of company. Can you come for tea?' Pam's voice.

It is dark outside. I look at my watch. It has just gone six o'clock.

'Pam. Yes. I'd love to. I've been asleep.'

'Thought so. I can tell from your voice. You know, that half-dead, where-am-I tone. You need livening up, kiddo. Bring your things and stay the night.'

I feel my spirits lift at the prospect of Pam's calm, clear-sighted company. She seems to have a sixth sense of knowing when I'm down, her offers of support almost uncanny in their timing. But in the taxi gliding through the darkened streets of Hawthorn, I decide that perhaps her intuition in my affairs is not really so surprising. Our understanding of each other is often instinctive, based more on a reading of subtleties than the usual, overt signals. We have been friends for years now. We know each other well.

Pam meets me at the door, her cloud of dark hair back lit from the hall like a halo. She is a tall woman, solidly built. Overweight, she calls it, forever wrestling between dieting and a love of food. She looks terrific. She kisses me warmly, her eyes appraising.

'Mm. Someone's under the weather. Let's see. You need coffee, food and wine. In that order.'

The coffee and the company revive me, and I help her with the food, chopping vegetables to make sauce for the pasta.

We eat in front of the fire, our meals on our laps. I tell her about my day, about Barry and Clarissa on the pier. Her deep, green eyes are watchful. 'Cat's Eyes' we called her at uni. Eyes that could see in the dark.

'How do you feel?' she asks.

I shrug. 'Amused. Angry. Amused at the stupidity of it all. Angry at being lied to. That's the worst part. It's such an insult.'

'Mm.' She nods agreement. 'But you can be too trusting, Lyn.'

'I was with him.'

Pam says nothing, waiting for me to run on, as she has at other times and in other places. But I am surprisingly calm, not really in need of the solace of words, a sympathetic ear. After today, the last lingering regrets of breaking up are firmly in the past.

Pam takes a sip of wine and looks at me levelly. 'Thank God you're out, Lyn. He was bad for you, he didn't let you breathe. I could see it more clearly than you.'

I shrug. 'I knew though. I was stuck in some sort of inertia, unable to make decisions. Hopeless.'

'We've all been there. Upheaval is always difficult. I guess that's why too many people stay in bad relationships.'

'Not you,' I comment.

'Well not now,' she agrees. 'But I've had my turn at being stuck, as well you know. You were the one then, who helped pick up the pieces.'

I raise my glass. 'Well . . . here's to being unstuck.'

We look at each other and smile. A log snaps in the fire, sends up a little spurt of flame. We don't speak for a while, our eyes drawn to the fire. The silence, like the room, is warm, endlessly comfortable.

Pam speaks first. 'When I was a kid I used to wish I had secret powers. You know the old story-book stuff. I still wish it sometimes. I'd like to turn him into a toad and squash him flat.'

I laugh. 'When Adele and I were kids, she would give me a choice. Always a choice mind, never both. Would I prefer to fly or to be invisible?'

'And what did you choose?'

'Invisibility every time. Adele would try and change my mind. She'd go on about the joys of flying. The sensation of it. You know, the feeling of the wind in your face, gliding through space, the freedom of it all. That sort of thing.' My glass of wine glows red in the firelight.

'And did you? Change your mind?'

'Not once. Invisibility won every time.'

'Stubborn, eh.' Pam raises her glass. 'So what's changed?'

I am glad to be there, already feeling better and brighter. Pam has offered solace and bed for the duration. The bed I refuse, on a permanent basis at least. There is solace enough in the offer. In the knowledge I can always rely on her.

# Chapter Three

*K.1, purl to the last stitch, K.*
*Rep. to the end 2 tog. and spurn*
*The passages where mad brasses bray*
*And turn, lady, turn.*
'On a Grey-haired Old Lady Knitting . . .', Furnley Maurice

In the morning I see the woman again. I am on the train, going into work after leaving Pam's. She gets on at Glenferrie station and takes the seat next to me, near the window.

She is younger than I realised. Late teens, perhaps early twenties. Her skin is pale, almost translucent, as though she is unwell. Her clothes are slightly ethnic: black ankle boots, a heavy black skirt that brushes against her legs mid-calf, a black jumper beneath an open purple shirt. A single heart-shaped earring dangles on a long silver chain, the heart thick enough to be a locket. She takes out a book and reads. Her smell is pervasive and unpleasant; a mix of perfume, stale cigarettes and the faint, sour smell of alcohol.

It is not until we have left Hawthorn station that I notice the man, notice his interest in her. He is sitting opposite her, looking fixedly at her. I look past him, out over the parklands near the Yarra. Through darkened glass they are deeply green, winterish and lush. The day is grey, heavy with cloud, no brightness anywhere. When I look back, his gaze has not moved. His eyes are riveted to her face and every now and then she moves, as if discomforted by his stare. He is dressed casually, almost scruffily: jeans, a thick black windcheater, old runners. He has long, light brown hair which falls untidily around his face. A pleasant face, slightly long-jawed.

His gaze moves from her to include the other passengers, to include me, watchful and, I sense, observant. His eyes are a pale hazel. In my bag I have the knitting that I always carry, waiting for these odd moments of stillness. I take it out, manoeuvre wool and needles into place. The jumper is a soft, pale green, growing slowly. He looks away, dismisses me. If he looked closer, I'm sure he'd see the interest in my eyes.

One row plain. One row purl. The movements are automatic, contained within my fingers and not my brain. My eyes are free now, can observe unrestricted, unnoticed, but even so I keep my gaze averted, watch their reflections in the window. In daylight the darkened glass gives a shadowy image, but in tunnels, each movement is clear, as though seen in a mirror. Her body is rigid, her eyes glued to her book, but I can tell she isn't reading. Her eyes are too still and she forgets to turn the page. That fixed stillness is disconcerting.

Outside the Tennis Centre the train slows, moves uncertainly towards Flinders Street. She looks out at the dense network of tracks, the spidery threads of overhead wires, as though to consult where she is. In the Swanston Street tunnel, she closes the book and puts it away in her bag, but not before I see the cover. An early Penguin with its orange cover and distinctive logo. *Middlemarch* by George Eliot.

The train shudders to a halt and she stands up, not quite steady, a small wallet in her hand. There is a beading of sweat on her upper lip, a faint flush to her cheeks, a wariness in her eyes. The man is already at the door. I hurry ahead of them, up the ramp, and wait at the top, pressed against the wall, hopefully unnoticed. The woman leads the way but he follows closely – too closely – almost on her heels. She doesn't stop or look around; her pace doesn't change. She seems oblivious to his presence in the crowd, but I am not so sure. There is a stillness about her, an air of concentration. I suspect she is aware of his every step, of his breath on the back of her neck.

On the concourse at Flinders Street, she stops at a kiosk and buys coffee. He buys a *Herald Sun* and stands away from her, reading the sports pages. Even from my position, out of sight behind a news stand, I can see the bold headlines announcing: MAGPIES TO WIN and underneath, a photo of two footballers training. Melbourne's love affair with football is in full swing; the lead-up to the grand final.

She sits facing towards Swanston Street and stares into her coffee cup, seemingly oblivious to the streams of commuters ebbing and flowing on the tide of trains, and to the two people watching her. When she has finished her coffee, she tosses the empty cup into a bin and moves off down Flinders Street, her handbag over her shoulder.

The watcher doesn't follow. His gaze sweeps across the intersection and suddenly he moves off in the other direction, blending in with the flow of pedestrians. I can still see the woman. Her purple shirt and frizz of blonde hair stand out in the crowd. Her stride is long and easy. She is already half-way to Elizabeth Street.

I am torn between curiosity and the demands of time. Should I follow? It is ten minutes to opening time and I have never opened late yet. But I am intrigued by what I have just seen, by the tension in the carriage, the fear in her eyes. Curiosity wins and I run to catch her, to see where she goes, what she does. She confounds me though by re-entering the station. I am just in time to see her showing her ticket to the guards at the Elizabeth Street entrance.

I walk slowly to the shop, wondering about the purpose of her journey. A cup of coffee at Flinders Street station? Some rendezvous with a man she didn't speak to? Hardly. But among the familiar jostle of pedestrians, I begin to doubt my reading of the situation. After all, what have I really seen? A man looking at a woman on a train. No other facts, save fear in her eyes, intent in his.

In the shop doorway is a single rosebud. A pale, apricot rose, bright against the grey concrete step. No note. No clue as to who left it. I smell its fragrance and look around, remembering the roses in Smithy's vase the other night, almost expecting to see him in the street. But would he? Roses? Not his style surely. Barry? A gesture of friendship or a gesture of guilt? I can't decide.

I put the rose in a glass and place it on the office table. I have had enough of puzzles for one morning and turn my mind to the familiar task of processing books. A small collection that I bought, on impulse and by proxy from a private sale, a deceased estate. A mixed bag of classics: gardening books, bird books, children's books. All of them saleable and worthy of shelf space, but nothing out of the ordinary. I shelve them according to category and price range.

Between customers, I chase up orders and return outstanding calls. Among them are the calls from Friday evening. Vanessa's and Ruth's. Vanessa is my publisher, the manager of Vane Publications, a small company that took a chance on my one and only book, a slim volume on the Australian poet Adam Lindsay Gordon. A new company, beginning to ride high on accolades of innovation and quality of presentation.

'Lyn, I'm so pleased to hear from you. Where on earth have you been lately? And how's that gorgeous man of yours?'

Her speech is fast, as though she is in a hurry. But Vanessa is often in a hurry, moving efficiently from one conversation to the next, one meeting to the next.

'The gorgeous man is no more,' I say matter-of-factly. 'I've been getting over it Ness, like a cat licking her wounds.'

She pauses. 'And are you . . . over it, I mean?' Her tone softens in concern.

'Definitely. And yes, I would love to come to your party.'

'Good. It's not just a party, you know. We're launching a new book. There's going to be some publicity about it in one of the newspapers. And there's someone I want you to meet. His name's Peter Ireland. He's working for me now, a sort of junior partner. Very junior.' Her tone is dry.

'I'll look forward to it,' I say. 'Congratulations Vanessa. It sounds as though you're branching out.'

I am pleased with her success. Pleased the frantic workload of establishing herself has been worthwhile.

'I am with your help.' She continues in a little rush of pleasure, her voice as brisk as ever. 'I should be congratulating you. *Gordon* is on next year's reading list for Year Twelve.'

I look out at the shop, at the high shelves and cabinets filled with books. The books that helped me with the months of research, kept me company through the infinite hours of writing.

'But that's wonderful,' I say.

'Yes,' she replies earnestly. 'And just think of the increase in sales, let alone the prestige. It's a credit to you, Lyn. Listen, I must go, but I'll talk to you about it all soon. Saturday, eight o'clock. I'm pleased you can come. And I'm pleased you're okay. You take care of yourself.'

I hang up, excited by the news on *Gordon* and moved by Vanessa's concern on my behalf. The unexpected glimpse of a softer side to this brisk, successful woman.

I return Ruth's call, but I already know what she wants. Ruth lectures in the English Department at the university. When my book first came out she invited me to be a guest speaker in a series of lectures focusing on Australian poets, an invitation extended to this year.

'Lyn, how are you? Thanks for calling. Any more books in the wind?'

'Only an idea for one, Ruth. A collection of poetry on Melbourne. Different poets, different times, a lot of early stuff. What do you think?' I ask.

'I think it sounds great.' Ruth replies enthusiastically.

'It's early days yet. I've been slack.'

'Hardly that, I'm sure. Too busy, perhaps. Like us all. Which makes me feel guilty for even asking you, but . . .'

'Yes, I'd love to. Please don't worry, it will be a pleasure.'

This is almost true. Last year, my foray into academic life was a distraction after Adele's death. At the time it provided me with a sense of going forward, a feeling of achievement. Twelve months on, nothing much has changed.

'Bless you, Lyn. It's 7 October, a Wednesday. Eleven a.m. Does that suit you?'

This fits in with Jordie's work schedule. I don't even have to ask her to cover me.

'Perfectly. Looking forward to it. I'll see you then.'

After work I swim at the City Baths in Swanston Street. This is something I do regularly, enjoying the glide through water, the pull of muscles, the feeling of activity after the long day in the shop. Afterwards I walk down the hill to the State Library and work in the domed reading room. A vast octangular room, its long tables spread out from the central dais like the spokes of a wheel and everywhere pools of light shining on old timber. A spacious hall, airy and quiet.

There are not many people late in the evening. I browse both physically and electronically through the different collections of Australian poetry, looking specifically for the poetry of Melbourne, and, further afield, the Victorian countryside. I photocopy work from various sources, work on undisturbed. The work at this stage is a gathering of disparate ideas, a collecting of resources. I like this early time of writing, ideas emerging, but the body, the main part, remaining amorphous, structureless, not yet formed. A book stirring into life. A beginning.

At closing time I head for home, my strange transient home, the office of a city bookshop. Outside the library the great statues cast crooked shadows across the concourse and down the narrow flight of stairs to the street. Swanston Street is quiet on a Monday night. I stride past bookshops and sex shops, past the brighter lights of Bourke and Collins Street, fairy lights in trees, the city growing festive. I turn at Flinders Street and, beyond the station, the lights become less frequent, the buildings smaller, the street emptier. I turn in at the side alley next to the shop.

I wonder how many of these old buildings will be taken over by developers. What modernisation will take place. I try and imagine the alley as it could be in the future: modern façades, attractive street-lighting, the grime removed. Instead the passageway between the high bluestone walls seems narrower, the recessed doorways deeper than ever. The high arched windows are blinded by sheets of tin and solid bars. Modernisation seems a gigantic leap of faith.

I stride down the long dark alley, glad to get inside and lock the doors behind me. Before I go to bed I check the answering machine. There are no messages.

# Chapter Four

*O mystery! as I learn thee more,*
*the more thy deeps are dark to me!*
*'By the Camp Fire', Ada Cambridge*

I stay at Pam's for a few nights and in the mornings, on my way to work, I look for the woman on the train. I see her, or what I think is her, only once. She is coming out from a different city platform, but is too far away and gone too quickly for me to be sure. For the rest of the week, when I finish work, I swim. Afterwards I visit the library, going through old papers and journals, gathering resources for my book.

On Friday, when I open up, Jordie is, as usual, precisely on time, her arrival uncannily timed to the moment of opening the blinds on the windows, unlocking the door.

She is an attractive woman, tall and slim, with a cap of dark, shining hair. She is wearing a black miniskirt, black stockings and ankle boots; an outfit totally inadequate for the weather. Over her shoulder is the black attaché case that she always carries and, dangling from the strap, a silver whistle on a silver chain. An added piece of equipment to the armoury that is Jordie.

Jordie Armstrong is twenty-two and single. She works for

me by arrangement, usually two half-days a week, more on request, less sometimes if the situation arises. She works for other small city businesses: a few, regularly like mine; others when and if she wants to. She is good at her job, efficient and hard-working. I am lucky to have her.

She has worked for me for nearly a year now, but for all that I sometimes feel I hardly know her. At first when I tried to draw her out, I hit a barrier, a reluctance to open up. Polite but definite, reinforced by a certain crispness in tone and manner. Since then little has changed, but sometimes I sense a slip in her reserve, almost a thawing before the barrier is reinstated. For all her reticence about her own life, she seems quite interested in mine.

She looks briefly around the room, at the business of living here, the clothes and possessions cluttering up the work space, and, as usual, makes no comment. She summed up the situation weeks ago, but today there is an expression on her face that I can't quite read. She makes a small, reaching gesture with her hand and then smoothes it against her side. The automatic response checked before it is full-born.

I wonder what emotion she has stifled. Sympathy. Disapproval. Disbelief. Disbelief probably, for it is impossible to imagine Jordie, with her air of quiet efficiency, getting into this sort of mess. Any sort of mess.

'Have you seen the paper, Lyn? There's an article on Vane Publications.' She unlocks her case and hands me a newspaper cutting. I read the small print and think of Vanessa putting it all in place. Her energy and organisational skills, a small whirlwind of activity.

*Well-known local publishing house Vane Publications is launching the new work of up-and-coming writer Georgina Stavros. Her latest book is titled* The Stirring *and consolidates this writer's promising career. Among the invited guests are others who have published with this house, including such notable writers as Max Spurelli, Judith Weaving, Lyn Blessing and Daryl Earle.*

24

'Moving into the big time, Lyn.' Jordie says when I have finished reading.

'I'm on the list of notables, Jordie. Hardly notable myself.'

She sets the laptop up on the central table.

'You're too modest. It's a feather in your cap. You deserve it.'

Her tone is crisp, invites no comment. She collects the accounts and invoices, the tray of correspondence.

I think about telling Jordie about the woman in the shop, about seeing her again on the train, asking her opinion. Before I can frame the sentence, she has pressed the play button on the answering machine and we listen to Barry's voice, distorted by static.

'Lyn, I must see you. Ring me. I'll be home all day. Please.'

Jordie is silent, but she flicks me a quick, assessing glance.

Smithy's voice next. A repeat of last time. 'Lyn, come and have a drink tonight if you can. I've designed a new one.'

Jordie is curious. 'Someone new, Lyn?'

'Hardly new.' I smile. 'That was Alex Smith, my neighbour. I've known him for ever.'

She nods. 'I saw him this morning on my way to work.'

'Really. Where was he?'

'At the station. Most people wait under the clocks. It's almost an institution, standing there in the open, large as life. You can't miss them really. But not your Mr Smith, tucked away behind a pillar somewhere. At least I think it was him. I've never really met him, you know, but I have seen him once or twice in the shop. I don't think he knows who I am.'

'Perhaps a romance?' I say, interested in this unexpected glimpse of Smithy's life.

The rose from Monday is in Jordie's way. The tight orange bud has opened now, it is almost in full bloom. She moves it to one side and settles down at the desk.

The doorbell interrupts our conversation and I go into the shop. I can see Jordie through the open door, her head already bent down over the accounts, her air of quiet concentration.

'Good morning, Mrs White.' A frequent customer this,

adding to her collection of filmed books as often as her finances allow. A small, frail woman.

'Good morning, my dear.'

She smiles at me expectantly, knowing from a phone call earlier in the week that I have tracked down another book on her list. I retrieve it from the office and she reads the catalogue slip inside the cover, confirming the details and condition of what she now holds in her hands.

A Town Like Alice. *Dust wrapper, soiled and creased. End papers lightly foxed. Heinemann, 1956, eleventh printing. Special Film Edition. $20.00*

She hands me a crisp note.

'A small amount for so much pleasure. Thank you, my dear. I knew I could rely on you.'

I wrap it up and she cradles it lovingly in her hands. She is still smiling when she leaves the shop.

Twelve o'clock. Time to do the banking, to buy some lunch. I leave Jordie in the shop and walk briskly to Swanston Street. The streets are busy as always, city workers in a rush mingled in with the aimless pace of people shopping. Everywhere the light is grey, a winter light, the colours dull, heavy as grease.

On impulse I walk on Princes Bridge. The unfinished Southgate complex crouches expectantly at the river's edge. No customers yet, but plenty of activity, the workers finishing off. There are rowing boats on the river, their oars cutting through the leaden surface of the Yarra. I stop for a minute to enjoy the speed and silence of their progress, the quick dip and glide, the precision of the oars. But it is too cold for lingering. I buy lunch for two: hot roast beef rolls and mugs of soup. I hurry on, eager for the warmth of the shop.

The messages Jordie has taken are mainly work-related. Two enquiries regarding stock, two enquiries into progress on tracking down books. One has been easy. Daphne Du Maurier's *The Birds* is readily available. The other, for the same customer, Du Maurier's *Rebecca*, a first edition, has proved more elusive.

One o'clock. Jordie tidies up her work. When the table is empty she moves the rose back to the centre of the table.

'Must go, Lyn. See you Wednesday.'

'Thanks, Jordie. Enjoy the weekend.'

She turns at the door and hesitates before speaking. 'Look after yourself.' No crispness now but a touch of concern, a hint of sympathy.

'Yes. Of course,' I say, surprised at this slip in her detachment.

The clutter in the office must have got to her. She has seen a crack in the image of the successful businesswoman she believes in.

I smile. 'Thanks, Jordie. I'm fine. Really.'

She nods and closes the door behind her.

Almost immediately the door opens again and I look up, half expecting it to be Jordie, forgetting something. With a start I see Adele. No. Of course not. Not Adele, but the nameless woman from the train.

I check the clock. One-fifteen. Last week was the same. She comes after Jordie leaves. Two weeks in a row. One-fifteen Fridays. She is dressed in black and her skin seems paler than ever. Her actions are the same as last time. She walks straight to the classics section, straight to a book and flicks through the pages as though looking for something particular. She touches her head briefly, fumbles, closes the book and restores it to the shelves. The fumbling is familiar, the same as last week. She leaves with no backward glance, no attempt to scan the other shelves. I follow her to the door and watch her progress up Flinders Street, wondering what it is that she does. Her visits are too short for browsing. Her actions too determined. She walks hurriedly through the crowd and stops at the lights on the corner, lost in the cluster of pedestrians there.

Again I check the shelves. One book is slightly out of line, not quite pushed back hard enough. *The Mill on the Floss* by George Eliot, an Everyman edition. This book was Adele's favourite. She read it time and time again. I always found it tedious and dispiriting, such futile restrictions, such a waste of life. An unremarkable book, shelved among other editions of the same work. None of them rare or expensive.

The door bell clangs and I turn to the sound. A stranger this time. A man dressed in jeans and a bomber jacket. He moves quickly, purposefully through the shop towards me. Some instinct, something about his stride and demeanour makes me step away from the shelf. He nods at me as I pass, a quick cursory nod. At the classics section he pauses, stops to browse, uses a hand to guide him through the titles.

Another customer comes in – Mrs Hall, a regular visitor to the shop and a passionate collector of bird books. There are some new ones in stock from my recent purchase and I point them out, but keep an eye on the man. He is still there, still looking through the titles. His hand reaches up, takes down a book.

'This is just what I'm after.' Mrs Hall's voice is loud and piping, carries clearly.

The man turns to look at her for a moment and then turns back to the shelf.

She has *The Atlas of Australian Birds* in her hand. 'I'm thrilled to find it.'

'I'm glad,' I say. 'It's only just come in.'

He has put the book back now and is coming towards me.

'How much is this?' Mrs Hall asks.

I consult the catalogue slip. 'Fifty dollars, Mrs Hall. A first edition. You have a bargain.'

I write out the sales slip. He is at the door. He doesn't look my way. The door closes behind him.

'Don't forget, Lyn, if you get in any bird books, any at all, you must ring me, let me know straight away.'

'Yes of course. Don't worry, I won't forget.'

'Goodbye, then. And thank you so much.'

Again the door closes. After that brief flurry of activity, the shop is suddenly empty. Once more I check the classics shelf. *The Mill on the Floss* is pushed back now, the same alignment as all the rest. I take it down and turn the pages carefully. The book itself tells me nothing. There are no marks. No pages turned back. No clues. But even that small difference in alignment has told me something. The book that interested the woman also interests him. Something disturbing is going on in my own shop, going on almost in full view.

I stand there for a long time thinking about what I have just seen, aware of a complex mix of emotions: unease, curiosity, determination to know what's happening. And with the different shades of anxiety and resolve is a heady sense of anger at the audacity of it all.

# Chapter Five

*Thoughts flutter like butterfly wings*
*In Memory's folding web;*

'Memory', Furnley Maurice

Vanessa's house has been in her family for generations. An older house, built in the red brick of its period and set among established gardens. I park behind others in the wide, circular driveway. The house is spacious and elegant with that indefinable feel of welcome that only certain houses possess. Vanessa meets me at the door and kisses my cheek. The room behind us is already filled with people.

'Lyn! You look simply stunning.' Vanessa greets me warmly, takes my outstretched hand in both of hers and regards me frankly. 'How are you?'

'Fine.' I squeeze her hand. 'Honestly.'

'Good.' She is emphatic, pleased with my answer. 'And tell me, how's the writing coming along? We're waiting for something new from you.'

'Soon, Vanessa. Soon.'

She is a large woman, with an air of suppressed energy as though the stillness required in greeting people is not her natural state. Her dark hair is swept back from her face, severe but flattering. She is wearing black: a stylish three-piece outfit edged with crimson at throat and wrist. Black stockings. Black three-inch heels.

She takes my arm and steers me towards a small group of people.

'Have you met Max, Lyn? Max Spurelli. Max published with us last year. A huge success, wasn't it, Max? This is Lyn Blessing.'

He is a short, thick-set man, with wild eyebrows and darting eyes. He looks uncomfortable and when I shake his hand, it is soft and moist. Vanessa looks on approvingly.

'I'm so pleased that my authors are getting the chance to meet each other. Does you good to get out of those dull rooms you work in.'

'Not always dull, Vanessa,' I comment.

'Well, no, perhaps not for you with that shop of yours. I always think that a writer needs another outlet.'

She turns to Max. 'Lyn is author of the definitive text on Gordon. It's on display.'

Max makes appropriate noises and Vanessa smiles encouragingly. She draws me to one side.

'Congratulations, Lyn, on the success of *Gordon*. Who would have believed it?'

'You did,' I say, smiling. 'Or you wouldn't have published it.'

She nods happily. 'I always thought Gordon would make that list, but it's nice when things work out the way you've planned.'

'This is all terrific,' I say, looking around at the elegance of the room, the movement of waiters, the clusters of people.

'I meant that about your next book, Lyn.' Vanessa looks pointedly at me, taps her foot to emphasise the remark.

'Yes. I know,' I say. 'I have made a start.'

'Good. We'll have lunch soon, Lyn, and discuss lovely things such as new print runs and increased sales.' She pats my hand and extends her focus to the wider group. 'I must leave you for a moment. Georgina has just arrived. She'll be worried if she's left alone. We'll get the speeches over soon and then we can all relax.'

Vanessa's voice rises, addresses a man in a nearby group.

'Peter, this is Lyn. You know. Lyn Blessing.' She squeezes my arm and moves off purposefully to greet her guest of honour.

Peter regards me calmly and extends his hand. A flamboyant mix of casual and formal, a dinner jacket over jeans; a mass of curly brown hair, slicked down for control. He looks crisp and fresh and attractive. A junior partner Vanessa had commented in dry tones and now I understand why. He is young, somewhere in his twenties, two decades younger than Vanessa.

'Peter Ireland.'

He shakes my hand warmly and we find ourselves following Vanessa into the main function room and standing near the displays. Georgina's book is the focus of attention. There are large posters of the front page, the title, *The Stirring,* in crimson script, standing out big and bold against the silver dust jacket. There are large photos of the author, an attractive woman, blonde and well groomed. In front of the posters are deep piles of her book.

'Looks good,' I comment.

'Vanessa always does things well. She's one of these rare people with an innate sense of style. She's told me all about you,' Peter says.

This is disconcerting. I wonder fleetingly if their conversation included a run-down on my love life. I fall back on formula.

'All good I hope.'

'Nothing but praise.' He looks at me steadily, the interest showing in his eyes.

'What was the title of your book?' Max asks, unexpectedly at our side, his tone peevish.

I tell him, but he has the air of someone who has never read it and has no intention of changing the situation.

'Lyn's book is on the side table, Max, near yours. You should read the press clippings.' He points him in the right direction where other Vane Publications are displayed, with blown-up commentaries by newspaper reviewers. I watch Max's back as he makes his way across the room, a thick back, hesitant in the crowd, unsure of its way. I have read his book: a fluid, well-written satire, full of changes of pace, thought-provoking and lively. Hard to connect this author with his own work. Someone with more to say in print than in life.

'Would you like a drink?' Peter asks.

'Thank you. A glass of white wine.'

Peter weaves his way through the crowd and removes two glasses from a nearby waiter. He looks comfortable and self-assured.

'Well done,' I say. 'You didn't spill a drop.'

'Plenty of practice. Sign of a misspent youth.' He smiles and raises his glass. 'Good luck.'

The wine is sweet and cool. The room is filling up around us and we are in danger of being jostled. We follow Max to the safety of the wall, to the displays of books and reviews. Max is absorbed in one of the many press clippings. I look over his shoulder and exchange a grin of amusement with Peter. It is one of his own. Peter takes up one of the more garrulous of mine and reads it out loud.

'"Well-known Melbourne businesswoman Lyn Blessing has added another string to her bow with the publication of her work *Gordon*. *Gordon* is an unusual volume in that the collection of poetry is accompanied by excerpts of biography and relevant contextual notes, offering clear insight into the creative process and another life and time. In publishing this work, Lyn Blessing is once more following in her grandfather's footsteps. Matthew Blessing established the family business in Flinders Street in 1937 and was heavily involved in Melbourne literary circles. We wish Lyn well in her new endeavours."'

'My grandfather was an interesting man,' I say.

'It must run in the family,' he says, regarding me frankly. 'I loved the book, Lyn, so fresh and clear. Vanessa was telling me she wants you to write another in the same vein. You know, choose another poet, fill in the background.'

We stand close together against the side wall, our voices loud over the noise of conversation. I am aware of his warmth, the interest in his gaze.

'Yes. She has mentioned it, once or twice,' I say, matter-of-factly.

He grins. 'Ah. An understatement if I know Vanessa. Did it take you long to write?'

'Ages. The research is the thing. Much too time-consuming.'

'Yes, but worthwhile.' He is earnest, looks over his wine glass at me, waiting for my reply.

'Research is about energy. You need to have the energy to keep going. At the moment my energy levels are low.'

'I could help you,' Peter continues. He is slightly too eager. 'It's in my line, that sort of thing.'

After the mess with Barry, it is pleasant to be flattered by an attractive man. Pleasant to have such an interest taken in my work. But his gaze is slightly too familiar and I sense that there is something more to his offer than an interest in my work. I look away.

'It's kind of you, Peter, but I work better on my own.'

'Fair enough. But let me know if you change your mind.'

The crowd is thicker now, the noise level louder. Vanessa's parties are traditionally huge affairs with no expense spared. Plenty of food and drink passed around quietly and efficiently by a team of waiters. I recognise some of the faces in the crowd. Not instantly identifiable faces but seen often enough to be familiar. Society faces, political faces, business faces, literary faces, media faces. A mix of the up-and-coming and the rich and influential. A soft click of cameras among the voices, the clatter of glasses, the clack of high heels on polished timber.

Vanessa is still busy with Georgina. She is a willowy, blonde woman, older than her photos and heavily made-up. At her side is a young man, dressed formally in a dinner suit and ruffled white shirt. He wears glasses, thin-rimmed and circular. His hair is light brown, almost blond, and worn long, slicked back from his forehead. He too seems familiar.

Across the room Vanessa is gesturing to Peter.

He turns towards me. 'Excuse me a minute, Lyn. Looks like speech time. I'll see you soon.'

Max hovers next to me, shifts his weight from one foot to the other.

'Do you know him?' I indicate the young man at Georgina's side.

'Some actor on TV.'

He sounds definite, as though he knows. Somehow I don't think so, but as I have no better knowledge I let it go.

Vanessa rings a tiny bell and the noise level drops until only the tinkling sound of the bell remains. She casts a beaming smile around the room and we all wait for her to speak. She introduces Peter as her new colleague. He makes a confident reply, expressing his delight at being in Melbourne and at working with Vanessa. Georgina is next. A short speech to thank Vanessa for her care in the process of publication. Vanessa replies, expresses her delight in the book, which she is sure will be a bestseller. She invites everyone to purchase it, to drink up and enjoy the party. Wine glasses clink, cameras click. There is an orgy of congratulation. Speeches over, the guests resume where they left off, the noise level rising sharply.

I detach myself from Max and drift off, mingling with some old acquaintances. From time to time, I see Georgina and her young man mixing with different groups of people. Georgina smiles freely, accepting their congratulations gracefully. Her companion is attentive, smiles often at her, at the conversations going on around them. Once when I turn unexpectedly I see him watching me. His gaze slides away.

I am disconcerted, the little bubble of enjoyment fading as though it had never existed. The noise of the party is suddenly deafening, the room close and hot. I am restless, in need of solitude, of time and space to work out cause and effect. A sliding glance. A jolt of unease. I seek out Vanessa to say my goodbyes, but find Peter first. He looks warm and slightly flushed.

'Lyn, I was just coming to find you. Can I get you another drink?'

'No thanks, Peter. Time for me to go.'

'So early? And you so popular.'

'How so?'

'Someone was asking me about you. Who you were . . . what you did.' There is a faint glimmer of sweat on his upper lip.

'Oh. Who was that?'

Vanessa arrives at my side in a cloud of perfume and good humour. She looks as fresh and cool as when I first arrived.

'Lyn. I've neglected you. I hope Peter's being taking care of you.' She slides her hand under my arm.

'Yes, of course. And Max.'

'Good. A success, then. Never underestimate the power of a good party, Lyn.'

'I don't,' I say, smiling back. 'Not with you in charge.'

She laughs in genuine delight.

'It's been a lovely party, Vanessa. But I'm feeling a bit under the weather.'

'Look after yourself, Lyn. You're looking wonderful, you know. So fit and healthy. You must be doing something right.' She kisses me on the cheek and I feel the brief softness of her skin against my own. 'I won't forget our lunch. I'll be in touch.'

She flits off with a little wave of her fingers. Peter watches her go, his eyes following her like a magnet. I'm not surprised. Vanessa has that effect on lots of people.

'Who was it?' I ask, drawing his attention. 'Who wanted to know about me?'

He blinks at my insistence. 'Um. I'm not sure of his name. Georgina's man.'

They are at the other end of the room surrounded by a cluster of well-wishers. Georgina and her familiar man. An attractive couple, both fair-haired and tall. He has his hand lightly on her arm and is laughing at something she has said, his head thrown back.

'Can you find out for me? Let me know.'

'Yes. If it's important.' A touch of surprise in his tone.

'Not now,' I say quickly. 'I'll ring you. Goodnight, Peter. Thank you for everything.'

The garden is lit up, subtle lighting illuminating a careful beauty, years of growth and work. After the noise of the party, the outside world is quiet and calm, and I pause for a moment to enjoy the stillness.

The front door stands open, gives off a rectangle of thick, yellow light against the outside darkness. As I watch there is a flicker of movement as someone passes through it. The dark figure of a man stands there unmoving, looking out at the garden. Back-lit, his face is in shadow and I cannot make him out. The anxiety of earlier strengthens, as though for some unknown reason it is me he is watching. At the gate I look back. The figure has not moved.

I park the car in my space in the back alley and use the rear entrance to the shop. There is a bunch of flowers pushed into the alcove, hard up against the door. A huge armful, tied together with rubber bands, wrapped in florist's paper. In the office I read the card, the familiar, cramped writing. *Lyn. I understand how you feel about what happened. I can only hope you will forgive me. Barry.*

I breathe in the scent, the sweet, cloying scent of roses. Perfect pink buds nestle among feathery sprigs of gyp and heather. Where, I wonder, is Clarissa? Barry has moved from apologies over the phone to apologies with flowers. The stakes are going up. A bunch of flowers as compensation for lies and infidelity. Roses to wipe the slate clean. I put the flowers in the office sink, weary of the situation. Tired of meaningless apologies.

I go to bed, but I am anxious, keyed up by uncertainty, and sleep is slow to come. My thoughts leap from one subject to another. Barry. The woman in the shop. The man who followed her in. The man at the party with his evasive eyes. I am tired, though, my body heavy with fatigue, and ironically it is in the last drifting moments before sleep that realisation strikes. I sit up with a start, my heart thumping in my chest, the shock of recognition, sudden as a hammer blow.

Georgina's young man with the furled white shirt and slicked-back hair has transformed in my mind. It was the formality that put me off, because as a rule I am good with faces. I know without doubt where I have seen him before. The young man, scruffily dressed in old jeans and a windcheater, his eyes boring into the girl, flicking over the passengers. Watching me as I take out my knitting, and turning away. Georgina's man. The watcher on the train.

# Chapter Six

*Those mountain ranges, far and near, enclasp me, – sharply pencilled there,*
*Like blackest sea-waves, outlined here, like phantoms in the luminous air,*
*Between that cold and quiet sky, and the calm river running by.*
*'By the Camp Fire', Ada Cambridge*

On Sunday I go home. I bundle up some things I won't be needing, clear some space in the office. Home is the old family home, a farm of sorts, where I grew up. After Mum died, Adele and I shared it. We didn't live together but used the house as a convenience, time out when needed. A space of our own away from Melbourne. Sometimes our visits coincided, mostly they didn't.

On the Eastern Freeway, driving out of town, I am aware that I am doing this still, using the house as convenience, as a refuge. This is only the second time I have been back in the eighteen months since Adele died, since the day of her funeral.

The first time was about a month ago. Even operating in a fog of disbelief and betrayal, I knew it was a mistake, that Barry himself was a mistake. The trip was quiet, both of us sunk into our own thoughts. Where Barry's were I don't know. With her, probably, the ecstasy, the swinging moods of infidelity.

'We're adults, Lyn. These things happen. Can't we still go away as we planned? Talk things through, sort it out.'

My thoughts were busy with the relationship, the futility of it all. It had been a prop after Adele, something to keep me afloat. But the mutual support had faded early, the relationship sliding easily into habit. And no, these things don't just happen, like an earthquake or a flood, but people like Barry *make* them happen, let them happen. Basic rules of honesty and fidelity broken when it suits. I had made the firm decision that I didn't want a relationship like that.

We didn't stay. We didn't even come into the house, but walked around the garden, overgrown and neglected, talking it out. It was raining, a thin drizzle that found its way down the back of necks, and the long grass soaked our shoes. We drove back to Melbourne in damp, unpleasant silence. At the flat I collected my things and left.

My feelings now are mixed, difficult to analyse. Sadness, of course, a sense of reluctance at coming back, at opening this particular can of worms and yet basically I am glad. A churning gladness deep within, like a child at Christmas. For some reason it is time. Time to come home. Time to recoup. Time to go forward.

Kangaroo Ground. The road sweeping upwards, higher now in altitude. The air changes, becomes crisper, fresher. The day is clear, sparkles beneath a thin winter sun. On a high crest of hill I catch a glimpse of the distant city, the road winding back behind me. The cubes and blocks of far-off buildings thrust upwards to catch the sun. Light glistens on spines of concrete, shines in a million chinks of glass. The city seems unreal, hovering Houdini-like above the unseen bedrock. The road turns again and rises higher, winding towards the distant looming ranges, flecked with patches of snow. I am nearly home.

I park the car in the garage and walk around the veranda, looking out at the familiar swell of hills. The land rolls gently away in all directions, rising up to meet the distant ranges: Dandenong, Macedon, Warburton. I have always loved the names themselves, fluid names, resonant, like the song of birds.

In the frail winter light, the hills are starker than I remembered, an intense cobalt blue. I had forgotten how beautiful they were. I stand there for a long moment, swallowing at the sudden lump in my throat. It stays firmly in place.

The front door swings open when I turn the key. There is an envelope pushed under the door. I pick it up and open it, delay the moment of impact, the moment of meeting the house. Inside the envelope, a note and an electricity bill.

*Dear Lyn*
*This was delivered to my house recently. Does a bill from the* SEC *indicate a return? Please forgive an old Nosy Parker, but I do hope so. We all miss you and the family. Pop in when you can.*
*Lucy*

Lucy. My nearest neighbour, half a kilometre away. Someone has made an error, though. I have not used any electricity. The power has been turned off at the mains. I check the details: the date, the address, the billing period, the amount. The bill is for the current period and totals $17.65. It makes no sense. I put it in my bag and turn back to the house.

It stands before me, expectant but hushed, as though it too is unsure after this long period of isolation. I walk through the empty rooms, lingering here and there, waiting for the kick of recriminations, the whisper of voices, the ghosts of sadness and loss.

Mum is here of course, as she often is in my thoughts, but in this house her presence is almost tangible, felt in every room, in almost every memory. In my mind's eye she is smiling, holding out her hands to welcome me back. Against this glow of warmth, I settle into the house, feel its presence around me, comfortable as old shoes, welcoming as a friend. But the atmosphere is cold and stale. I open blinds, windows, doors, let in light and air. Through each window a remembered composition of trees and plants and distance.

All the rooms speak of neglect, of dust, of a lack of care. In the lounge, paintings and photos look out at me from their accustomed positions. Among the family's pictorial history there is one of my grandfather and his friend George Smith, together with the children: Adele, Alexander Smith and me. Alex is almost as tall as the grown ups. Adele and I are small children, dressed in stiff dresses with stiff, photo smiles.

Smithy was a frequent visitor to the house in the old days. As a young man, he would stay at weekends and go off into the bush, studying the wildlife. Adele and I dogged his footsteps until Mum stepped in and directed us on to some task or other.

There are photos of us all on a gallery of occasions. My parent's wedding, graduations, anniversaries, sporting events, book launches. There is one of Adele after winning the State Championship. Adele the sprinter, fastest in Victoria over 100 metres. She is holding her trophy and smiling, her face full of energy. I wipe the thin sheen of dust from the glass and hug her to me.

My room, the room of my growing up, is as I left it. I sit on the floor next to my bookcase and flick through the old books. On the bottom shelf is a box of my own work, the stories and plays that I wrote as a child.

I am so engrossed in reading, I don't notice the passage of time. My head is full of old memories, old stories, old events, clear as yesterday. My stories are of ghosts and witches and improbable villains. 'Imaginative,' the teachers commented, usually in red biro at the bottom of the page. On one story is the cryptic comment, *Lyn's imagination carries her too far*. I had forgotten this, this concern with my imagination, considered then as overactive. How long ago it all seems and how improbable now. All those years in between, focused on the demands of business. No room at all for undisciplined flights of imagination.

And then suddenly it is almost too dark to read. A heavy, winter darkness, falling thickly, suddenly. I get up, stiff and cold, my mind fuzzy. I switch on the bedroom light, close the blinds and doors. I light the heater and feel the spring of instant warmth.

Adele's room is the last taboo, the last uncertainty. I hesitate at the door, unsure of the ghosts inside. Adele could be here. At any moment she could step out from her room, young and alive, her clear voice ringing with disappointment. 'Lyn, why didn't you come? I wanted you to come. Where were you?'

Coward-like, I don't go in. I have no answer save postponement.

I am aware of a small sense of unease that has nothing to do with Adele. A sense of something being wrong, a small but persistent undercurrent to my thoughts. I am tired, though, and preoccupied with other things, in no frame of mind to work it out. I make up my old bed and sleep easily, dreamlessly, and wake at first light, not to the alarm, but to the sound of birds. Somewhere outside a magpie is warbling into song, light and clear as a flute. I had forgotten this. The noise of it. I dress, ready for work, but there is time before I leave for a quick look around.

Next to the fence line is Grandad's old shed, and behind this, stretching away as far as the eye can see, are acres of uncleared land. Bushland, untouched and uninhabited. A flock of galahs sweep above my head, a blush of pink and grey.

The shed is a large one, but has been on the edge of bush for so long it seems to have blended into it. Adele and I always talked about having a garage sale, about getting rid of some of the old junk stored here for decades. Something we never got round to. I stop, surprised. There are tyre tracks at the door. Fresh tyre tracks through fresh mud, the imprints sharp and clear. The padlock looks all right, but when I test it to see if it is locked, the shaft twists uselessly away from its housing. The metal has been cut through. I twist the shaft back into position. The cut is unnoticeable.

I open the door and light floods into the interior, touches the disorganised clutter of generations. There are shelves on

43

both sides of the shed and a large workbench in the centre. All available surfaces are strewn with bridles, saddles, harnesses, tyres, ladders, tools, nets, seed, fertiliser, weedkiller, gold pans, table-tennis bats, dart boards, old bottles. The shed is a storehouse for assorted, homeless things.

It is impossible to tell if anything is missing. Who after all these years would know? The shed floor is earthen; soft, dusty earth undisturbed by wind and rain. There are no obvious prints and, when I walk across the floor to test my own footprints, the dust rises and settles indeterminately.

The tyre tracks are two sets of parallel lines. One coming in, one going out. A little way up the drive, they merge and become one. Near the shed, the car must have spun its wheels in the mud. There is a splatter against the shed wall, a tell-tale groove in the ground. The few footprints are deep indentations in the soft earth. I place my foot inside them. Mine are tiny in comparison.

I feel cheated and apprehensive. I have come to get away, to be free of problems and mysteries. The knowledge that something is going on in the shop is bad enough, but here in this old sacred ground, it strikes as untenable.

The bush stretches out beyond the fence line, still but not silent, for the bush is never silent. Unseen birds provide a mosaic of sound, and suddenly, unexpectedly, a flock of cockatoos squawk above me in mid-flight, a demoniacal screech that takes me by surprise, but fills me with delight. I watch them fly away, back towards the house. Their feathers are an iridescent white. Above the subdued colours of the bush, they seem to glow.

I close the house, switch off the power at the meter and understand, instantly and belatedly, what caused my sense of unease last night. In my room, I had reached for the light switch and the room had flooded with light. Yet switching off the power at the mains is part of the process of leaving this house, something that I always do, something I have never forgotten. At the fuse box, the lights and appliances switch had been on. I turn all the switches off now, and double check it. I worry about this all the way back to the city. Could I, in the distraction of Adele's death, have left it on? Or has someone else pressed the switch?

# Chapter Seven

*Have a care, lady, oh, have care –*
*How can you will what you will not snare?*
*'On a Grey-haired Old Lady Knitting . . . ', Furnley Maurice*

At half-past eight I buy coffee at Flinders Street station and sit on one of the stools, facing towards Swanston Street. I am in shade, but outside the wide roof of the station, the sun is out. In sunshine the city looks cleaner, fresher, almost festive. I sip my coffee, watching the endless streams of people. When I see the woman, she is coming from an unexpected direction, crossing over the road from Princes Bridge station. She has done something to her hair. It catches the winter sun, like Adele's use to, a blur of shining paleness. Her resemblance to Adele is more striking than ever. She looks young and pretty, more confident than last week. I check the time. It is ten minutes to nine.

She sits a few seats away and puts her wallet on the bench in front of her. I study the faces at the station, wondering if the man is here, standing somewhere out of sight, watching her. A train comes in and a mass of people surge over the concourse. New customers arrive and someone sits between us. She finishes her coffee, retrieves the wallet from the bench and moves off. I watch her walk down Flinders Street and turn in at the Elizabeth Street entrance. The same procedure as last time. No one follows her. There is no sign of the watcher.

At work, I ring Vanessa to thank her for the party. She is not there and her secretary tells me she is away for the week, a business trip, expected back on Friday.

'Can I talk to Peter Ireland please?'

A click and then piped music.

'Peter Ireland.'

'Peter, this is Lyn Blessing.'

'Lyn!' His voice lifts in delight. 'I wanted to ring you, but Vanessa's gone off to Sydney with your phone number in her book. For some reason the secretary hasn't got it. Or so she tells me.'

I laugh. 'Sounds efficient.'

'Well, hardly.'

'First day in?'

'Mm. Not a good idea with Vanessa being away. It was unexpected though, some contract or other that was in jeopardy without Vanessa's sure touch. But without her, there's only so much I can do.'

'Roll on Friday.'

'As you say. Lyn, I was wondering . . . would you have dinner with me?'

I hesitate, but the need to fill my time is still strong.

'A business dinner of course,' he adds quickly.

'Well, why not?' I agree.

'Any particular day?' he asks.

'Wednesdays are good for me.'

'Great. You can begin my introduction to Melbourne's restaurants. The only catch is, you'll have to choose the restaurant.'

I tackle the reason for my call. 'Peter, did you find out his name? Georgina's man.'

'Mm. I checked the guest list. Name of Jason.'

'Jason who?' I ask.

'Stavros,' he answers with a note of surprise, as though the answer were obvious.

A relative, then. I remember his doting attention, his laughter at something she had said, his head thrown back. An element of flirting. I had not thought of him as a relative.

'Peter, I need to get in touch with Georgina. Can you let me have her address?'

A small pause. 'Can't help you there, Lyn. We can't give out addresses.'

'Peter, it's really important. I wouldn't ask otherwise.'

Again he hesitates before answering. 'Is there anything I can do?'

'No. Not really, it's complicated.'

'She's a very private person, Lyn. I couldn't break the rule. Not even for you.'

I hadn't really expected anything else. Despite the delay it will cause, part of me is pleased at this policy of protection.

'If I write her a note, will you pass it on?'

'With pleasure.'

Better, then, than nothing.

'Fair enough. I'll send it through you.'

'About dinner, Lyn. Do you have a favourite place?'

The bell on the shop door rings. A customer comes in bringing with him a blast of cold air.

'Gertrude's in Collins Street is meant to be good. You'll need to book. I'll meet you there, if you like. Say seven-thirty.'

'Look forward to it.'

A voice at my shoulder as I hang up. 'Ms Blessing?'

'Yes.'

'Jack White.' He offers me his hand. 'My aunt directed me here. She says you may be able to help. I'm after a particular book, but so far I've had no success.' He smiles engagingly.

'What is it that you collect, Mr White?'

'Australian poetry mainly. I'm after a book on Adam Lindsay Gordon. A memorial volume. My aunt tells me you're something of a specialist on Gordon. She seemed to think you might have it, or at least know of it.'

'I think I can help you.'

I lead him to a display cabinet. The book itself emerges from the original box, a portrait of Gordon on the front. I unlock the cabinet and take it out. The price is $360.

'The very one! I've looked everywhere for this. And in better condition than I'd hoped.' He is delighted, holds the book gently. I feel a pang of regret at its sale, anything by Gordon is like an old friend, but this is one I have recently decided to part with. Even in terms of space I cannot afford to keep everything.

'My lucky day, Ms Blessing. Thank you so much.'

In the quiet moments I compose a letter to Georgina. After a few false starts I settle on this version.

*Dear Ms Stavros*
*My name is Lyn Blessing and I had the pleasure of meeting you briefly at your book launch on 29 August. I have also published with Vane Publications and would like to interview you regarding a work on Melbourne University and its successful women graduates. I would be grateful for your contribution.*

I enclose my card, the dark green script bold against pale cream.

> *Lyn Blessing*
> *Antiquarian Bookseller*
> *Flinders Street, Melbourne*

If I judge correctly, the publication lure should do the trick. As a new author, she wouldn't want to let the opportunity pass by.

# Chapter Eight

*Dressed is the beautiful city — the spires of it*
*Burn in the firmament stately and still;*
*'The Melbourne International Exhibition', Henry Kendall*

The restaurant is set high above the city. An elegant, spacious room, a show of flowers, white linen and careful lighting. Peter and I arrive together and he smiles in greeting, takes my hand in his own, holds it longer than is strictly necessary. He is dressed more casually than at the party, jeans and a beige cord jacket. His hair too is wilder, not so firmly slicked down. We are led to a table at the window and the lights of the city surround us, its endless buildings and spires lit up against the night sky. Our eyes are drawn to the view as metal to a magnet.

I find myself relaxing with the ease of our conversation, enjoying his company and the warmth and elegance of the room. When the waiter arrives we order racks of lamb, chocolate roulade and a bottle of Brown Brothers' wine. I point out the landmarks that I know: the inky blackness of parklands, the dark ribbon of river, the strings of lights lining roads and clusters defining buildings. Before our meal arrives I hand him the letter. The name, Georgina Stavros, written in large letters on the envelope.

'That was quick.' He puts the letter in his jacket pocket.

'Don't forget, will you? It's important.'

'Trust me, Lyn. First thing tomorrow I'll send it on.'

'What time did the party finish up?' I ask, pursuing an element in the puzzle.

'Late. Three o'clock, thereabouts. You were an early finisher, Lyn.'

'Peter, did you come to the doorway when I left? There was a man there about your height. I wondered if it was you.'

He doesn't answer for a moment and then shakes his head. 'No. After you left I was busy with Georgina. Something she wanted to discuss in private. Hardly the appropriate place, but you know authors. No sense of the conventions.'

'And her man. Was he in on the discussion?'

'No. He left soon after you. Georgina went home on her own. She wasn't too happy about it.'

'Well, no. She wouldn't be.' A disappointment. Something she didn't need on a night dedicated to her success.

'Did you see him leave?' I ask.

He shakes his head. 'No. Vanessa told me. Georgina was as mad as a snake about it. And after she got over being mad, she got worried, thought something might have happened to him. Not very fair on her, considering.'

So his departure was sudden and, to Georgina, inexplicable. Safe to assume it was him looking out, watching me leave. The mystery deepens and I feel a stab of anxiety. Why? What did he do after I drove away?

'What is it about this man, Lyn? Why all the interest?' Peter asks, staring at me. I must look as puzzled as I feel.

Our racks of lamb arrive, tempting and fragrant, giving me time to answer. 'Only curiosity. I've met him somewhere before.'

My evasion is too obvious, but I leave the silence empty, fill the awkwardness by concentrating on the food.

'I like your restaurant, Lyn,' he says eventually. 'A good choice.'

'Thank you. I like being so high up. A customer recommended it.'

'And tell me, what are you working on at the moment?'

I continue the lie I told Georgina. 'Two things really. A collection of poetry focusing on Melbourne's history. I'll do the context stuff again, find out what was making news at the time of writing. Try for an angle on the writers. And I'm also thinking of a work on female graduates from Melbourne University. The ones who are making their mark.'

'Two books, Lyn. Excessive, isn't it?'

'Known for it. And you? How are you liking Melbourne?'

We look again at the city sparkling around us, the distant lights flickering like stars.

'Love it.'

Despite the flow of conversation, there is a stiffness about him, a touch of formality. Against Vanessa's fluid briskness, I wonder how he will fit in. What role Vanessa has assigned him.

'How do like working with Vanessa?' I ask, following the thought.

He smiles then, a oddly sweet smile. 'She's a hard act to follow. A bit of a whirlwind. My role is to keep the home fires burning while Vanessa sets sail, sweeping all before her. The duller side of publishing.' Admiration in his tone, perhaps the barest trace of discontent.

'She's good at what she does,' I comment evenly. 'Exceptionally good.'

'And she inspires loyalty,' he says, smiling at my too obvious leap to her defence.

I laugh. 'She does.'

'To loyalty, Lyn.'

He raises his glass and I think fleetingly of Barry and his lack of loyalty. We linger over coffee and dessert, pass the time pleasantly enough with small talk, with only a few awkward lapses in conversation. On balance I am pleased I came. On balance I think Vanessa is lucky to have him as a partner.

'Can I see you home?' he asks eventually.

'I'm going back to the shop, Peter. I have some work to finish off.'

'To the shop, then? I'd like to see it if you don't mind. Vanessa's told me all about it.'

'Of course. I'll be pleased to show you.'

Again the walk through city streets. Collins Street, the trees illuminated by fairy lights, the grey open space of the City Square, the Cathedral, the station. With company I use the front entrance, lock the door behind us and switch on the lamps. The shop fittings gleam in soft lamp-light. Rich mahogany, leather bindings, fresh flowers.

'Lyn, it's beautiful. Can I look around?'

'Of course.'

I work in the shop, filling in time on the next catalogue, but as usual I become absorbed. When Peter arrives at my shoulder I am surprised to find that a whole hour has passed.

'Lyn, your shop is great. I'm knocked out by it.'

'Thank you. Yes . . . I love it too.'

'There's so much history here. I could spend a day and not get bored.'

'You're welcome any time,' I say, meaning it.

'Thanks, Lyn. And thanks for this evening. I enjoyed it. And don't worry, I'll send your letter on.'


He rings the next day.

'Lyn, I sent the letter off first thing, but Georgina has just phoned. She's coming in on Tuesday at twelve o'clock. I thought that, seeing as it was important, you could be here, meet her here. I'll introduce you.'

'Wonderful. Thank you for thinking of me.'

I make a note in my diary for Tuesday. In large letters I write Georgina Stavros. Twelve o'clock. And then I plan my strategy.

# Chapter Nine

*Can you snare, do you think,*
*The bell-bird clink . . . ?*
*'On a Grey-haired Old Lady Knitting . . . ,' Furnley Maurice*

By Friday morning I am ready, waiting for the woman's arrival.

'Jordie, this may sound strange, but can you stay late this afternoon. I need you to video someone for me.'

'What for? What have they done?' She sounds alarmed.

'There's two of them. A woman first, then someone follows her in. I want to see what they're doing.'

'What about the security cameras? Don't they pick it up?'

'No. It's the only place in the whole shop they don't.'

'Sounds convenient.' Her tone is dry.

At twelve o'clock I set the video up, ready to film. Jordie goes out to buy our lunch. We eat on the go, me between customers, Jordie while she works.

At one o'clock Jordie files the invoices and accounts, packs away the laptop. To get a stable position at the one-way glass, Jordie needs to use the bearer for support. The old filing cabinet is in the way. I try pulling it back from the wall but it is heavier than it looks. Jordie adds her weight and the cabinet slides easily away. She squeezes into position, camera ready. I go into the shop, clipboard and pen in hand as though stocktaking. I work at the back of the shop, close to the classics shelves, but as far away from Eliot as I can get.

One-fifteen. Dead on time the door bell clangs. Footsteps on the wooden floor, coming towards me. She hesitates when she sees me but I smile at her faintly and keep on with my audit. She is uneasy at my presence but I am boringly repetitive, engrossed with the details on my clipboard. She takes down the book and I see that it is the same one as last week. *The Mill on the Floss*. I hear the book being replaced. Again footsteps on wooden flooring, the clang of the door bell.

I flick through the book, looking for the clue, for what she is telling him. Again, there are no signs, nothing to show me what she is up to. The phone rings and I think of Jordie in the office, unable to answer it. With the book still in my hand I go into the office. Jordie is in position, the camera still running.

'Good afternoon, Blessing's Books.'

With the receiver crooked against my neck, I turn the pages slowly. I see then what I didn't see in the shop's duller light. A hair. A single strand of blonde hair, strong and wiry.

I remember the girl's fumbling action as she opened the book, the quick touching of her head. It is hard to concentrate on the call. An enquiry about books, an early edition of John Gould's *Birds of Australia*. I wrench my mind back to the stock. The customer sounds pleased, promises to call that afternoon. I replace the receiver.

A bookmark of sorts. I photocopy the double page. The hair makes a thin, wavy line between the pages. Pages 100 and 101. The dense text on both pages is preoccupied with the misbehaviour of both Maggie and Tom Tulliver. Is there is a clue in all this? If so, what?

'Lyn.' Jordie's whisper is loud. 'Is this him?'

I turn quickly. A man in the shop, moving slowly but surely towards the classics shelves. If this is him, he is earlier than I expected. I close the office door and go into the shop, leaving the book in the office. I work my way slowly to the back of shop, ostensibly checking the shelves as I go. He looks fleetingly at different books, but I can sense that he is not really interested. Most of my customers are after books in certain categories, books by certain authors, books by specialist publishers, and concentrate their search accordingly. This man picks out books at random, looks at them perfunctorily and replaces them on the shelf. Different books from different subject areas, no two the same.

A different man from last week, but a similar type: young, casual, unremarkable. At the classics shelves his search becomes more intent. This, I am certain, is what he is really after. All else is pretence. The same shelf that interested the girl interests him. The shelf housing copies of Dumas, Eliot, Fielding. He takes a book from the shelf, looks at it closely, turns it in his hand.

'Can I help you?' I ask.

He is preoccupied, uninterested in me, barely turns to look. 'No, thanks. Just looking.'

He puts the book back, takes another down, examines it closely, turns the pages. I think of the marked book still in the office and feel uneasy. He leaves soon after and pauses outside the shop. He looks up and down Flinders Street as if unsure of what to do next.

Jordie joins me at the window and we stand together watching him. I make an instant decision. When the man moves off, I slip out of the door, wave a quick gesture of goodbye. Jordie stares after me, open-mouthed.

The man is broad in the shoulders and his jacket has a distinctive stripe around the collar, easy to keep in view despite the crowds. I walk behind him up Flinders Street to the Swanston Street intersection. He stops at the lights as if ready to cross and then suddenly turns back, enters Young and Jackson's, the pub on the corner.

I follow him into the bar. It is lunchtime and crowded. He

places his order. I sit away from him on a stool at the far edge of the bar. He takes his beer to a table at the window and sits there drinking idly, looking out at the intersection beyond. He doesn't meet anyone. He doesn't talk to anyone.

My choice of seating is a bad one. An old man next to me turns and breathes alcohol in my face.

'Hello, love.'

The whites of his eyes are dull, etched with heavy red lines. I turn away, keep my eye on the man at the window.

'I said hello.'

The old man's voice rises, shrill and penetrating against the background noise of the bar. He looks at me with easy, drunken belligerence, a dribble of spit escaping from his mouth. Everyone turns to look, including the man at the window and I move away, any chance of anonymity gone.

'Bloody snob,' the drunk calls after me.

I am too late. By the time I get to the doorway, the man has already gone. I can see him across the road, blending with the station crowd. The light is red against me, the traffic already moving. I cannot follow.

Jordie is at the door when I get back.

'You were quick. What happened? Lyn, what is this all about?'

I tell her about the hair in the book, the anticlimax, of having got as far as the pub on the corner. The drunk. About how everyone turned to look. Her face is oddly still, as if the emotions can't quite show through.

'Lyn, I hope you know what you're doing.' Her voice is cool.

'Obviously not,' I say, stung by her remark.

'Was it deliberate?' she asks suddenly. 'I mean ... did he know you were following?'

I shrug. 'How can you tell?'

Jordie looks at me speculatively. 'Next time I'll go.'

'Thanks, Jordie. I think that, whatever it is, it is out of our league.'

'You should come with me to self-defence.'

Jordie has a black belt in karate. This is one of the few personal things she talks to me about. This is the first invitation into her life.

'I hope I won't need to.'

She puts her hand on my arm. The gesture surprises me, compensates for her diffidence earlier. Not like Jordie to show affection.

'Got to go. Sorry Lyn, but my next port of call waits. Look after yourself, won't you?'

'Yes. Thanks.'

She doesn't turn to go as I expect, but stays where she is, regarding me firmly.

'Lyn I don't know what's going on. I don't want to intrude but . . . you're the nicest boss I have. If you need any help, ring me.'

I watch her walk up the street, black hair, black clothes, black boots. A tall woman, slim but strong, light on her feet. She doesn't turn or look around but keeps undeviatingly to her path. People fill the space between us and I can no longer see her. Without her familiar presence I feel suddenly vulnerable. I shake my head in irritation at the thought.

# Chapter Ten

*How much terror, how much truth?*
*Here all the howling fates are loosed.*
*'On a Grey-haired Old Lady Knitting. . .', Furnley Maurice*

The video is there like a presence, waiting to be played. I resist the temptation. I want to watch it uninterrupted, to give it my whole attention. The rest of the day passes slowly.

Five-thirty. Closing time. I am just turning the sign on the door to CLOSED when I see the woman. She is standing just outside the shop, looking scared. I open the door. The air is cold with the promise of rain, but now a blustering wind stirs up dust and grit, blows it in my eyes.

'Come in a minute. Get out of the wind,' I say.

She is hesitant, but the wind is cold and the shop inviting. I close the door behind us.

'I saw a book here today. I wonder if you still have it?'

Her voice is low, the vowels flat and drawn out. Her face is colourless, the skin around her eyes and mouth tinged with blue. She is shivering with cold. The wind buffets against the windows, pushes hard against the glass. It is coming in waves, the initial blast, loud and thumping. She is nervous. I pull the blinds down, close out the darkening street.

'Which book was it?' I ask.

I am undecided, unsure of the best tactic. Now she is here, I long to know.

'*The Mill on the Floss*. Do you have it?'

She feels the locket dangling from her ear as if for luck, for reassurance.

'This way.'

She follows me to the back of the shop. I pick the book from the shelf, the same book I had taken into the office earlier. The book she had marked. She looks at it in wonder.

'He said it wasn't marked. He said I'm unreliable. He was angry. I've never seen him so angry. He said that because of me, they'd missed . . .'

Her voice trails off, she is confused, wary, lost in thought. The silence grows.

'It's a code, isn't it?' I ask.

She doesn't answer, doesn't seem to understand.

'What you do with the books. It's a code, isn't it?' I repeat. 'Some sort of message you are passing on.'

I see in her eyes that the penny has dropped, see the flash of instant fear.

'Who *are* you?'

She looks straight at me, her skin paler than before. Her eyes roll upwards, the whites glimmering in the dull light. She collapses into a crumpled heap on the floor, her breath fast and shallow. I bend down to touch her hand, to find the pulse on her wrist. Her skin is cold as ice, but the pulse beats strongly enough. She doesn't stir to my touch. She doesn't react in any way. I collect some bedding from the office, slide a pillow under her head, a blanket over her body. The smell of alcohol on her breath is strong. I put the kettle on, prepare some hot, sweet tea. While the water boils I go through the things in her bag.

There is little enough. A comb, a wallet with some money, a small Spirax notebook, the binder type, with most of the pages ripped out. On one page, in shaky writing, are the numbers '335'; on another, two phone numbers: 660 5859, 819 8118. There is nothing else. No driver's licence. No cards. No source of identity.

I go into the office and photocopy the numbers in the notebook, replace the originals in her bag. Her breath is still rapid, a shallow rise and fall. No change. Her locket earring on its long silver chain has been thrown away from her face and lies on the floor, close and inviting. Is there a photo inside? A lover perhaps. Do I dare risk it? The clasp is interwoven in the scrollwork of decoration, a clever disguise, but one I know because it is similar to my own. I touch the cool silver, feel its solid weight. On cue she stirs.

I pour the tea and stand over her while she comes to. Her lips are pale, but the tinge of blue has gone. She sits up with an effort. Her hands are shaking too much to hold the cup. I hold it for her and she drinks the tea thirstily.

'Sorry.' She is disoriented. 'I don't know why... I haven't eaten all day.'

'What's your name?' I ask.

She hesitates. 'Maggie.'

'Look, Maggie, stay here. I'll go down the road and get some food.'

She doesn't answer and I feel uneasy about leaving her, but there is nothing in the shop and first of all she needs to eat. I lock the door behind me.

I buy soup, sandwiches and a bar of chocolate from a café around the corner. The wind is as strong as ever. I walk fast, head down to keep the grit from my eyes, anxious to get back.

She is still there, sitting exactly where I left her. She seems to be in shock, incapable of decision. I hand her the soup. She holds the cup in both hands for warmth and drinks, slowly at first, and then greedily. She finishes the sandwiches and some of the deathly pallor leaves her face.

'You won't tell them, will you? That I've been here...' Thought processes are returning.

'No, of course not.'

'Who are you?'

'My name is Lyn. I'm a friend. I want to help.'

Her tone is contemptuous. 'Why? Why would you bother? You're one of them, aren't you? Of course, I should have known.' There is a wondering quality to her voice as though she is thinking out loud. 'They told me you weren't in it. Andy said they picked you specially. Old established business. Respected owner. No one would suspect.' She pauses for a minute. Her dark eyes are on my face, still and watching.

'I'm a friend, Maggie. Let me help.'

Some unspoken message passes between us and I know, in that instant, she trusts me.

'Have some chocolate.'

I offer her the packet. Her hand shakes slightly as she unwraps the silver paper, but she is much more in control.

'Who's Andy?' An attempt at casualness that doesn't quite come off. I'm not sure whether she takes it in or not.

Her voice is low and flat. 'At first I thought he knew what he was talking about, that he was clever. But he's changed. He follows me sometimes. He thinks I'll . . .' She breaks off.

'Andy follows you?'

'No. Not Andy.' She is doubtful at my lack of understanding, looks at me with huge, dark eyes.

'Maggie, let me help. Whatever it is you're involved with. Let me help.'

There is a sudden blast of wind against the glass. She jumps with fear, struggles to her feet.

'Maggie, don't go.' I grasp her wrist. My hand closes around it, encircles it completely. It is as thin as bone. 'I want to help you.'

I see the fear in her eyes waver, a flicker of indecision. She regards me steadily as though trying to make up her mind. And then another gust of wind, stronger than the last, and the moment is lost.

'Let go,' she hisses in sudden and compelling anger.

Her eyes are dark as coal. I drop her arm as if stung. She

struggles with the lock, slams the door behind her. The bell clangs loudly with her force.

'Wait, Maggie,' I call after her, but my voice is lost in the wind and the rumble of trams. Someone moves away from a window display further up the road. I can see Maggie still, a small figure in the distance. I lock the door and follow her. She crosses at the Swanston Street lights and enters the station.

And everywhere, crowds and confusion, a cold darkness. I lose her, or she loses me. I'm not sure which. There are too many platforms, too many exits. I look at the banks of terminals, city platforms, suburban train lines. Times and destinations. Which platform is she on? Which line? Screens full of information tell me nothing.

# Chapter Eleven

*Thro' dismal vapours in the west*
*The weary Sun went down to rest;*
*Chill soaking rain, fell thick and fast*
*And loudly roar'd the southern blast*
*'Adventures on a Winter's Night in Melbourne, 1841', George Wright*

Back at the shop I watch the video, but I am edgy. The wind still blusters against the windows, rattles at the door, and I have Maggie's haunted face in my mind, feel some of her fear. The film winds on, shows me the unaware faces, the movements and procedures, normally clandestine, caught on film. Maggie turns the corner, comes into full view of the office, turns side on at the classics shelves. She takes down a book, places the hair and turns away. The films runs on, waiting for the man who follows. And then he too rounds the corner, comes closer to the office. I pause the tape to study his face more closely. But he is no one I know. No one I have met before, save for those few fleeting minutes in the shop.

I look at the photocopied pages. Different sets of numbers. I pass over '335' because it tells me nothing. The phone numbers: 660 5859, 819 8118. A city number. A Hawthorn number. Maggie got on the train at Glenferrie. I noticed the man some time after Hawthorn. Does he live there? But he could have been on the train all the time and I just hadn't noticed.

I think of Maggie, of the name Andy, of my 'being chosen'. I think of the man who scares her. The man who follows her, his watchful eyes. Not Andy, but someone else. I think of the shadow unpeeling itself from a shop front as I followed Maggie up the street. I think of the man I followed, the quiet elusiveness. The wind is strident now, blows relentlessly against the glass, no let-up, no periods of remission. I think of Smithy close by, the safety of his flat. Even now, whoever it is that so terrified her could be waiting, watching. Do they know about me? Do they know Maggie was here? I am out of my depth, unsure what to do.

I gather the pieces of evidence, the video tape and photocopies, stuff them into a large hold-all, my sleeping bag on top. I leave by the back exit and lock the door behind me. The wind pushes at my body, its dull roar mixed in with the sound of distant traffic. Too late I remember the torch. I hesitate but I am used to the alleys, can find my way easily without it. I move off into the darkness.

Tonight the alleys seem more a comfort than a threat, their darkness offering the protection of invisibility. I feel safer here than in the shop, safer than in the street. I turn out of the alley into the wider laneway just beyond and here the wind dies, kept at bay by the complicated barrier of the walls. A welcome stillness, an oasis of calm. But in that sudden silence I hear another sound. A sound that turns my knees to water. A footstep behind me. And another. And then a noise I can't identify. A sound like a baby's cry, muffled and unformed.

I pause, my heart loud in my ears, trying to be rational, to disobey the instinct of flight or fight, trying to decide on the safest thing to do. And again I hear footsteps, but closer now. Fear takes over and I run.

I take the longer way, the way I have been only once before, years back with Adele. The entrance, though, is close by. A doorway into a disused walkway, and further along an entrance to a shaft of sorts, a dark entrance offering the sanctuary of invisibility. A steep downwards slope into a tunnel that runs underground. What it was used for Adele and I never knew and couldn't ask. All these old passageways were out of bounds. I am no wiser now. I enter the narrow passageway, aware of the musty smell, growing thicker and more unpleasant as I descend into the bowels of Melbourne. The floor slopes steeply downwards, and then levels and turns into complete darkness.

I remember suddenly, as children, Adele and I playing here, her small, serious face caught in the light of her torch. How could I have forgotten the darkness? The heart-in-mouth feeling as we switched our torches off and stood there, darkness pressing in on us like a physical force. Between us the unspoken dare. Who would give in first? We waited for our eyes to grow accustomed to the dark, for the pupils to widen, to let in what light there was. It took me a while to realise that there was no light. We could wait for ever and the darkness would not lessen, would not change, because here the darkness was absolute. I gave up first, glad to snap on the switch, flood the tunnel with a bright beam of light. The grins and giggles of relief.

I don't stop. Impelled by fear, I use one hand to guide me, to feel my way along the rough, brick walls. I try not to think of rats and spiders or concentrate on the smell, thicker now and nauseating. My feet make no noise. The only sound is the rasp of my own breath and the blood pounding in my temples. I inch my way along the corridor, moving slowly in the darkness, trying to remember the way out. How far was it? But memory is fickle and no recollections stir.

I strain my ears, listening for footsteps, but hear only a muffled sound, a gentle gurgling, like running water. And then my hand reaches into nothingness. I feel around me. The wall I have used as a guide, the wall on my right, stops. I find the wall again and feel around, feel where it ends. But it doesn't just end, it turns. A corner of some sort. I take a pace straight ahead, but can feel nothing. I step back. I take a pace to the left. Nothing. Arms spanned, I feel about me, taking in the composition of the tunnel, and begin to understand. The tunnel I was in ends, branches off in two directions. A 'T' intersection. I have a choice, a blind choice because I have no knowledge to guide me. Adele and I never came this far. Left or right. I choose right.

In the new section, the floor seems to slope slightly downwards. I stop again to listen and the sound of running water is closer now. With luck an exit. I move more quickly, anxious to be out. A mistake, though, because my foot slips out from under me and I fall heavily on my side. A sharp bolt of pain runs through leg and hip and shoulder, and I feel myself slipping, falling. Then suddenly the shock of icy water. I am fighting for air, floundering, struggling to get upright, to get my head out of water. At last I break through, gulp in great mouthfuls of air.

I am standing waist deep in water. Slowly moving water, numbingly cold. Now I understand the reason for the slope, the reason for the tunnel itself. The thing that Adele and I never knew, never even guessed. The sloping floor leads to a central gutter, deep and narrow, and full of water. I feel a wave of revulsion. I am in a city drain.

I try and pull myself up, but the wall is too high. I press my palms against its edge and attempt to lever myself up, as if this were the local swimming pool. The strong, deft movement, the spring of the feet. But the ledge is too high and the drain walls offer no foothold.

Slowly I inch my way along, feeling for a grip, for a toehold, for any irregularity in height that I can use. I walk a step, feel with hands and feet. Walk a step, feel with hands and feet. I am cold, icy to the bone, and my legs are numb. And then, finally, a small miracle, a bar of sorts, smooth and reaching down into the water. With a heave, I haul myself out, and lie trembling and exhausted on the tunnel floor.

I am cold, deathly cold, and almost too tired to move. There is a dull ache in my side and my knees and elbows sting in the bitter air. I pick myself up and stand still for a minute, gathering the strength to go on. I hear nothing. I move closer to the wall, stumble against the rough bricks and jar my arm painfully. My eyes sting with tears. There is no sound anywhere save my own breath, faster now, and jagged as I fight the urge to cry. And all around me the unbroken darkness, thick and oppressive, closes in on me like a tomb.

How long I stand there, close to tears, gathering the strength and nerve to go on, I don't know. I think of the city, the clean bright lights not far above me, and begin to move. For ages it seems there is no change in the light, no easing of the darkness. But then I hear a small change, as though something has been added to the sound of moving water. At first I cannot place it, and then, moving on, I feel it. The air around me stirs. And I understand.

It is wind. I can hear it now, a low moan that sounds almost human, blowing somewhere outside the tunnel walls. I must be nearly there, near some exit, some way out. My hand moves off the rough brick, and touches emptiness. Here the floor slopes slightly upwards and I can feel the air stir against me. A long uneven slope, and the sound of the wind grows louder with every step I take. The tunnel turns sharply and the wind roars close by. I run to the sound.

Suddenly I am out. The wind presses against my clothes, moulds them around me like sheets of ice. I am standing outside the tunnel, standing in wind and open air. Above me stars and a half-moon; a remote, cold glitter that has never been so welcome or looked so beautiful. I fill my lungs with clean air. I know exactly where I am. The other end of this alley opens out into Smithy's courtyard. I am almost safe.

Around the next corner the streetlight casts its warm glow, splinters the courtyard into light and shadow. Again I hear a sound like a voice in the wind, a small moan, or is it just the wind itself. I hammer on Smithy's door, and the skin crawls on the back of my neck.

He opens the door promptly and I slip inside, gasping for breath and totally incoherent. He looks at me, bewilderment showing in his face. He closes the door behind me and passes a blanket from the cupboard.

'Stay here.'

He locks the door behind him with a key. I pull the blanket around me and sit on the carpet in the lit stairwell, trying to imagine what he sees, where he goes. The minutes pass slowly, uncertainly. My wet clothes cling achingly to my body. I cannot stop shivering. I hear his footsteps first, a soft pad on concrete, and then the key turning in the lock. He bolts the door behind him.

'Was there anyone?' I ask.

He puts his fingers to his lips and I see that he has been running. There is a faint sheen of sweat on his face, and his breath is short. We go upstairs and I stand dripping, next to the heater. He turns off the light and we look out over the deserted, dimly lit square. There is no one.

'He ran off when he saw me. Back through the alley. Back towards the shop.' Smithy looks at me questioningly. 'Who was he?'

'I don't know.' I shake my head. 'I didn't dare look around. What was he like?'

He shrugs. 'Taller than me, I think. I guess around six feet, maybe less, difficult to tell when you're running. Slim build, moved well, reasonably fit I'd say. I followed him back to Flinders Street. He bolted straight across the road, dodged behind a tram, and was gone. Almost killed himself.' A note of undisguised satisfaction in his voice at the thought. 'What was he doing Lyn?'

'He was following me. I heard someone behind me when I left my place, and then after, in the tunnel . . .'

'The tunnel! Bloody thing should have been bulldozed in years ago. What on earth were you doing there?'

'I was trying to get here, to get away from him. I thought it would be safer.'

'Safer! Christ, Lyn. It's a death trap. Listen. You're freezing. We'll talk later. Shower first.'

In the bright bathroom light, my face is pale against a dark line of bruising that extends from cheekbone to ear. There is a gash below my knee where I fell and my shin bone is scraped raw. My whole left side aches and, looking down, I can see the start of massive bruising. The shower is blissfully hot. I stand under its jet for ages, feeling the sting of water on cuts, the eventual thawing of cold in my bones. I wash my hair and wash it again. I scrub every part of me.

Smithy is still standing in the window looking out. When he sees me he pours coffee. I think of Maggie and, like Maggie, I cradle the cup for warmth. The coffee is hot and strong, hits my stomach with a jolt of warmth. In every mouthful a touch of fire.

'I added brandy,' Smithy explains. 'Strictly medicinal of course.'

'My bag!' I cry, suddenly remembering. 'I dropped it. In the tunnel somewhere. Maybe where I fell. It had everything in it.'

'Well, that doesn't matter too much, does it?' he asks, slightly mystified at the extent of my dismay. 'You can always replace whatever it is.'

'But you don't understand. It had all the information.'

Smithy is deep in thought. He looks at me directly. The kindly avuncular expression is no more, replaced now by something unfamiliar, something hard and assessing.

'What's happening, Lyn?' he asks. 'What is going on?'

I nod in acknowledgement of the question and sit on the couch, make myself comfortable before I begin. I take my time, collect my thoughts. I am careful of the chronology, making sure the story is told in sequence. Smithy is methodical, makes notes of dates and times and places as I speak, organises the information into a chart. I talk for a long time.

'The man in the shop today. Could he have followed you tonight?'

I can only assess the man's height and build from Smithy's estimation.

'It's possible, I suppose. But why would he? He barely looked at me in the shop.'

'But if he saw you following him.' he smiles.

That episode at lunchtime seems like a million years ago. I remember it with a sense of disbelief.

'I don't know if he saw me. How can you tell? I'm no detective, I admit.'

'No-o. I wouldn't say that. You've done amazingly well. Pity about the drunk.'

I laugh at the absurdity of it. I am beginning to feel warm and safe and it is good to talk. To share the fear and worry of it all. He reaches out and touches my arm, strokes the skin where the wide rough sleeve of his dressing gown ends.

'Feeling better?'

'Mm. Almost peaceful.'

'Don't get too comfortable. We've got things to work out.'

He doesn't say anything for a long time.

'What about the woman? She could have told whoever it was about you. What you said about the book being used as some sort of code.'

'Not much time. There would have been a period of about five minutes when I watched the film. Another five to get the shakes. Ten minutes maybe.'

'Plenty of time. He could have met her at the station. But anyway, let's work from the other end. Let's work out why. What's it's all about.'

I shrug. This is my own private stumbling block. The same question I have asked myself a thousand times, is still unanswered.

'Drugs?'

I am doubtful, though. My knowledge of drug smuggling is gleaned from books and television dramas. High stakes, high rewards, high degrees of professionalism. Too professional, surely, for messages passed on in a bookshop.

Smithy shrugs. 'As good a supposition as any at this stage.'

I glance quickly at his face. It is unreadable, but I wonder for a moment if he is patronising me.

'I have a video, Smithy,' I say evenly. 'I have them on tape.'

71

'You filmed it?'

'Yes. Well, Jordie did.'

'Jordie?' He looks blank.

'Yes, you know. Jordie Armstrong. She works for me.'

'Jordie filmed it?' he repeats quietly.

'Yes. But that's what I'm trying to tell you. I did have evidence, but it's gone. The video, everything. All the information. I lost it in the tunnel.'

'Where in the tunnel?'

'Where I fell, I think. At least I had it up to there.'

He shrugs. 'He's either got it by now or he hasn't. Morning will do.'

I think about the tunnel, the close darkness, the sickening surges of fear. I don't argue the point.

'The problem,' he continues thoughtfully, 'is why? I mean, why so complex? Why the cloak and dagger?'

We study Smithy's chart of times and dates as if we will find some answer there.

'Looks pretty hollow, eh? The only definite thing is that it's always Monday on the train, Friday in the shop, and the book is always the same one,' Smithy comments eventually.

'A code?'

'If it is a code, whatever is on the page must tell him something.'

'Obviously. If she goes to all the trouble of marking it,' I agree.

'Does the chart help in any way?' he asks.

I look at it carefully, but there are too many gaps in our knowledge, too little information. My attention wanders and I begin to yawn. Smithy looks at me and brings blankets and a pillow, throws them on the couch.

'Come on. Time for bed. We need to sleep on it. And by the way, Lyn, I'm glad you're okay.' He hugs me briefly.

'Thanks, Smithy.'

'Glad to help. Goodnight, Lyn. See you in the morning.'

The couch is deep and comfortable and I drift off to sleep.

Despite the bruises and abrasions, I sleep soundly, only vaguely aware that outside, some time in the night, the wind dies and is replaced by the sound of steady rain. A soft drumming on the roof, comforting as a pulse.

# Chapter Twelve

*But soon, like flowers, they're done*
*And leave no husk.*
*But the mind's things pass*
*Not readily away;*
'The Agricultural Show, Flemington, Victoria', Furnley Maurice

I wake slowly, reluctantly. Smithy is standing over me with a cup of tea in his hand. I feel sluggish and my whole body aches. I take the cup from his hand and drink the hot, sweet liquid thirstily.

'Sleep well?'

'Mm. Too well, too much brandy in the coffee.' I yawn.

'Ready to go soon?'

It takes me a minute to collect my thoughts. To remember last night, the sequence of events. I struggle to get up but my limbs are heavy and unwieldy.

'Your clothes are ready, they're on the back of the couch.'

I had forgotten about my clothes. Smithy must have stayed up after me, washing and drying them.

He is standing in the doorway, watching the rain. It has lessened now, falls as a thin drizzle. The umbrella is already wet, draining at the alley door and, on the small table, there is a damp copy of *The Age*. The front page a mix of politics and sport; more on St Kilda's Grand Final win, and the Labour government in trouble in the run-up to the election.

'Ready?' Smithy asks. He puts the umbrella up over our heads and smiles at me.

'I'm going to the shop to get my torch,' I say.

'I've got two,' he says, rummaging in pockets. 'You know me, Lyn. Something of a Boy Scout, always prepared.'

It is hard in daylight and in Smithy's company to remember the fear of the night before. In the clear morning light, the alleys and walkways no longer seem sinister, but merely dingy and depressing. The walls are high and grimy, the windows boarded up, doorways locked up with iron grilles, a scatter of rubbish, an erratic spread of weeds. We make our way to the back entrance of the shop, retrace the route I took the previous night. We meet no one.

We come to the shaft, the downwards slope to the tunnel. This time the heavy darkness is kept at bay by torchlight, two beams moving independently, lighting our way. At some stage, Smithy takes my hand and squeezes it as a gesture of reassurance, but I am okay. The whole episode last night seems unreal, as though it happened to someone else.

We walk close together, following my passage of the night before. Torchlight reveals unrealised dimensions that had been invisible last night in the darkness. The passageway is narrower than I had imagined, the roof lower, only inches above my head.

Torchlight on brickwork. Bricks of blue stone, the occasional vent, and every now and then a grille at our feet, a cover over a narrow gutter. On the floor, a dense layer of dirt and grime. We leave no footprints.

'Christ,' Smithy says, his voice echoing unnervingly down the tunnel shaft. 'Nightmare of a place. I haven't been in here since I was a kid. To think of you in here last night without a torch. You're braver than me.'

'No. Just more desperate.'

My voice too seems disembodied, echoes as Smithy's has

done, caught within the tunnel's solid walls. And surprisingly the smell is worse than I remember, as though the sheer panic and fear of last night left little room for other sensations. Today the smell registers fully, a choking, nauseating foulness that fills every breath.

We walk on, breathing shallowly and saying nothing. Every now and then Smithy touches my arm for reassurance. We find the place where the shaft ends and the tunnel branches in two directions. I guide Smithy into the right passageway and suddenly the light from our torches picks up the glint of water at our feet. For a brief second, it strikes me as a thing of beauty, like moonlight on the sea. We stop and look. This is the central drain, fed by a network of smaller drains and gutters leading into it. The water is sluggish, scum on its surface, like a dense layer of oil. I feel a return of the revulsion from last night. This is what I fell into. This, in my hair, my nostrils, my mouth.

I shine my torch on the ground, looking for the place where I fell in, for some mark or indication. I find it soon enough. An inconclusive groove, but probability suggests the mark of a heel skidding into the large drain. There is nothing else. And further along, but not much further, we find the bar reaching down into the water. A bar of smooth dark metal.

Last night the wade through waist-deep water had seemed interminable, but in reality it was less than thirty metres, less than the length of the city swimming pool.

'Nothing,' Smithy says, shining his torch around, looking for the bag. His voice is low and close.

'Unless it's in the water somewhere,' I say.

We walk back to the groove mark and play our torches into the murky water, moving slowly along its edge. There is nothing. We give up, find my point of exit, the upward shaft, the opening into the alley.

I blink in the bright daylight, my eyes adjusting to the difference in light. Despite the cold air, there are beads of sweat on Smithy's brow. We stand without talking for a minute. I can't quite grasp the fact that it has really gone, that all the evidence has really disappeared. No back-ups, no copies. I feel a sense of impotence and futility. Around me the alley walls look bleaker than ever.

'No copies?' Smithy asks, as though reading my mind.

I shake my head.

He puts his arm around me as he used to when I was a child.

'Never mind, Lyn. Something will turn up.'

It is when we go back into the main alley again that I see the rose. A splash of colour out of the corner of my eye. It is pressed hard against the wall and is almost hidden in weeds. The stem has broken, but the flower itself is perfect. An apricot rose, tight curled in bud, a scatter of raindrops.

'What is it?' Smithy asks.

I show him the rose. He looks at it blankly.

'Not yours?' I ask.

'Mine. God, no. Should it be?'

'I think it's from Barry,' I mumble.

'Barry? Your ex. That Barry?' Smithy snorts in surprise. 'Lyn, what on earth is going on?'

'I don't know. Someone left one on the doorstep of the shop. I thought it might have been you.'

He looks at me steadily, waiting for me to go on.

'It's like a trademark,' I explain. 'A calling card. I was here. You know the sort of thing.'

'But Barry?'

I can see the disbelief in his eyes. 'What are you saying, Lyn? That it was Barry who followed you last night?' He is having trouble getting his thoughts together, his sentences straight. 'That Barry is the person you ran from and nearly drowned yourself for?' His voice rises.

'I don't know,' I shout in sheer frustration. 'How am I supposed to know?'

He stops suddenly and comes towards me. 'Sorry, Lyn.' He puts his arm around me. 'I'm confused, that's all.'

'You're confused! How do you think I feel?'

And now the nagging thought, did I run for nothing? Were the footsteps in the alley last night only Barry? A friend of sorts. A meeting gone wrong. A meeting that I misinterpreted as sinister. A case of the spooks after Maggie? I look at the rose, blurred now with tears. A stupid, bloody rose.

# Chapter Thirteen

*I stop. I go again.*
*The bell commands above my head.*
*Next stop the province of the mad.*
*Twelve elephants are climbing on –*
*A lady, sad,*
*Who should be dead.*
*Hold on. Hold on.*

*'Tram Driver's Song', R. A. Simpson*

I catch the tram to St Kilda.

'What the hell did you think you were doing?'

Barry's doorstep. He blinks at the sudden attack. The hangdog look of surprise and hope already fading, but for all that he studies my face closely.

'Lyn! What happened...? Come in.'

'No thank you. I'm safer here.'

'Why are you acting so hostile...?'

'I *am* hostile, you bastard. I nearly died because of you.'

His heavy lids open and close in surprise. A flicker of fish eyes.

'What, Lyn? Tell me what I am supposed to have done.'

The curtains twitch in the next-door flat. The neighbours are interested. An aroma of coffee wafts out on to the doorstep, a safe, familiar smell.

'You know very well. Last night. In the alley.'

'What alley? Behind the shop?'

The man from next door comes out and locks his door

slowly. He nods as he passes, moving slowly, listening in.

'Come inside, Lyn. Please. We can talk more easily.'

I stand my ground.

'Christ. What is this? This is me, Lyn. Barry. You know, the man you slept with all those months. I'll leave the door open if you like. You're free to leave at any time. It's just that I think we should get this sorted out. Don't you?'

It makes sense. Standing here on his doorstep, I cannot really see him as a threat. I follow him inside. There is no sign of his new love, no female presence.

'Would you like some coffee, Lyn? I've just made some.' He is all efficiency, no touch of the personal. The only solution to this whole situation is to be businesslike, communicative.

'Thanks.'

While he pours the coffee, I wait in the lounge, read through the titles in his bookcase as I have done many times before. The morning sun slants through the curtains and it strikes me suddenly that I always felt safe here. A feeling that I took for granted, a feeling that has almost disappeared now.

I look around the room at the few possessions I left here, things I have no room for at the shop. Two old family paintings on the walls, a coffee table, a favourite chair. Barry carries in two steaming mugs. The coffee is as always, hot and strong. Barry sits in a lounge chair, I remain standing.

'Last night I left the shop late. Six-thirty maybe. Almost seven. I left by the back entrance. Someone was there. I heard their footsteps behind me. Whoever it was followed me. I went into the old tunnel and nearly drowned.'

'The tunnel?'

'Yes, you know. An underground drain.'

'Christ Lyn. You fool.'

'You do better when someone follows you.' My voice is angry.

He pauses. 'Did you see who it was?'

'Obviously not.'

He smiles. 'Sorry. Stupid remark. But, Lyn, why me? I mean

. . . why did you think it was me?'

'I stayed the night at a friend's. We went back this morning. There was a rose in the alley. An apricot rose.'

He whistles, a low sound of expelled breath. 'I see.' He gets up and paces the room.

'Look, Lyn. I don't know what's going on. I can assure you that it honestly has nothing to do with me.'

'Assurances come easy, Barry. Where were you last night?'

He blinks again and raises his hands, palms up, a familiar gesture. He doesn't take offence at my doubting him.

'Last night I was out with a client. A seven o'clock meeting. Dinner at Edward's. I didn't get home until after eleven.'

There is nothing unusual in this. Barry entertains regularly for work. Edward's is a restaurant we went to together sometimes. Good service, slightly upmarket, slightly pretentious. The perfect restaurant for impressing clients.

'I see. Just tell me one thing. Did you leave a single rose under my door the other day?'

His gaze shifts.

'No, Lyn. Not me.'

I finish the coffee, put my cup on the table.

'I'm sorry, Barry. It's seems as though I've made a mistake. Goodbye.'

At the door I turn back. He is standing in exactly the same place, looking after me, the forlorn, spaniel expression firmly in place.

I go to Pam's for tea and sympathy. She opens the door in her dressing gown. Her cloud of black hair is tied ruthlessly behind her head and her skin is the baby pink that speaks of long immersion in a hot bath. Her smile of welcome fades to disbelief when she sees the damage to my face, the stiffness of my movements.

'Lyn! What on earth's happened to you?'

'It's a long story. I thought I'd tell you over lunch.'

'The comment is reassuring if not the face,' she says drily.

'Okay. Make yourself a drink. I won't be long.'

She is back in fifteen minutes, dressed in stylish jeans, a blue jumper under a jacket a few shades darker. Her hair is back to its usual cloud. She jingles the car keys in her hand.

'Ready?' she asks.

We don't need to consult about where to go. Carlton has always been our stamping ground, the Italian district, next to the university. A district full of restaurants. We park the car in Rathdowne Street and walk to an old favourite on the corner. Good food, low prices, fish net on the ceiling. A haunt of university students past and present. I am unable to keep up with Pam's brisk stride, because my body is too sore. She slows to my pace, regards my stiffness with interest and a few shakes of her head and tucks a hand under my arm.

We order and I tell Pam about the tunnel, about the rose, about confronting Barry. We make our way through plates of pasta and salad, elegant domes of crème caramel and a bottle of wine before I have finished.

She looks at me quizzically. 'You don't do things by halves, do you? What do you think now?'

'At first, I thought that perhaps I'd panicked. That the sound of footsteps was only in my imagination. You know what it's like,' I say. 'The sound of the wind in the alley is really weird. It's possible to imagine anything you like.'

She nods agreement.

'But the fact remains, my bag is missing,' I say. 'Fact, not imagination.'

'And Barry? Do you think it was him?'

This is something I have thought about a lot, despite the swiftness of his denial. Denials come easily to Barry and I have no faith left in his honesty.

'I don't think Barry would have the imagination or the guts to be involved in anything shady or mysterious. Do you?' I ask, interested in another opinion.

'Hard to imagine, certainly,' Pam agrees thoughtfully. 'But

you never really know what people are capable of.'

'That's always the trouble. On the face of it, though, it seems unlikely. I think he was probably telling the truth about where he was, but I think he lied about leaving the rose at the shop. He wouldn't look at me.'

'What are you going to do?' Pam asks.

'I could ring the restaurant, confirm it with them.'

She nods. 'Good idea. At least then you'd know.'

There is a couple at a table in the corner. They are holding hands, gazing into each other's eyes. Love, I think. After Barry, who needs it?

'Pam. I hate to ask, but can I stay another night?'

'No.' Her gaze is serious, steady.

'No?'

'It's enough, Lyn. Something is going on out there. Something scary and you're involved in a way that we don't understand. You're either moving in with me for the duration or finding yourself some sensible accommodation. No more sleeping in offices. No more mad flights at night down city alleys.'

'I'll be in the way.'

She shakes her head with emphasis. 'As it happens, you won't. I've finished that software project I was working on. My time is now my own.'

'Software?' I ask, only vaguely aware of the details of her recent project.

She pulls a face. 'You obviously haven't noticed, but I have spent every available hour lately designing a software project to help students with reading problems.'

'I didn't know,' I say, feeling guilty at my preoccupation with my own affairs.

'Why should you? You have been busy with other things, or so I believe.' Her tone is dry. 'The software is aimed at students who can't differentiate between "b"s and "d"s, or "p"s and "q"s. The idea isn't new, I've just adapted colouring into the screen. I'm counting on a larger hand movement needed to

83

operate the mouse and some sound reinforcers to get the idea across. I'm rather pleased with it, even if I do say so myself.'

'What will you do with it?'

'I've sold it, Lyn. To an educational company. They were delighted with it. Want me to design something else.'

'So all those hours paid off.'

'Educational software is a growth industry. I'm in on the ground floor.'

In my turn, I tell her about *Gordon*, about the sales set to rocket, and she smiles in genuine pleasure, her face lighting up. There are no half-measures with Pam. There is nothing mean about her.

'Anyway, getting back to where we were,' Pam says, 'I could do with some company. And after all those hours in front of a computer screen, a bit of intrigue sounds appealing.'

'Thanks, Pam. I'd like to stay. I think last night unnerved me more than I thought. But are you sure? I'd hate to crowd you.'

'And I'd hate to lose you. Lyn, have you told anyone else about all of this?'

'You now. And last night Smithy.'

'Ah. The notable Mr Smith,' she says with a flicker of something unreadable in her eyes. 'And what did Smithy have to say?'

'We went through things. What it was about, tossed some ideas around.'

'What did he think?'

'We talked about drugs.'

'His idea or yours?'

'Mine.'

'Seems a bit convenient, doesn't it? Rescued from death's door and a bag of vital evidence goes missing.'

It takes me a minute to follow her drift.

'You think Smithy took it!' I ask incredulously.

'Why not? Simple enough for him to slip back and get the bag while you were asleep.'

I don't answer for a minute, seeing again Smithy's wet

umbrella, the damp copy of the morning's paper on the hall table. But at the same time I remember his unspoken reassurances in the tunnel, the squeeze of my hand. Smithy as suspect. This is something I had not considered and the idea strikes as untenable, unthinkable.

'You've been watching too much TV,' I say in amazement. 'Alex is an old family friend. I've known him all my life.'

Pam looks at me intently, choosing her words carefully. 'There was an interview in the paper the other day.'

'Oh, yes.'

'It was a friend of John Murray's. You know, the man who murdered that little girl in Collingwood, last week. She said she couldn't believe it. She had known him all her life.' She pauses before going on. 'And as I said before, you can never really tell what people are capable of.'

The waiter brings out coffee in small white cups, places them ceremoniously before us.

'Pam, I can't believe Smithy is involved. I mean, why? What does he have to gain?'

'But that's just it, Lyn. That's my point exactly. We don't know what it's about, so how do we know what he, or whoever it is, has to gain? What do you know about him?' She watches me intently. 'Lots of friends, has he? Do you know them?'

'Well . . . no, not really.'

'Precisely.' A note of triumph in the word.

'Okay. Spit it out. Tell me what you think.'

'Only that there's more to your elusive Mr Smith than meets the eye. I've always thought so. It's not natural, the way he lives. No friends, too much desire for privacy.' She stops and looks at me steadily, raises one eyebrow.

'What?' I ask.

'You've got that stubborn look on your face again.'

'Sorry.' I smile. 'It just seems inconceivable somehow . . .'

'What does he do all day in that flat of his?'

'Well, he paints . . .'

'All day, every day? Hardly a full life.'

I look at her for a long moment, unconvinced but trying to keep an open mind.

'I'll think about it. When I get back to your place, I'll write everything down. Reconstruct the chart we drew up. Begin a new file. See what you think then.'

We call in at the shop on the way to Pam's. She looks taken back at the clutter in the office but, like Jordie, says nothing. I collect some clothing and necessities, create slightly more office space. Jordie, at least, will be pleased.

I dump my belongings in Pam's spare room. A comfortable, warm room, overlooking a park. After the office, it looks both immense and luxurious. Pam pours liqueurs. I make a phone call.

'Good afternoon. Edward's Restaurant. Michael speaking.'

'Michael, this is Lyn Blessing.'

'Ah, Ms Blessing. How nice to hear from you again.' A trace of accent, a recognisable voice. The head waiter.

'Listen, Michael, I wonder if you can help. My partner, Barry Eastlake, has asked me to ring you. He had to go interstate this morning. He's made a mistake with filling out his expenses for work and his boss is cracking down. He wants me to confirm the date of his last reservation with you.' It's weak, but it passes.

'Certainly, Ms Blessing. I'll just be a minute.'

The sound of the phone being laid down, the turning of pages.

'According to our records, the last time Mr Eastlake dined here was on Friday 14 August.'

'I see. Nothing more recent. He mentioned something about last night.'

Again the turning pages, the pause before answering.

'No. He had a reservation, but cancelled at the last minute.'

'That's probably the problem. Thanks, Michael, for your time. We'll see you soon.'

I hang up. So he wasn't where he said he was. His reservation cancelled. That particular door swings open again. Where, I wonder, was he? In the alley behind the shop perhaps? Or with Clarissa?

Pam hands me a tiny glass of fiery liquid. She has overheard the one-way conversation, followed the gist.

'Barry Eastlake still head of the suspect list?' she asks.

'Seems so,' I say thoughtfully, tapping the pen on the back of my hand. 'At least he wasn't where he said he was.'

'All that proves is that Barry's a habitual liar and we knew that anyway.' She laughs.

'True,' I agree, and begin documenting the sequence of events, drawing up a new version of Smithy's chart.

Pam reads over my shoulder for a while.

'So what do you think?' she asks after a while.

'It's far too inconclusive to think anything. The only thing I know is that someone was there last night. No trick of the wind or imagination. The bag is gone. Someone is up to no good, and whoever it is must be involved with what's going on in the shop.'

She nods thoughtfully, her eye on the chart. 'Someone and something unknown. You're right, Lyn. We need to keep an open mind. There's too much we don't know, and that's why *you* have to be careful.'

I feel a sense of dread at her words. A feeling that has been growing all day, nagging at me insistently from the moment I realised that my bag had gone missing. It is likely that the man watching Maggie is watching me. A shadowy figure somewhere out there. Watching me. Following me. Waiting. But for what I have no idea.

# Chapter Fourteen

*The darkness gather'd all around is full of rustlings strange and low*
*The dead wood crackles on the ground,*
*and shadowy shapes flit to and fro;*

*'By the Camp Fire', Ada Cambridge*

On Sunday I go home again. I need to get away. I need somewhere to think, somewhere to be on my own. I want to sort the house out, take refuge in the tedium of cleaning, of creating order out of chaos. I fill the boot with necessities: cleaning stuff, coffee, tea, food.

When I get there I check two things, the electricity and the shed. The power is still off. I switch it on. The definite prints and tracks to the shed are no more. Instead there is a mish-mash, an area of churned-up mud, a suggestion of prints and tracks which tells me two things: that it has rained and that I have had visitors during the week.

I have had enough of mysteries. I feel a growing sense of outrage, a heady flare of anger. I ring the police. While I wait, I begin on the house, attacking the work with furious energy.

A police car in the driveway. One officer on his own. I watch him through the window walking towards the house, looking about with interest.

'Ms Blessing?'

He is thin-faced with high cheekbones, a definite set to his chin. He shows me his badge and looks at me intently, a smile hovering.

'It's Lyn, isn't it? I couldn't believe it when I got your call. I thought you'd moved away.'

I must look blank, because he hurries to explain.

'I'm Joe. Joe Mileto. You might remember me. I used to come here in the holidays to play with Billy.'

Bill is my younger cousin. A constant guest in school holidays, married now and living in Queensland.

'Joe! Of course I remember you. You look so different. No, not really different...'

'But older,' he finishes, smiling. His eyes are a soft blue.

'Exactly.' I grin back. 'I thought you were the one who moved away.'

'I did for a while. A posting to Mildura. I'm back for a short time, and then who knows where.'

'It's good to see you, Joe.'

'How is Bill?' he asks.

I fill him in on family news. Children and a promotion. He brushes some hair back from his forehead. A familiar gesture that recalls more vividly than words the young boy who used to visit.

'Down to business, I s'pose. You rang to report a robbery.'

'Well, not exactly a robbery. At least I don't think so. But someone's been here in the week and the week before.'

I take him down to the shed and show him the driveway, the churned-up, inconclusive mud.

'Last week there were footprints, definite tyre tracks.'

'You should have rung us then,' he remarks.

This is so obvious I don't even bother to reply. He checks along the outside of the driveway and stops to examine an impression of a heel. A deep, wide depression in a clear patch between gravel and grass. He places his own foot beside it, like I did, and compares the two.

'Bigger foot than mine. Looks like oversize gum boots to

me, impossible to tell actual foot size. Most people buy them far too big, especially out here in the sticks.'

'I haven't really been here for over a year. This place is usually unoccupied. No one should be driving in and out. I'll be coming up more often now. I don't like the idea of people being here when they shouldn't.'

'Better buy a padlock for the gate.'

'Talking of padlocks,' I say, indicating the padlock on the shed door.

He twists the shaft and it swings away from the locking device. He twists it back.

'Useful... How long has it been like this?'

'I have no idea. I can only swear to the last week or so.'

He twists the shaft back and forwards in his hands.

'So are you coming back for good?'

'Intermittently at least. Weekends and breaks, you know.'

'Weekends and breaks,' he repeats.

'I thought about selling up, after Adele died. But some-how...' I gesture at the land rolling away to the distant hills. The bright cold day, the air clear and still around us.

He nods and follows my gaze.

'I was sorry about Adele. Car crash, wasn't it? I had quite a crush on her for a while.'

'Yes, I know.'

He smiles again, an easy smile.

'Cup of tea?' I offer.

'I'd love to see the old place again.'

I make the tea and hand it to him.

'Go anywhere you like. Feel free.'

He nods and wanders off. I leave him for a while and find him in the family room, where he and Bill used to spend hours. The old cricket posters are still on the wall, and on the shelves, piles of old newspapers, the sporting pages, full of scores from test matches. He is studying them, head down, deep in concentration.

'I'd forgotten these. Bill and I spent all one summer

collecting them. Working out averages.' He looks at his watch. 'I'm late. I'll report the break-in and check at the station to see if there are any other reports. Ring me if anything else happens.'

'Come back any time, Joe. Any time you want to visit, any time you want to read through, just give me a call.'

I take his cup.

'You know, I used to have quite a crush on you too.' His eyes regard me steadily, blue eyes, a soft blue like the hills. 'Goodbye, Lyn. I'll be in touch.'

By late afternoon I sit back and admire where I've been. The house sparkles around me, fresh and clean. I make another cup of tea and browse, as Joe did, through the old cricket reports. It makes interesting reading. The papers focus on the summer tour of the West Indies and the Australian heroes of the day, names from the past: Bobby Simpson, Jeff Thomson, Kim Hughes. But I am just wasting time. It is time to take on the last ghost.

Surrounded by the things of her childhood, of our shared childhood, the things of our growing up, I thought Adele might accuse me of letting her down. Of not being there when she died. But there is only silence. Around me are her possessions; her collection of teddies, her desk, her papers, photos, books, curtains, bedspreads, paintings. All these things are quiet. I close my eyes and let my thoughts wander.

I am ten years old. Adele is twelve. The older sister interpreting the world. Our father is dead and the house is full of grief. We shared the bed that night, a habit given up but resumed for the duration.

'Del, do you believe in ghosts?'

'No. Of course not.'

'Julie says the ghost of her grandfather visits her at night.'

'Ghosts aren't true. Ghosts are just unpleasant memories. Something we think about because we've done something wrong to someone who has died.'

'What?' My voice sounds small in the darkness.

'I don't know really, it could be anything. We might have let them down in some way, or just never told them that we love them. And then they die. And we feel guilty. That's a ghost. Now go to sleep.'

I don't, though. I listen to Adele's breathing growing deeper and heavier, falling into the regular pattern of sleep. I lie there in the darkened room and wait for the ghost, my father's ghost. It does not come.

Twenty-five years later I am waiting for another ghost. Adele's ghost. And again it doesn't come. Her room is full of memory, but the memories are safe, do not accuse me, do not confront me.

I clean first. Dust the shelves and paintings, vacuum the floor, clean the windows. When I have finished, I sit at the foot of her bed. Adele's desk is in front of me, with all the business of her life. As good a time as any to lay the last ghost once and for all, to try and come to terms with my sister's death. I ring Pam to let her know I am staying on, but there is no answer. I leave a message on her machine.

Adele's desk. I open the drawers one by one and go through her personal papers, the scatter of bills and papers and receipts. In the top drawer is a slip of blue paper, dated 6 February 1991. Adele's name written in large letters at the top. A single box marked positive is ticked. It takes a minute to sink in. This is a pregnancy test. Adele was pregnant.

A wave of grief and loss washes over me, fresh as the day she died. But among the sudden blur of misery, I remember that at some time I had suspected this. At some level, I had known it, but dismissed it. The clues were all there. Preoccupation, sickness, unhappiness. She must have wondered at Christmas, been worried by it. She didn't tell me about it and I never asked. The distance between us strikes like a smack in the face. How little we really confided. When she needed me I wasn't there. At the end, we were as far apart as the poles.

It is getting too dark to read. I switch on the lights and go through the bookcase, find her stack of diaries. One for each year since she was ten, recorded and kept for ever. A habit forged and unbreakable, a habit we both grew up with. The diaries form a neat row of books, uniform sizes, different colours. They take up little space on the shelf. I pull them out, sit on the floor and begin to read through my sister's life.

The writing is like my own slanting, roundish letters. I flick through the different journals, read brief extracts from her past, the threads of friendships begun and continued, begun and ended. The recording of our family history, the chronicling of events. The progress of her growing up. As she gets older the entries become fewer, less detailed, used more as appointment lists than detailed recollections. The last diary, the diary for 1990, tells me the least.

Towards Christmas time, though, the entries begin to fill out again, but without Adele's usual lightness. It is as though she is bored or depressed. The writing is dispiriting.

*24 December. Home again. Or not home. Without Mum . . . well, it all seems pointless. At least it's peaceful here. Spent the day on a report for work, hope at last to get that finalised. I wonder if Lyn would like to sell up and buy a unit in town. She arrived mid-afternoon, loaded with food. She looks dreadful.*

*25 December. Christmas Day. Felt sick all day. Without Mum and without Paul it seems empty. Lyn and I rattled around here together all day and drank too much wine. Lyn preoccupied. Paul rang. A guarded call though, unsatisfactory for us both. He'll ring again New Year's Eve.*

I remember that Christmas Day reluctantly. A dreadful Christmas. Our first without Mum. My last with Adele. The smell of roast pork and Adele dragging herself away from some monumental project to come and eat. A heavy dinner, a traditional Christmas dinner that we didn't want, cooked and eaten as a concession to 'the done thing'. What a senseless waste of time. And later, with our thoughts elsewhere, the day disintegrated into wine and arguments and headaches.

It was my first year of managing the shop single-handedly, without guidance, without help from Mum. I remember the feeling, like a wrung-out rag. The new year's catalogue was due at the printer in three weeks' time; the work scarcely begun.

Adele had the gift, the flair, of being able to negotiate the complex and infinite variables of book collecting and selling. Of knowing innately which defects detract and which enhance. Of knowing the trends, the history, the trade. We all deferred to her opinion. Some of this knowledge I now have, but it was knowledge achieved painstakingly, with many errors, some of them spectacular.

And the flaring row when I asked for help. Her blunt refusal.

'But you know the trade backwards. I can't do it on my own.' I argued.

'Lyn, I have a job I love, an exhausting, demanding job. I can't. I simply can't.' Her words were slow and carefully articulated, as though explaining something to a slow child. Which perhaps I was.

'But couldn't you . . .'

Her dark eyes were determined, her square chin set and stubborn, a flush of anger on her cheeks.

'No. I haven't got enough time. If you can't do it, employ someone or sell.'

She flounced out, slammed the door behind her.

But in those days there was not enough money to employ anyone. It is only now that I have the luxury of Jordie, two half-days a week. And curiously Jordie was Adele's recommendation. A note Adele left on my briefcase after the fight. *Jordie Armstrong, 784 6563. Office work. Reasonable rates. Reliable. Efficient. Easy to get on with*. A barb in the last sentence.

The discussion ended, but resentment lingered. At the end, though, it was me who let her down. This is something I have always known.

*27 December. Sick again this morning. Lyn left this morning. I was glad to see her go. She is impossible to talk to. Her anger takes up too much energy. I don't have the time.*

And I was glad to go. A parting shot about working on the catalogue. She didn't answer. Just closed her dark eyes against my anger and felt what? Impatience. Disgust. Resignation.

This is the last journal on the shelf. I flick through the empty pages given over to the last week of the year. Whatever we did, we did it separately. Adele died six weeks later. I search the shelves for the new diary, but it is not there.

I realise where it is. After I made the formal identification, the police gave me her possessions; the things she carried the day she died. They were all in a large plastic bag, her jewellery, her clothes, her bag and its contents: keys, diary, wallet. The day of the funeral I put it in her wardrobe and closed the door.

I retrieve the bag now and upend it over the bed. A purple diary, the same size and style as all the others. With unsteady hands I take it up and begin reading eagerly, edgily.

*1 January. So much for resolutions. Mine is broken already. I couldn't wait for Paul to ring, so I rang him at home. He was there of course and hostile at the call, made out I was ringing about work. When he rang later, he was distant, putting me off. All those promises. At least now I know where I stand. At least I know what to do. All those lies. How I hate being lied to.*

The last sentence has been dug deeply into the page. I sit down on the bed and think of Barry, of the parallels between Adele's life and my own. The unsatisfactory relationship. The insult of being lied to. I think back to that last Christmas. The general misery. Adele hovering near the phone, pouncing whenever it rang. I should have known. Should have seen beyond my own preoccupations. I should have helped.

*2 January. Have written to Paul finishing things. At least it's settled. That report for work is finally done. So much work for so little achieved. I only hope they appreciate it. I'd like to... No. I don't know what I want any more.*

The next entry is for 6 January. The effect the break with Paul has had on her is evident. There are references to things I don't understand, people I don't know of. At the end she writes:

*This house is lonely on my own. Everything is wrong, even work. I need to make plans, to get going, but I have lost direction.*

The next day is slashed through in large letters, a single word. Work. She goes back to her flat in town, back to the office after the Christmas holiday, most of it spent working. Outside the darkness is solid, the heavy darkness of a cloudy night. No moon. No stars. No light anywhere.

I stretch, ease the stiffness from my neck and read on.

The entries thin out again. Recede into appointments and mere jottings, indecipherable. She mentions Paul only once more.

*20 January. P came in to work to see me today. He looks dreadful, thin and gaunt. He has left his wife and wants me back. It's too late, though. The trust has gone and it's finished. I've changed my mind about selling up. I need somewhere to get away. Somewhere safe.*

In early February, she comes back home for a weekend.

*6 February. The doctor has confirmed I am pregnant. He expected me to be happy about it. Am I? I can't think. I can't decide. Two nuisance callers in two days. How I hate that. No heavy breathing, just a pause before they hang up. I wonder if it's Paul.*

*7 February. The shed has been broken into. Nothing missing, at least I don't think so, but the padlock is cut through. I rang the police. That thick Bruce Spence is in charge. I could tell he thought the whole thing was a waste of time. Got nasty when I asked for Joe. Joe has been posted to Mildura. How far away can you get? The other end of the state. It would have been nice to see Joe again.*

The sentence leaps out from the page. The padlock cut, eighteen months ago. The shed broken into. Again. Still. A small wind springs up, rustles unseen in the trees, moves the curtain cord in Adele's room. I read on but there is nothing else of interest. Just a growing depression, a sense of confusion, an inability to decide. The only definite thing, the break with Paul, holds firm. She has made a clear decision, there is no turning back.

*8 February. A phoned to ask me for a drink in the week. Next time I come here I'll ask Lyn. We need to talk, to get things straight. I need to tell her about the baby. I need to tell her what's been happening. This house isn't safe any more. I'll give A a key to check the house, and then I won't need to come back. I don't feel like coming back.*

This was the last entry. Adele died on 10 February, two days later. The day she died, she asked me to meet her at Lacey's for dinner. I refused, made some excuse, pleaded overwork. It was our last chance.

I was the one who let resentment linger. I let her down when she needed me. I should have gone. This is something I regret every day. This is the thing I have to come to terms with. This is my ghost.

I close the book and begin pacing the room. Trying to come to terms with what I've just read. Who is A? Did Adele meet A for a drink or did she die before that? The thing that sticks, though, is the shed. Whatever was happening then is happening now. And Adele didn't feel safe.

The phone rings, shrill and sudden in the silent house. I let it ring for a moment, reluctant to answer it. But I remember the message I left on Pam's machine and pick the receiver up.

There is only silence. Adele was right. I can't hear them breathing, just the small pause and the replacing of the receiver. I hang up slowly. Another mystery. Coincidence? Not likely. I don't really believe in coincidences.

Outside, it is dark as coal, great banks of cloud obscure the moon. I go through the house, switch off lights, check the locks on the doors. I use the phone in Adele's room to ring the local police station. At this time of night there is a recorded message, directing me on to the Regional Office, half an hour away. I ring Pam again. Her answering machine clicks on. I hesitate before speaking.

'Pam. Me again. I'm still at the farm. There's something going on up here. Can you ring me please.'

I think about what to do. The phone calls have taken time and have been no help at all. I stand there listening. I am torn between going and staying. Part of me wants to run, to hide somewhere out of sight, to keep safe. Another part, a more resolute part of me, wants to stay. Wants to know what is going on. Wants an answer to it all. I think of the tunnel and have my answer. I will not repeat that mad and terrifying flight from unknown danger. This time I will not panic.

The swish of tyres on wet gravel, no accompanying sweep of lights. A car door closes. They are here already. I had not thought they would arrive so soon. Adele's room has the best view of the shed. The night is paler now. A three-quarter moon has escaped from behind a bank of clouds, casts its strange green glow, enough light to see by. The car is large and square, a four-wheel drive, a gleam of silver in the moonlight.

Too late I dial the Regional Office. The phone rings at the other end. I should have gone. Safer to have gone. The phone rings on. A scraping noise close by, too close. A key in the lock. I step back, replace the receiver silently, push myself behind the gathered curtains. Silence everywhere, save my heart thumping in my ears.

Torchlight and footsteps. Someone is in the room, but my eyes pressed to the open weave curtains can make out only movement and shadow. The beam of light plays around the room, settles on the bookcase, travels slowly across coloured spines. I count silently, trying to make sense of the time, trying to keep calm. The torchlight swings away, stops at the desk. And then a rifling through papers. A pause. An absence of sound or movement that seems to go on for ever. And then through curtains I see the dark bulk of a body moving swiftly towards me. One arm swings high above their head, and in their hand the barrel of a torch. Arm and torchlight swing down towards me. I hear the swish of air. And then a flash of light and pain and after, nothing. Darkness, solid as a cave, black as the tunnel.

How long I lay there I can't tell. A phone rings somewhere in my sleep, a long way away, and then silence. When I come to it is morning, and the house is cold and quiet. My head pounds when I breathe, pounds when I move. I move my arm first, slowly, but even that small movement brings tears to my eyes. I feel my forehead gingerly, feel where the blood has flowed and stiffened, trickled down my face and into my hair. I bring my hand to my eyes. The blood on it is red and moist. I am still bleeding. A wave of nausea sweeps over me. I close my eyes, willing it to pass.

When I wake next, it is lighter outside, the sun higher. There is movement and sound somewhere. I struggle up through black layers, struggling to meet the voice. Someone is talking as though through a tunnel, a long way away. Footsteps loud and strong, and close by a small cloud of steam, a touch of warm water, the weight and warmth of a blanket.

'Pam?' I can barely talk.

'Yes, darling. Shhh. Don't talk now. The ambulance is on its way.'

She begins wiping at my hands and face, rinsing the blood

away in the bucket.

'Pam, is it really you?'

She dries my hands with a towel, rubs them softly between the thick folds of cloth.

'Yes, darling. Of course. Everything's fine. You're going to be fine.'

'Only ... I thought you were my mother.'

She smiles then. She is so close I can see the light in her eyes. The facets of green. Cat's Eyes. Eyes that can see in the dark. I close my eyes against their brilliance.

# Chapter Fifteen

*How will you govern this wild thing fraught*
*with the abracadabra of dread?*
*'On a Grey-haired Old Lady Knitting...', Furnley Maurice*

The lights are white above my head. I drift between cool darkness and an arc of blinding light. In the light, someone is waiting for me. I cannot see her face, but her hair is a halo of shining silver, quite brilliant.

'Adele?'

But something has gone wrong with time because Adele is dead. She takes my hand and bends down to whisper and I see then that her hair is dark, almost black.

'It's all right, darling. You're going to be okay.'

No, not Adele. Pam. Cool hands, a cloud of dark hair. And again, darkness.

Sometimes I think I am in the tunnel and the pain in my body seems to rise and fall with my breath. Sometimes a nurse is there, her hands cool and comforting on my skin, and I slide back into sleep; deep, peaceful and solid.

When I wake next the overhead lights have been turned off

and the room is dim. The cloud of dark hair is still with me. And eyes, green eyes, deeper than the sea.

'Pam, is it you?'

'Yes, darling.' She squeezes my hand, bends down close to my face. 'I'm still here.'

'Where am I?'

'You're safe now, Lyn. You're in hospital. The doctor's been to see you. She says you'll live.'

'Oh. That's good, isn't it?'

'Of course, silly. Go back to sleep now.'

I sink down easily into a soft, muzzy, pain-free world, drifting in and out of sleep, aware in increasing bursts of the hospital routine, of Pam sitting close by and of a deep and numbing headache.

'Pam?'

'Mm. What is it?'

'What happened?'

'Someone broke into your house and attacked you. The police assume the motive is theft, that you got in the way of someone intent on robbery.'

'Do they? Robbery?'

It doesn't seem right, but I am too tired to think.

'Shhh now. Time enough in the morning. Go back to sleep.'

'Pam?'

'Yes.'

'What day is it?'

'It's Monday night, Lyn.' She consults her watch. 'Sorry, early Tuesday. You've missed a whole day. We've been worried about you. Now will you get back to sleep or do I have to call a nurse?'

Tuesday. Something was happening on Tuesday. Something important. I close my eyes and drift off again.

When I wake next the sun is low in the sky. Rectangles of light find their way through the blinds and lie as stripes on the floor. It is early morning and Pam is asleep. Her cloud of dark hair is against the bedspread. I can't quite see her face.

I sit up carefully, trying not to jar my head. She stirs at the movement, opens the one eye that is visible, looks directly at me.

'Welcome back.' She yawns and stretches. 'God, the things I do for you. I'm totally wrecked.'

'How long have you been here?'

'I rescued you Monday morning, early.'

I reach for her hand. 'Pam, what can I say?'

'Nothing. For once in your life say nothing. Here, drink this. Small sips, mind.'

The water is cool and welcome. I drink it eagerly, thirstily. She wets a flannel at the tap, washes my hands and wrists, passes it over my neck. I touch my head gingerly, and find the roughness of a bandage. My skin crawls beneath my fingers, and the numbing ache intensifies down one side of my face.

'Pam, where am I?'

She looks at me assessingly. 'You're in hospital, Lyn.'

'Yes. I know, but where? Which one? Melbourne or the bush.'

'Oh, I see.' She grins in relief. 'I thought . . . The bush, Lyn. Yarra Hills.'

The hospital closest to the farm. The hospital I came to as a child to have my appendix removed. A hospital with its grounds set on a hill above river flats. And close by, the coil of the river. The Yarra winding back on itself, on its immense journey to Melbourne and the waters of the bay.

'How's the pain now?' Pam asks.

I grimace, but only slightly, because movement hurts too much.

'Manageable.'

She grins. 'Serves you right. Next time I'm coming with you. I think you need a bodyguard.'

'Next time! There won't be a next time!'

'Ah. Sense at last.'

There are flowers on the shelves and on the cupboards.

Bouquets of flowers. She follows my gaze.

'Someone loves you, you know. The pretty pink and white carnation one is from Jordie.' She hands me the card. *Dear Lyn. No more excuses. You're coming with me to karate. Get better soon. Jordie.*

'Sensible woman, don't you think?'

'Very,' I say drily.

She indicates another bouquet, a native selection: blue gum and bottle brush.

'Smithy's. Hand-delivered, but he was sent home.'

Again she hands me the card. *Dear Lyn. What can I say? Get well soon. Your friend, Alex.*

'Nice of him. Did you meet him?'

She looks at me steadily.

'Yes, I introduced myself. He seems quite charming. This elegant, golden one, spikes of white gladioli and yellow roses is from your publishers.'

*Dear Lyn.*
*Devastated to hear what happened to you. All our best wishes for a speedy recovery.*
*Vanessa and Peter, Vane Publications.*

'They obviously don't know I've developed an aversion to roses, especially yellow ones.'

Its not funny. But we laugh anyway.

'What's happened to the shop?' I ask. 'I've missed a whole day.'

'I knew you'd be concerned. I phoned Jordie yesterday, first thing. She was going to do what she could herself. It's all taken care of. Nothing for you to worry about.'

'Pam?'

'Mm.'

'How do I look?'

'Pretty bloody dreadful. Here, have a look.'

She passes me a mirror from her bag. The face that looks into it is hardly recognisable as my own. My head is bandaged, a thin strip around temple and forehead. My skin is white, and down the left side of my face is a bruise, deeply purple, swelling around a tiny eye. My hair springs up from the bandage, dry and brittle.

'Told you.'

Pam is matter of fact, shuts the mirror away in her bag.

She stays with me for a while, until the nursing staff come to sort me out.

'Got to go, love.'

Pam holds me for a minute, but gently as though I might break.

'Pam?'

'Yes.'

'Thank you.'

'Just don't do it again! The doctor was worried about you, you know. She said if you hadn't been quite so fit, well . . .' She trails off, unable to finish the sentence.

'All that swimming,' I say lightly. 'Improved lung capacity, etc. etc.'

She smiles. 'Yes. All that. Listen, I'm going home now. I'll be back tomorrow. I need some sleep and so do you. Besides, you've got people to talk to.' She bends down to whisper. 'There's this lovely-looking policeman keeps popping in. Wait until you see him. Be back tomorrow.'

She blows me a kiss from the doorway and is gone.

I lie back down and fall asleep. When I wake Joe is sitting by the bed. He sits without fidgeting, his notebook still in his hand.

'Sleeping beauty,' he says when I wake.

'Well, hardly.' I smile at him, remembering my face in Pam's mirror and aware for the first time that Joe must be Pam's 'lovely policeman'.

'Good to see you, Joe.'

'And you. The sergeant thought you'd be more comfortable with me, seeing we're friends. I think the thought of you lying at death's door was a bit much for him.'

'So he sent you.'

'Yes, but I would've come anyway. Have come anyway. The doctors wouldn't let me in before. They said that unless my name was Adele or Pam, there was no chance of me seeing you.'

'Adele?' I ask.

'Apparently you were asking for her. Adele and sometimes Pam.'

'Poor Joe.'

'Poor Lyn.'

He takes my hand and squeezes my fingers gently, over and over. His touch is warm and soothing, oddly familiar.

'Bit too close for comfort, eh?'

'Mm,' I agree. 'Pam tells me that you think the motive was robbery.'

'Well that was the assumption, but now, with what Pam tells me, who knows?'

We say nothing for a few minutes.

'There was someone here to see you earlier. He was pretty upset about you,' he tells me, breaking the silence.

'Who?'

'Bloke by the name of Alex Smith.'

Smithy. Well, yes, he would be.

'What happened?'

'We sent him away. The doctors and me. You were too ill for visitors.'

'Yes.'

'We've been through the house, but there's not much to go on. The only thing we've really got is some new tyre tracks. We've taken an impression. A four-wheel drive of some sort, which doesn't mean a lot. Out here they're pretty common.'

An orderly comes in pushing a tea trolley. Joe doesn't release my fingers, doesn't reach for his book as I half expected.

She smiles at us like some doting big sister, charmed by the sight of young love. I want to tell her it's not what she thinks, but the effort is too great.

'Tea? Coffee?'

'Tea, please. And you, Joe?'

'Yes. Tea for me too. Thanks.'

We drink our tea peacefully and at leisure. The ache in my head is slowly subsiding and the day outside looks sunny, almost warm. A touch of spring. Joe puts his cup down, wipes his mouth with the back of his thumb, picks up his notebook. Interlude over, we are now official. The police mask resumed. All traces of the ten-year-old firmly banished.

'I checked on recent disturbances around your place. Nothing.'

I'm not surprised. Surrounded by acres of bush and pasture, who would see, who would hear?

'I had a long talk with Pam. She told me some of the things that have been happening. About the message you left on her machine. About the other attempt on your life.'

'I don't think you could call it an attempt on my life. Someone followed me and I panicked.'

'A bag went missing, Pam says?'

'Yes. A bag went missing.'

'And something about a woman in your shop. A messenger, she called her. Maggie. Surname unknown. Can you describe her?' His tone is different now, official and precise.

'Blonde, square-faced. She looks like Adele, but not as nice.'

I repeat as accurately as I can the story that I told to Smithy and to Pam. He listens attentively, making notes as he goes. His writing is bold, easy to read, no loops or flourishes.

'And another thing ... I don't think her name is Maggie.'

'Oh. Why?'

'She was scared, so scared she fainted. I just can't imagine her giving her own name. And all this business with the code. The book in the shop – *The Mill on the Floss*. Maggie was the name of the woman in the book.'

'I see.' He stops writing momentarily, his pen hovering above the page.

'What about Sunday night. What did you see? What did you hear?'

I tell Joe what I can remember about that night. It is vague, though. Snatches of consciousness well up from shadowy depths, vague stirrings that I can't quite grasp. I remember cleaning and sorting and deciding to stay on. I remember ringing up. But who did I ring? I remember the sound of the phone some time in the night and Pam in the house, washing my hands.

'Don't worry. It'll come to you.' Joe says. 'We need to know if he took anything. What he was after. When you feel better, we'll go to the house together. Don't worry, you'll be safe.'

He says it without doubt, as though it is written in stone. He gives me a small tape recorder.

'When you're up to it, talk into this. Anything you can remember.'

He squeezes my hand, kisses my cheek and leaves.

I fiddle with the tape recorder, testing it out, thinking back, but find nothing to say. But after lunch a different sort of memory stirs. I remember what was so important about Tuesday. Georgina Stavros was coming into Vane Publications and Peter Ireland was going to introduce us. Twelve o'clock. Two and a half hours ago.

I slide out of bed gingerly, careful of my head, and find my legs are surprisingly weak. I cross slowly to the window and the view is as I remember it. The sweep of manicured lawns. The Yarra River coiling away in the distance across flood plains lined with Manna gums. In sunlight the river gleams with flecks of silver, intricate as snake skin.

The doctor interrupts my reverie and I cross back to the bed.

'Feeling better?'

'Yes, thank you. Much.'

She takes my blood pressure, shines lights in my eyes, examines the wound.

'You had us worried, you know. A nasty crack on the head.'

'I can't remember much of it,' I tell her.

She sits on the bed. 'That's very common, you know. When

you lose consciousness a lot of people lose time. Some dramatically so, hours and even whole days. The brain just shuts it out. You may remember, or you may not. All I can tell you is not to worry.'

She stands up.

'You'll need to take it easy for a few days. You know, rest and recovery, that sort of thing. If I let you go home tomorrow, have you got anyone to stay with?'

'Yes, with Pam.'

'Excellent. A very sensible person. And don't let the police worry you about remembering everything. Worrying won't help your memory come back.' She pauses at the door. 'I almost forgot. You've got another visitor. Feel up to it?'

'It depends on who it is.'

'Barry someone.'

I nod.

He puts his head around the door, like a puppy unsure of its welcome. He smiles and comes in. Not roses this time, but a small spring bouquet.

'Lyn, I'm so sorry. I'm so glad you're okay.'

'How did you know I was here?'

'I rang the shop and they told me you were ill. So then I rang Pam. She'd just got back from seeing you. I came straight away.'

He hands me the flowers and sits down on the visitor's chair. He makes no attempt to touch me. He looks instead at the damage to my face.

'Poor, poor face. I just couldn't believe it when Pam told me.'

'Believe it. None of this is a game.'

'No, I can see that. I just hope I haven't made things worse.'

He hangs his head, avoids my eye. He twists the ring on his finger. A signet ring, the letters B and E entwined intricately on a flat platform of gold.

'I should have told you when you asked. I've ruined everything.'

'Told me what, Barry?'

'I only wanted to talk.'

Suddenly I understand where this conversation is heading.

'You were there, weren't you? All the time, you were there in the alley.'

He nods. 'I waited across the road for you to finish work. There was this woman outside the shop. I saw you let her in. I gave up then, and went and had a coffee down the road and something to eat. I had to walk past your place again. I knocked at the front door, but you didn't hear me. By this time it was really late, well after closing time. I didn't know whether you were there or not. I waited around a bit, getting more and more fed up. I was about to go home, but I thought I'd try around the back, in case you were in the office. I just turned into the alley at the back and there you were. I couldn't believe it after all that waiting. I called out but you took off so fast. I tried to catch you. You wouldn't stop.'

'What did you do?' My tone is cold and he flinches slightly.

'I waited for a while, for you to come back. I was worried about you, but I didn't want to go too deep into the alley. As it was I was scared. I couldn't hear you and it was so dark. It's eerie there at night, especially with the wind . . . I don't mind telling you, Lyn, I got the creeps.'

Could I blame him really? The alley has unnerved me more than once and he's right about the eeriness of the wind. He senses that my hostility has lessened and takes my hand.

'There was someone else there.'

I am not surprised. I say nothing.

'Two of them.' He looks at me for my reaction.

'Two of them.' I stare at him steadily. 'Why didn't you tell me before?'

He looks down in discomfort. 'I felt a fool. A grown man scared of an alley. I thought that if I told you, well, you know . . . You see, I still wanted you back. But I know now that you won't, I know that it's really over. And at least you deserve the truth, such as it is.'

'Thank you,' I say carefully, keeping contempt from my tone. 'What did you see?'

He shrugs. 'First off, it was too dark to see anything really. There was someone with a torch. Only a faint glow. They kept it down, trained it on the ground. They walked right past me.'

'Didn't you see anything? A shadow, a profile, anything?' I ask, fascinated.

'Not really.' He is hesitant, though, unsure. 'I heard footsteps, quiet ones, and the light from the torch.'

I don't say anything, wait for him to continue.

'I stayed where I was. You know, where the alley turns. I squashed into the corner there. That must have been where I lost the rose. I suppose, thinking about it later, that he or she couldn't have seen me even if they'd been looking. It was the darkest place of all. I didn't think that at the time. I was just scared.'

'She?' This is something I haven't considered and yet why not? 'Why she? I mean why did you think it could be a woman?'

'I'm not sure really. An impression, no more. Whoever it was was light on their feet. Apart from that . . .' He shrugs, breaks off momentarily. 'It was so dark that if it wasn't for the torch I wouldn't have seen them at all. Funny, though, one minute nothing, and then suddenly I saw the torch. As if whoever it was materialised out of thin air.'

Or had been waiting and watching, torch switched off.

'Which way were they going? Away from Flinders Street, or towards it?'

'Away from it. Past me and deeper into the alley.'

'And then what did you do?'

'I stayed where I was for a while. I don't know how long, but it seemed like ages. I didn't want to be seen. There was something menacing about the whole situation. When I thought it was safe, I headed back to Flinders Street.'

'And the second person?'

'I was half-way down the alley next to the shop when I

heard footsteps, someone running behind me. I guess I showed up in the light from the road. It was a man. He called out. 'Oi, you.' Something like that. I thought it was the first one. The one in the alley. It was only when I was in Flinders Street, I realised it was someone else.

'Did you see what he looked like?'

He nods. 'I watched him from behind a truck. He couldn't see me.'

'And?'

'Jeans and a flannel shirt. Not quite as agile as the first one. Heavier. He was tall and thin. He waited for a minute or two and then went back up the alley. I went home and stayed there.'

This at least is concrete – Smithy, without doubt.

'And the other person. The one you saw first. What did you see?'

I make him go through it again. He has my full attention, because at last I have the hope of something definite. I sit up and the sudden movement jars my head, sends messages of alarm down the side of my face.

'Steady, Lyn.' He strokes my hand and continues. 'You know where it turns towards the big loading bay at the end and there's light from a streetlight somewhere?'

'Yes, I know the place.'

'I caught the merest glimpse. They had their back to me. And then, well nothing. There's nothing to describe really, I've thought about it a lot. They weren't tall and they weren't short. A slim build. Dressed all in black. Black shoes, trousers, gloves, the lot. And they were silent. So very quiet.'

I see. So nothing definite after all.

'I'm sorry, Lyn. I've let you down badly.'

He leans against me and snuffles like a spaniel. It is only later, when he has gone, that I realise that, despite all my injuries, he was the one seeking sympathy.

An orderly comes in dispensing tea and I drink it thoughtfully. Barry's story doesn't tell me very much, doesn't really give me any concrete facts to run with. But even so, it tells me something. I think about the figure glimpsed briefly in a patch of pale light. Someone dressed entirely in black. Someone watching me in the darkness. Not Barry. Not Smithy. No chance meeting this, but something cold, calculated and professional.

# Chapter Sixteen

*So weave them, lady, weave them in,*
*Horror and sunshine, laughter and sin.*
*'On a Grey-haired Old Lady Knitting . . .', Furnley Maurice*

I am eating breakfast when Pam arrives, clutching a small hold-all and a bunch of flowers. She smiles when she sees me.

'Nothing wrong with your appetite I see.'

Hospital food: scrambled eggs on toast, orange juice, a pot of tea. Lovely.

'I'm so hungry I can't believe it.'

'Good. Here's another contribution to your garden,' she says, handing me the flowers. 'This time to celebrate your coming home.'

No roses, but a brilliant bouquet of daffodils. She empties a bag of clothes onto the bed. My clothes from Sunday: brown trousers, underwear, boots, my bright green jumper. Everything washed and ironed.

'Joe rang. He's glad you'll have company. He's concerned about you.'

'Sweet of him.' I sniff the jumper.

'The blood came out okay. I left it to soak.'

'Thanks.'

'Joe wants us to meet him at the house. You need to go through things. To see if anything's missing. Feel up to it?'

'Of course. I can't wait to leave.'

Pam drives. The day, like the daffodils, is fresh and bright. The road winds around the mountain, offering breathtaking glimpses of the valley below. And then miles of bush, the road sweeping up through cleared hills.

The farm again. A police car in the driveway. When we pull up, Joe unwinds himself from the driver's seat, kisses me on the cheek.

'How's the patient this morning?' he asks Pam.

'Co-operating. Fragile. Some signs of showing sense.'

'Ah. Things are looking up.'

They smile, the easy smile of conspirators. We walk onto the veranda. I close my eyes against the day's brightness. My head feels fuzzy.

'How did you find her?' Joe to Pam.

'When I got here the house was locked and the garage. I tried all the doors. You know this place, outside doors everywhere, all opening on to the verandah. Anyway, I walked all around the veranda, and the last door, the kitchen door, was open.'

'Open or unlocked?'

'No. Open. Wide open, that's when I knew ...'

She links her arm through mine and gives me a squeeze.

'I checked the obvious places: lounge, bathroom, your room, Lyn. I thought ... The last room I checked was Adele's.'

I unlock the front door and we all go into the house. As Joe says, everything seems to be here, televisions, videos, all in place. There are no signs of disturbance, no vandalism.

'Apart from your head you've been lucky.' Joe says.

My teeth have stopped aching, but my eye is still half closed. I look at him from under the swelling.

'Very lucky.'

He smiles at the irony in my tone. 'Take a good look through. Check the small things, the things of value.'

I go through the house, but it all seems the same. Only Adele's room is different, for here there is blood on the carpet, blood in the curtains.

Pam takes up her story.

'When I got here, it was just light. At first I didn't see you. Believe it or not, I noticed the bloodstain on the carpet first. It had spread, you see, and then I saw you half hidden behind the curtains.'

'We think the curtain probably saved your life. That whoever it was couldn't get a good enough swing at your head,' Joe adds.

'You were here, Lyn. Your head here.' Pam indicates with her hands.

It feels strange to be discussed like this, almost as though it is something that happened to someone else a long time ago.

'Okay.' Joe takes a deep breath. 'What I want you to do, Lyn, is go through it, act it out. Everything you remember, impressions, the lot.'

I sit down on Adele's bed. My headache is worse. No coherent thoughts stir. The silence grows.

'What about a car, Lyn? Whoever was here had to get here somehow. I can't see them walking.' Pam prompts.

'Starting with the knowledge that you were in this room, what did you hear?' Joe adds.

I close my eyes against the fuzziness in my head and, like clouds parting, I see again a square and solid car. No colour but the cold gleam of silver.

'Yes,' I say into the expectant silence. 'A car. A four-wheel drive and then the sound of someone at the door.'

They both grin with delight as if I have answered some obscure quiz question and won a small fortune. It is infectious. I smile back. Joe closes the curtains, the dense open-weaved curtains that I hid behind. The room darkens and I take up my position.

'Don't worry about the blood. It's only yours,' Joe says.

The bloodstain is rust-coloured, immense.

'Very funny.'

Behind the fabric my voice is muffled.

'How long after the car arrived did you hear them at the door?' he asks.

'Not long. I was surprised how quick they were. You see, I thought, I hoped, that they would do whatever they do in the shed and not bother with the house at all. Minutes, less than minutes.'

Joe goes outside.

Pam puts her hand on my arm and together we wait. A car door slams. And then, almost immediately, the sound of the door opening and closing. Soon the bedroom door opens and light seeps in from the hall.

'Did you hear footsteps?' Joe asks.

'No, Joe. Nothing except the door . . .' I pause, the memory flooding back. 'But it wasn't just the door opening, I heard a key in the lock.'

Joe whistles slowly. 'So he had a key!'

I nod. I think back to that night, to my careful checking of the locks. How futile. Absurd against a villain with a key.

Joe closes the bedroom door and again the room darkens.

'Now what?' Joe's voice in the darkness. 'Did they have a torch?'

Did they? I close my eyes and think.

'Yes. They were looking at the bookcase.'

And again torchlight moves across the coloured spines.

'And then?'

'The desk, I think.'

Torchlight snaps upwards, moves across the room.

'Like this?' he asks. 'Of all the bloody stupid things . . .'

'What is it?' Pam's voice, sharp in the darkness.

'Come and see. Lyn, stay there. You'll see why in a minute.'

'Oh, my God. The mirror, Lyn. They saw you in the mirror. Your jumper stands out like a neon light.'

I am silent for a moment, thinking it through, remembering back. I open the curtains, again and the room fills with light.

'It wasn't like this. I stood behind gathered curtains Joe. A whole bunch of material.'

Pam closes the outside awning and once more the room darkens. We try different variations of gathering in the curtains, but the result is the same. No matter how much bulk I stand behind, the tell-tale gleam of bright green jumper is visible through the open weave.

'But it was night-time, darker than this,' I protest, still doubtful.

'Sunday night wasn't pitch black, though, Lyn. A three-quarter moon. Enough light to see you by.'

Of course, I remember now. The darkness and how I thought I was safe. The black night offering protection, the safety of invisibility. A false security, the moon sweeping out from behind great banks of cloud.

'Not quite invisible, hey, kiddo?' Pam follows my thoughts, the link to Adele.

I put my arm around her shoulders, touched by her perception. Joe looks at us enquiringly. We don't explain.

'What were you doing here, Lyn? I mean, why Adele's room specifically?' Pam asks.

'I'd been in here all afternoon, cleaning, vacuuming, going through her things. Reading.'

'What exactly?'

'Her diaries mainly. She kept one for each year.'

'Oh I see. The family trait.'

Joe goes through the diaries on the shelf.

'All here, save Adele's last year.'

'But that's it. That's the one I was reading.' And then realisation, sharp and flooding, the last memory intact. 'It was in the diary. The shed had been broken into, and the phone calls. Someone ringing and hanging up. The same thing.'

They both look at me.

'You mean that happened on Sunday?' Joe asks slowly.

'Yes. The phone call first. That's what terrified me. And then silence and hanging up.'

Pam shakes her head in disbelief.

'I rang the police. I rang Pam. No one home anywhere. Slack lot.'

Joe's thoughts show on his face. He is having trouble keeping quiet.

'Why on earth didn't you ring the Region.'

'Brain gone to mush,' Pam jokes, and Joe looks slightly shocked.

I grin. 'I should have. I did, I think. Yes, I did, only . . . I guess I ran out of time.'

'And you're missing the essential point,' Pam continues.

'Which is?'

'Where's the diary now?'

We all look. I hunt through the papers on the desk.

'Did you leave it anywhere? When you rang me. By the phone perhaps.'

I indicate the extension on the desk. 'I never left the room. Wait. I did once, to check the locks, but I used the phone here.'

'Why on earth would anyone want a diary that's been here for eighteen months?' Joe asks.

No one answers. No one knows.

'Do you remember anything she had written?'

This part is crystal clear. 'The padlock had been cut. She mentioned the phone calls. She was going for a drink with someone she referred to as "A",' I say matter-of-factly. I don't mention the pregnancy, not sure if I can cope with saying it, the enormity of the loss.

They look at me.

'A,' Pam repeats. 'Who is A?'

Another moment of silence. Too much is uncertain. We make coffee and drink it on the veranda, looking out towards the distant ranges. Line and shape are indistinct, blurred by morning haze.

I leave my car at the farm, unable to concentrate on the long drive home, glad to be a passenger. Joe and Pam make arrangements for the delivery of my car to the shop, a conversation that goes on without my participation, save for the passing over of keys. One of the few benefits of being incapacitated is that the small details of life are taken care of. Before he leaves, Joe hands us both a card. His name and the police station are on the front. On the back he writes his home phone number down. He gives one to Pam.

'Ring me if you need anything at all.'

The other one he gives to me. He presses it into my hand, holds it there with his own.

'Same goes for you. If you think of anything, anything at all. Or if anything happens. Promise me you'll ring.'

'Promise.'

He bends down and kisses my cheek.

'Wait, Joe,' I say.

He turns expectantly. I dig deep in my bag, find the small tape recorder he gave me.

'I haven't used it,' I tell him. 'I couldn't remember any of it until just now.'

The police car pulls out of the driveway. Pam and I watch it drive away.

'What do you think of him?' Pam asks.

'He's nice,' I say, noncommittally.

'And good-looking . . .' she adds.

I make no comment. Barry is good-looking.

'And an athlete,' she continues.

'Is he? What sort?'

'Ah, interest at last. A runner. Long-distance. The marathon.'

His body is small, almost slight. He doesn't look strong enough.

She takes a folded newspaper article from her pocket.

'Last week's local,' she informs me. 'I read it at the hospital.'

I unfold the paper and Joe's face grins happily out from above a short report.

*Country police officer Joe Mileto, twenty-six years old, from Yarra*

*Hills, came first in the marathon at the Athletics Championship held in Stawell last week. He will represent Victoria at the National Championships, to be held later in the year.*

Only twenty-six. Almost ten years between us, half a generation.

'Plenty of endurance there,' Pam comments.

'I didn't know.'

She nods as though in agreement with something she has thought.

'Modest as well.'

# Chapter Seventeen

And shadows of the silver bridges quiver
Faint in the friendly torrent of the river;
'The Gardens', Furnley Maurice

Melbourne again. The uncertain spring morning through which we travel. One minute sun, one minute cloud. At the flat Pam carries my bag, orders me to bed.

'What about your work? You can't look after me for ever.'

'I owe myself some time off. And you need to sleep.'

'Pam, thanks for your concern, but I'm all slept out.'

'I'm following doctor's orders and so are you.'

I hold my hands up in defeat. 'Okay. Promise.'

'At last some sense.'

I do sleep. The fuzziness in my head has compacted into a tight band of pain that presses at my eyes. The short journey and the events of the morning have tired me. I doze the afternoon away and wake to the sound and smell of cooking.

'Hungry?' Pam asks, whisking eggs efficiently in a bowl.

'Mm. Starving.'

'Good.' She smiles. 'Situation normal. I thought an omelette was appropriate. Standard patient food.'

The omelette when it comes is light and fluffy and cooked

to perfection. I eat it hungrily, curled up on the couch in front of the TV, feeling spoilt and warm and safe.

I sleep again until morning and wake feeling rested, almost well. I stretch in delight, aware of the pull of muscles, a glow of energy. Half past six and light is streaming in through the window.

I have a shower and wash my hair. My face in the mirror is only slightly less hideous than yesterday. The swelling is settling down but the bruises are spectacular – a patchwork of blues and purples against the older line of bruising from the fall in the tunnel.

I leave a note for Pam and catch a train into town. The streets are filling, the city stirring into life. I want to walk, to stride, to feel alive and thankful. The great arch of the station yawns at my passing, and the row of clocks and platform indicators gives out the times of numerous trains. I stop and turn back, eyes riveted. Train lines. Platform indicators. Trains! This whole business with Maggie has something to do with trains. I feel a surge of excitement as the idea takes hold.

I re-enter the station and study the diagram of the railway network. Railway lines stretch out from the city like threads from an erratic cobweb. I have seen Maggie on different platforms, different train lines. Perhaps that itself is an answer of sorts.

The first time I saw Maggie she was coming out from platform nine. I look around for the platform indicators. Platform nine is the Frankston line. Another time, she was coming from Princes Bridge station, the Epping and Hurstbridge lines. Perhaps the train lines themselves are part of a code.

The day I travelled with her on the train from Glenferrie, she was reading *Middlemarch*. An unusual choice of book. Perhaps the book she reads is also some sort of clue, but if so, what? It doesn't indicate the book she marks in the shop. This I know because she read *Middlemarch* on Monday, and on Friday she marked *The Mill on the Floss*. Could it have something to do with setting up a meeting place, a certain train line?

I take the idea further, fantasising, speculating. *The Mill on the Floss* could indicate the Melton line. Or equally the Frankston line. Both these lines stretch away from the city to a far point on the diagram. I study the railway diagram again and give up, the excitement fading. Too much is unknown. The puzzle as elusive as ever.

I walk towards the river thinking things through. More profitable perhaps to follow up the marked pages in the book, these at least are fact and not conjecture. *The Mill on the Floss*. Dense pages of text marked in an old novel. Is the text itself some sort of clue? And if so, what? My head is full of ideas that seem to start promisingly but lead nowhere.

I lean over the railings of Princes Bridge, gazing fixedly at the river below, as though in that flat surface I might find some answers. The river is undisturbed by wind or movement and shines in the still morning light like a band of polished silver. This is the same river I looked at from my hospital room, my head bruised and bandaged. The water flowing at my feet now could be the same water I saw then.

And looking into that glittering surface I find within myself, not the answer to any puzzle, but a steely resolution. A fresh determination to solve the mystery. I have had enough of uncertainty, the vulnerability of not knowing, the dangers of ignorance. Twice now I have hidden. Taken refuge in the darkness, expecting safety in invisibility. The tunnel. Behind curtains in Adele's unlit room. Twice now I have come to grief. If my choice is ever again between flight or fight, between hiding or confronting, then next time I will fight.

# Chapter Eighteen

*So I have forgotten the day's duress,*
*The dungeoned offices, the liftmen pale*
                    *'The Gardens', Furnley Maurice*

Inside the shop everything is in order, everything tidy, surfaces clean, fresh flowers in vases. I might never have been away. There is a parcel on my desk. Black and silver wrapping paper. Jordie's handwriting on the card. Small concise writing, easy to read. *If you won't come to karate with me, this is the next best thing. Effective as mace and not illegal to carry. Spray it at their eyes. Keep safe. Jordie.* I open it, intrigued. A slim, black can of hairspray. Attached to the can is a silver whistle.

I laugh until I cry. Jordie, urban dweller, has given me some of her own protection. I think of using the whistle in the bush. No one to hear. No use at all.

I go through the in-tray. There are some personal letters for me that Jordie has not opened. One is written in unfamiliar loops and flourishes. I slit the envelope open and read.

*39 Peter Street*
*Fitzroy*

*Dear Ms Blessing*
*Thank you for your letter and your desire to include me in your research project on Melbourne University graduates. I was sorry to miss you last week and wonder if Tuesday 15 September at twelve o'clock would suit. Please ring to confirm.*
*Georgina Stavros*

I read through the messages that Jordie has taken, both in person and from the answering machine. Among the work enquiries are a jumble of personal ones. 'Peter Ireland. Lyn, where are you? Where were you? Georgina came and went.' 'Ring me' messages from Smithy and Barry.

Jordie, efficient Jordie, has managed without me. The diary entries for the previous days filled out, the dockets and paperwork up to date. The diary explains the week.

Monday 7: Jordie's neat concise hand.

*9.05 Query. Collector trying to track down* The Adventures of Sherlock Holmes. *First edition. 1892. The Strand Library series. Believes we bought it at a recent auction. Can you confirm. Please ring.*

*Can you call Mrs De Lacey. She wants to sell a collection of children's books left to her by her mother. Unsure of what exactly is in the collection, but unhappy with a bookcase full of smelly old books. Says undamaged. Please ring.*

At the end of the day, the sales slips tallied and recorded. The books done. A list of queries set in train.

Tues 8: The messages are in a different hand. A temporary, employed by Jordie.

*Ruth Stone. Melbourne University. To confirm lecture, 7 October, eleven a.m.*

*Ambrose Mallet phoned. He wants you to hold a book he saw here recently. Charles Dickens.* The Life and Adventures of Nicholas Nickleby. *Chapman and Hall. 1838. A first edition.*

This is one already in the cabinets under lock and key. A rare book, with minor stains and foxing. A good sale. Price $3,000. And again the sales slips for the day tallied and recorded, the books written up. Jordie trains her staff well.

Wed 9: Jordie's writing again.

*Alex Smith called in person. And as charming as he sounds on the phone. Seemed very concerned about you. Wanted to know where you were. When will you be back. Told him I didn't know, but possibly tomorrow.*

And a note pinned to the back:

*Denise looked after shop yesterday and is working for me permanently now. Any time you want extra days covered, just let me know. Thanks mainly to you, I'm branching out, starting up my own agency. A small one to start off with. Wish me luck. Jordie A.*

Good for Jordie. Her air of quiet efficiency will go down well in the business world. I file through more queries, making notes in the 'Want Book' of titles requested by collectors, matching them in my mind with possible sources. Later I will begin the process of tracking them down through the usual channels, the bookseller's network.

Eight-thirty. A knock on the door.

'Lyn, thank God you're here.'

Smithy on the doorstep, looking anxious. He is dressed casually, jeans and a winter-weight shirt. He looks thinner than ever, the slump of his shoulders more pronounced.

'You're an early visitor,' I say lightly.

'I saw the light on and hoped it would be you. I'm so pleased you're back, Lyn. But your face. Your beautiful face.'

He stands close to me looking at the damage with still eyes.

'Relax. I'll be okay.'

He shakes his head. 'I came to see you but they sent me away. I didn't know what to think. They said you were too ill.'

'Well, I was. They let me out yesterday.'

'But when I rang the hospital they said you were still too sick for visitors.'

'Hospital inefficiency,' I say. Or more likely the official police line.

He shrugs and brightens. 'Anyway, you're here now. That's the main thing.' Uncle-like, he pats my hand.

'How did you hear about it?'

'Oh, oddly enough I heard it on the news ... Well, sort of. A woman attacked in her own home at Yarra Hills. Recovering in hospital. That sort of thing. I just wondered and then, when I couldn't get in touch with you, I put two and two together. What did they take?'

'Nothing. At least nothing obvious. The police think I disturbed them, scared them off.'

'You didn't see them?'

I shake my head.

'No. No idea. The police think I'm hopeless.'

'Well, I don't. I think you're very brave.'

'They seem to think I got off lightly.'

'Lightly! Lyn, when I see your face ...'

'Smithy, please don't fuss. I'm okay. I can't stand it when people fuss.'

'No, I don't suppose you can. You never could, even as a child. I'm just so glad you're really all right.'

'Yes, Smithy, I really am.'

Finally he looks convinced and turns to go.

'I'll look in on you this afternoon.'

I nod and he leaves, turning to wave at the door, like he has a thousand times before. Just before nine, Jordie arrives.

'Lyn, you're back.' No crispness in her tone now, but genuine delight. 'I've been so worried about you.'

'Thanks for the flowers, Jordie. And the present, it's great.'

'Just, next time, follow instructions.' She imitates holding the can, pressing the nozzle. 'I must say, he did a good job on your face.'

'Mm.'

'And the police, what do they think?'

I repeat what I told Smithy. She shakes her head in disbelief.

'You've done a wonderful job in the shop. Thank you for covering for me.'

'No problems. I was pleased to help. Any time.'

'I love the idea of your agency. I'd like to take you up on the offer of more time.'

'Good. Just let me know when.' She emphasises her words with a smile.

I smile back, feeling pleasure at the prospect of more time to myself.

'I'm not planning on staying today.' I say. 'I just wanted to see what was happening.'

'Whatever you want, Lyn. You're the boss.'

She goes into the office and I use the phone at the front desk to ring Pam.

'Lyn.' Pam's voice, relief in her tone. 'What on earth do you think you're doing? Don't you realise people get worried about you? I do think you could show some consideration.'

I smile, but guiltily. This is Pam at her stuffiest.

'Darling, thanks for worrying, but I'm fine. I just needed to see the shop.'

'Now listen, Lyn. If you insist on working there, I think you need to hire some sort of security. And what about Jordie? Is she safe?'

'Pam. I'm sorry. I shouldn't have gone off without telling you. But it was so early. I didn't want to wake you. I'm not staying long, I just felt the need to get on with life.'

'Always provided that whoever attacked you lets you keep your life.'

'Pam, please don't worry. I need to pick up the pieces. I'll do what you say. I'll look into some sort of security. But I'm safe here, Pam, honestly.'

'How you can possibly know that?' Her voice rises in frustration.

'Pam, I can't hide for ever. Don't worry. I'll take care. I'll check out the security guard. I'll be so careful you won't believe it. And don't worry about dinner tonight. I'll get something on the way in.'

I ring Georgina Stavros and confirm our meeting. I ring Ruth Stone and confirm the lecture. I ring Peter Ireland and apologise for not being at the meeting on Tuesday.

'Lyn. We were just so shocked. We couldn't believe it.'

I change the subject. 'Thanks for the flowers. And thank Vanessa for me. They were lovely.'

'Yes, I will. How are you now?'

'I'm fine. Please don't worry.'

But not so fine, I think, feeling an unreasonable surge of irritation at the frequency of the question.

'Lyn, I was wondering. Would you like to come out for dinner again soon?'

Peter is pleasant enough company, but for some reason the prospect doesn't appeal. The ache of loneliness is fading and I remember our last meeting, those few awkward moments of silence.

'That's kind of you Peter, but I'm really busy at the moment.'

'Another time, then,' he says. 'Good to hear from you, Lyn.'

In the office Jordie is intent upon her work, her black cap of shining hair falling forward, covering her face.

I ring Mrs De Lacey about her mother's collection of children's books. She is not sure of exactly what is in the bookcase, but thinks mainly her own books from childhood. Mary Grant Bruce, Ethel Turner, and yes, as far as she knows, undamaged. I make an appointment to inspect them.

I feel restless, superfluous. I don't really need to be here. I decide to walk along the river.

'I'm going out, Jordie. Stretch my legs.'

She looks up distractedly. 'Do you good.' The crispness is back in her tone. By the time I get to the door, her head is already bent down over her work.

# Chapter Nineteen

*But thou hast graces of thy own,*
*In silver light and golden*
                    *'To the River Yarra', Richard Howitt*

'Excuse me, miss, but does your employer know you're slinking off like this?' Joe is standing beside me, dressed in jeans and carrying a bunch of flowers.

'Joe! I thought you were at work.'

'Day off. I thought I'd visit the patient, see if I could take the patient out to lunch. Give the patient flowers to add to her collection.'

'They're lovely. Thank you for the thought.'

'And last but not least, return the patient's car. It's behind the shop, courtesy of instructions from Pam.'

I take the offered keys. 'Wonderful. Thank you for the trouble. You've only just caught me. I'm off for a walk.'

'Sounds just what the doctor ordered. Am I invited?'

'Of course. Pleased to have the company.'

'Good. You can show me round.'

I put the flowers on the front desk and close the door. As we cross the river, the sun breaks through cloud, shines warmly on our backs, its light cutting through dullness like a knife through grease. The air sparkles.

The Southgate complex is finished now and the fragile warmth has brought some early customers to the outdoor cafés. The bruising on my face attracts a few sideways glances.

'I feel like a wife beater,' Joe says, interpreting the interest in my appearance.

'Then let's confuse them,' I say, linking my arm with his.

He looks at me and smiles and we walk together along the river's edge, stopping at an outdoor café to order pasta and drinks.

We sit without saying much, watching the sun play on the river. The light is golden, shot with silver from the wakes of river craft, from dipping, flashing oars. On the far bank the city soars, haphazard and immense and everywhere small flickers of movement: seagulls, people, boats, trains.

'It's good to see you, Joe. In fact you're just the person I wanted to see. I have an idea I want to try out on someone.'

'Nice to be in demand. But I have something to say to you first.' He is serious, quieter than usual.

'Oh. What is it?'

'I've let you down, Lyn.'

'How?' I ask, surprised.

'When you reported the break-in at the farm, I checked the reports for disturbances.'

'Yes, I remember.'

'Well, the thing is, I didn't check back far enough. I looked through the recent reports. What I should have done was go back longer. Eighteen months longer.'

'Adele?'

He nods. 'There in black and white. I should have checked.'

'Oh, rubbish, Joe. You're not a mind-reader. How could you have known, and what good would it have done anyway?'

'But perhaps, if I had taken things more seriously, you wouldn't have been hurt.'

'And if I'd bothered to read Adele's diary some time in the

last eighteen months ... And anyway Joe you're not responsible for me, for any of this.'

'Somehow I thought you'd say that. You're strong, Lyn.'

'For strong, read single-minded. And if I am it's only because I've had to be. There's not much choice sometimes.'

I don't finish the thought. The painful process of loss. Mum, Adele, the head-down industry of running the shop. Not much scope there for self-indulgence.

Our food arrives: deep bowls of creamy pasta, thick chunks of homemade bread. I change the subject.

'Pam tells me you're a runner. A marathon runner.'

'Yes. Among other things.'

'I never thought of you being a runner.'

'Oh. Why not?'

'Too slight, I guess. Not muscly enough.'

'It's the wiry ones you have to look out for, didn't you know? And what about you, Lyn, is there anything else in your life apart from books? The selling and the writing of.'

'I've always wanted to go hot-air ballooning – I knew you'd laugh. It's the closest I've ever wanted to get to flying.'

There are sparrows at our feet. Fat sparrows squabbling over breadcrumbs.

'Tell me your idea,' he says.

I tell Joe some of the more complex details of the mystery, go on to explain my recent ideas. The idea of the book itself setting the scene for the next meeting, indicating a certain train line. I show him the reconstructed version of Smithy's chart that I drew up the first night I stayed at Pam's. The train lines that I'm sure about filled in.

'I know it's hard to make sense of, but all that coming and going on trains with books, has to mean something. The time she sat next to me reading *Middlemarch*, she went straight back into the station. I mean, there had to be some reason for the journey. This whole thing has to be about something, but I can't seem to make anything fit.'

'Okay. But for that theory to make sense, the person on the

train checking out her reading material has to be the same one that turns up for the next meeting.'

'And twice in the shop it's been a different guy,' I confirm.

'What's the purpose of all that secrecy? Why not just have a meeting? Setting up a code sounds to me like there are lots of different people are involved. What's the point otherwise?'

Joe scatters the remaining breadcrumbs on the ground, to the greedy delight of the sparrows.

'Unless there's someone else. Someone working out of sight somewhere,' I say.

'Who knows?' He shrugs. 'It all seems too complex.'

On this I agree. The facts, as I know them, just won't turn into an acceptable, understandable theory. The glimpses I have had into whatever it is are too random, too few for certainty, too haphazard for conjecture.

'Does it have to be simple?' I ask.

'Most things that work well are. Tell me, when did you come up with this idea?'

'This morning on the way to work. Why?'

'I just wondered if it had anything to do with a serious bang on the head the other day.'

I make a face. 'Too much imagination on my part? Sounds like something one of my teachers said.'

'I'd say, trying to read too much into what you know. Trying to make the facts meet the theory,' Joe says.

'Theorising without enough attention to data.'

'I'd say not enough data to theorise on.'

'Well, in that case I need more data.'

He grins, a sudden easy grin. 'You haven't changed. Still as emphatic as ever.'

I calculate the years since I last saw Joe. Fourteen years, fifteen?

'What garbage you talk, Joe. Tell me, was anything ever done about Adele's report?'

'They did a few follow-ups, but nothing was ever seen, nothing else ever reported. A country shed is pretty small stuff.'

'What do you think about it all?' I ask.

He considers. 'One of the few things we know is that the time is probably fixed. You've seen the woman each time, close to nine. And that does make sense for some sort of clandestine meeting. Peak-hour crowds and all that. And at the shop, she's there at the same time each week.'

'The woman's the link,' I agree. 'The man on the train was with her, the receiver follows her into the shop.'

'The man on the train, what's his part in all this?' Joe asks, looking at me over his wine glass.

'Don't know,' I say.

'He hasn't been into the shop?' Joe asks.

'Not that I know of.'

'And he hasn't done anything to talk of. I mean, apart from staring at the girl on the train, and being with someone at a party.'

'No,' I agree. 'Nothing at all.'

'You're sure it's the same guy? Most people I've come across aren't too good at descriptions, at recognising people.' He smiles. 'When I was at Mildura we had this guy come in to report a robbery. An eyewitness. Someone who'd actually seen the robber, and when we asked for a description he remembered everything possible about the clothes, even the brand name of his runners, all of it, but when it came to the face and build, he went vague. Average height, average build, brown hair. We thought he was useless. Funny thing was, though, we arrested someone soon after that, a robbery that we got to, and there he was in the same runners, same clothes exactly. His thieving clothes we called them.'

'Perhaps any description is better than nothing,' I say, thinking of Barry and his description of the figure waiting and watching in the darkness, the night I went into the tunnel. No real facts, the details minimal, but adding together to form an oddly vivid picture.

'Well, in that case it was,' Joe says.

'Would it be enough to convict him?' I ask. 'On clothes alone?'

'Probably not,' Joe answers. 'But we caught him red-handed.'

'And anyway, I'm not your usual unreliable witness,' I say, changing the subject back to where we were. 'I'm good at faces.'

The waiter removes the crockery from our table. The mood is broken.

'Come on,' Joe says. 'Let's forget all this mystery for a while. Too much brain work on top of a head injury is definitely not a good idea. Feel like showing me around?'

We are in a holiday mood and walk upstream, under Princes Bridge and past the boathouses. Our route winds with the water's edge, along footpaths and bike tracks and soft grassy verges. We cross the road at the Swan Street Bridge and wander through parklands to the Botanic Gardens.

The gardens are another world. A dense green world, untouched by the nearby city. We meander along paths lined with ancient trees, their immense trunks towering above us, opening up into vast canopies of leaf. We buy coffee and cake in the tearooms overlooking the lake and watch the industry of the water birds, the collection of kids trying to catch the eels that squirm thickly just beneath the surface.

Joe is a pleasant, undemanding companion. I feel a sense of ease in his company. The same calmness that I felt when he visited me in hospital. There is no need to fill in the gaps in conversation, for they are easy, pleasant gaps. I feel myself relaxing, the jangle of nerves unwinding another notch.

'I haven't been here since I was a kid,' Joe remarks. 'I tried to catch eels then too.'

'And did you?'

'No. But not for want of trying.'

A child grabs hold of one, lifts it above her head in delight, but the eel squirms and she shrieks and lets it go. We laugh.

'Lyn, I'm on leave soon.'

'Oh. Going away?'

'Queensland for a short time. To see Mum, and then, after that, I'm free.'

'Sounds good.'

'Perhaps we can do something together. See a show. Dinner.'

'Sounds good,' I say in exactly the same tone, but feeling pleasure in the prospect.

He laughs.

'Come on you,' I say. 'I've got to get back. I've got some books to buy.'

'Too much rush and hurry. Typical city dweller.'

'You sound as though you're already on holiday.'

'I wish.'

We wander quietly back through the gardens and across the bridge to the shop. I introduce Joe to Jordie. They shake hands and make appropriate greetings. Jordie has arranged Joe's flowers and placed them on the coffee table. They give a rich glow of colour against the polished wood. Joe turns away, uses his mobile phone to check in at work.

'Lyn, Vanessa rang,' Jordie says, passing me the written message. 'She wants you to ring her. Something about celebrating both a return to life and a new print run of *Gordon*. Congratulations.'

'Thanks, Jordie.'

Joe touches my shoulder. 'Something's come up, Lyn. I have to get back. Thanks for today. I enjoyed it.'

'Yes, it was nice,' I agree.

He kisses my cheek and leaves.

Jordie looks on, her expression admiring.

'Where did he come from?'

'Yarra Hills. I've known him for ever.'

'That's what you said about the last one.'

I make a face and she smiles.


I buy Mrs De Lacey's books with pleasure. They are clean, intact, saleable. I load them carefully into the boot. On my way back to work I stop off to make some purchases. Among other things, I buy a selection of bolts for the next time I visit the house. At five o'clock Jordie gets ready to leave.

'Are you all right if I go?' she asks.

'I'm fine, Jordie, I'm leaving too. Thanks for covering for me.'

'No problem.'

Clouds have covered the sun. The day is grey now, with a cold, restless wind. Just as I am about to leave the phone rings. I answer it automatically.

'Blessing's Books.'

It takes me a minute to realise that this is not a bad connection. That the sound I am listening to is silence and the scratchiness of a faulty line.

'Who is this?' I demand, but there is no answer. No sound at all. I drop the phone back into its cradle. My stomach heaves and I feel a surge of nausea, sudden and almost overwhelming. This then is definite. Shop and farm connected. No doubts. No coincidences. No other possibilities.

I drive to Pam's wondering if whoever it is was outside the shop, waiting for Jordie to leave, waiting for me to be on my own. The watcher. Someone out there, out of sight, blending in with the crowd. I hold the steering wheel tightly to stop the tremor in my hands.

'Problems?' Pam asks, seeing my face.

'The silent phone call trick.'

'Christ. Again?' Dismay, clear as light, on her face. 'I'm ringing Joe.'

Before she picks up the receiver, the phone rings and we look at each other. Her expression a mirror of my own unease.

'Hello.'

Her voice is quiet and calm but her eyes don't move from my face. She doesn't say anything. She doesn't need to say anything. I know what she is listening to. The same thing I listened to earlier. The sound of silence.

# Chapter Twenty

*The gruesome samples here displayed*
*Make me afraid.*
        *'Upon a Row of Old Boots . . .', Furnley Maurice*

The road again. A heavy darkness. Steady falling rain. Pam at my side, a comforting, competent presence.

'Come up. Come straight away. I'll be at the crossroads in one hour. I'll meet you there. Don't go into the house on your own.'

Joe's voice on the phone earlier. He is as good as his word. The police car pulled off the road, the city side of the intersection. I flash my lights at him and he pulls in behind me, follows me into the driveway.

Joe uses his radio and checks in. We go into the house together, switching on lights and heaters as we go. Despite the knowledge that the intruder has a key, we check windows and doors. All are securely locked. I take the bolts from my bag, the screwdriver from the tool box and begin the process of adding bolts to all the outside doors.

'I've put in a report at the station. They know I'm here. Don't worry. No one's going to try anything with a police car in the driveway,' Joe says, but joins in anyway with the process of installing bolts.

With my help, Joe fills out an incident report, rings it through.

'What do you think, Joe?' I ask when he has finished on the phone. 'What's it all about?'

'Some process of intimidation. Whoever it is wants you out of the way.'

'Well, they've succeeded,' I say, and voice the nagging thought that has dogged me ever since the phone calls. 'Whoever it is knows about Pam. Name and phone number.'

'Someone close, Lyn. Like I always said.'

Pam is pale although steady, but to me this feels like the last straw. The danger spreading out relentlessly, catching Pam in its flow.

'I think it's time we had a good talk with some of your friends, Lyn. Start an official investigation.'

Pam's tone is definite. 'Alexander Smith for starters.'

I don't say anything. I seem to have lost touch with reality. I tell them about my conversation with Barry at the hospital. The impression he formed, waiting in the darkness in the alleys behind the shop. Someone slim, light on their feet. Perhaps a woman.

I leave them to it and wander through the house. The bloodstain is still on the carpet, a browner shade of rust. I can hear them talking in the other room. They stop, though, at my tread and turn to look at me as though I am an intruder.

I am suddenly overwhelmingly tired. The patient not yet recovered, not yet able to cope. Pam wanders out, collects pillows and blankets, dumps them on the couch. Joe makes coffee, undrinkable black coffee. None of us thought to buy milk.

I lay my head on the couch. We leave lights on but even with Pam and Joe's company, I am restless and uneasy.

'Do you know if it was on the news?' I ask, thinking about what Smithy had said. 'The attack on me, I mean.'

'I didn't hear it, but then I wouldn't. I was with you most of the time.' Pam says.

I look at Joe.

'No idea,' he answers. 'Is it important?'

'Could be. Could you find out, Joe, through police channels?'

'No problems. Do it tomorrow.'

'Anything we should know?' Pam asks.

'No. Nothing.' My tone is brisk, too brisk, and Pam turns sharply to look at me. We regard each other as if from opposing sides of a gulf, our thoughts racing.

'Lyn ...'

I shake my head impatiently, my tone dismissive. 'No. Leave it.'

Her eyes glitter for a moment but she turns away, catches her bottom lip with her teeth.

Joe continues, seemingly unaware of the tension. 'Whatever's going on has something to do with here. Perhaps a good place to start is to find out which of your city friends knows about this place. Does Jordie?'

'Jordie was Adele's friend originally,' I answer evenly. 'Yes, she often stayed here in the old days. But you can't think ...'

'Jordie Armstrong. A slim woman, light on her feet. And Adele was going to have a drink with someone named A.'

I say nothing.

'And Smith. What's his name? Alex. Another A. Does he know this place?'

'Yes, of course he does. He stayed here often, years ago. Look, nearly everyone has. Before Adele died we used it lots. I had guests stay over, parties, you name it. After the book was released, people stayed overnight. We had this huge party. Remember, Pam?'

She looks at me distantly, her voice flat, dismissing me. 'Yes, I remember.'

I think back to that party. The celebration of a book launch. Adele at my side, dressed elegantly in black. Her hair a blur of pale gold, her face alight. 'And we always thought your first book would be fiction,' she whispered in my ear, her arm

141

around my waist. A reference to my imagination, the old family joke. Funny how long these things from childhood last and how unexpectedly they pop up.

'Did Barry ever come here?' Joe's voice is carefully expressionless.

'Yes,' I reply, not bothering to explain the circumstances.

There is a small pause.

'Everyone then?' Joe taps his pencil against the back of his hand.

'Why not?' I snap. 'It's no crime. And this house is no secret. Anyone could know.'

I close my eyes to shut them out, to hide the surge of anger and irritation. This is the worst part, the pervasive suspicion that seems to touch everyone. My friends as enemies. Smithy, Jordie, even Barry.

The whole business of mistrust and fear and guilt is getting me down. But despite myself some of it sticks. Jordie's unnatural privacy. Her reticence to talk about herself. A female version of what Pam saw in Smithy. I think of her strength, a quiet strength, somehow understated. Strong enough to wield a torch as weapon, to inflict a savage blow. Yes, of course, but why would she? Why would Smithy? Why would anyone? Round and round it goes in my head. All questions unanswered.

Joe and Pam talk on, an interminable, droning discussion on probabilities, possibilities. I fall asleep without meaning to. Some time in the night I am aware of Joe somewhere close by. His steady breath, the warmth of his body.

I wake with the first light. Joe is asleep at the other end of the couch. He is uncomfortable, though, his body twisted around the arm of the couch, his head slumped awkwardly to the side. I slide from the couch, stiff and cramped. Pam is asleep on the other couch. We have slept the night through undisturbed. I wonder whether we have had visitors.

Outside, the world looks fresh and clean with that just-washed look after heavy rain. Everything seems ordinary, familiar, safe. I wander down to the shed, the fresh mud pulling at my boots. There are no footprints, no tyre tracks.

The padlock on the shed has gone, removed by Joe after the attack. I should replace it. I should have done this from day one. Got in their way. Made them aware that, if nothing else, I knew about the padlock. I slide the shed door open. Inside the usual clutter is seemingly unchanged, an untidy gathering of junk.

I am restless. Feel the need to do something constructive. To make order out of chaos. I collect kitchen gloves and begin what Adele and I had planned to do long ago.

Working with energy born of anger, I throw things out. All the rubbish: the half-empty boxes of fertiliser and seed, the old paint tins and oil containers end up in a pile near the door, dislodging little puffs of dust from the floor as they land. When I have created enough bench space I sort out the more useful things: old tools, bridles and saddles, gold pans, dart boards, table-tennis bats.

A bottle of turpentine slips from my grasp. I watch it roll away, the track of its passage on the earthen floor, the dust smoothed out. In its wake something flickers and dies. A small, upwards movement. A gleam of pink.

It's the colour that intrigues me. That inexplicable flicker of pink. Not a leaf. Not a bone. Not a stick. Not anything obvious. I squat on my heels and run a finger through the dust. As soon as I touch it, I know what it is.

A feather. A long, curved feather. I blow the dust from the plume and flex the spine. A blush of soft pink extends upwards from the base, fading into dense white, like a plume of smoke. The feather feels springy and fresh. I wonder how long it has been here.

Colour and size give it away. No common garden bird this, but something more exotic. In the house, I look up one of the family's books on Australian birds. A thick book sectioned off into bird types. In the section on parrots I find what I am looking for. A glossy photo of a pink and white cockatoo

143

looking out from beneath an intricate crest of red and white feathers. A pink cockatoo. *Cacatua leadbeateri*. More commonly known as a Major Mitchell, after the explorer who had first seen them on his travels, had first commented on their beauty. The text informs me that their status is under threat, their numbers diminishing due to loss of habitat, the effects of smuggling.

Birds. The answer to the puzzle clicks inevitably and finally into place. I hold the feather like some sort of prize. Smugglers, yes. But not drug smugglers, as I had discussed with Smithy. Not drugs, but birds.

# Chapter Twenty-one

*How will you know what spells are caught*
*In the nooses of endless thread?*
'On a Grey-haired Old Lady Knitting...', Furnley Maurice

I wake Pam first. The touch of a feather on a cheek is a sure way of gaining attention. She rubs her cheek to brush away the feel of the feather and opens her eyes reluctantly. She looks at me as though I am an annoying child.

'City dweller,' I say, and turn to Joe.

A similar reaction out of sleep that makes me smile, but as he begins to focus, he follows my train of thought.

'Birds. Bloody birds.' Joe's tone is dismayed. 'I should have known.'

'All this agony and aggravation is about birds?' Pam is disbelieving.

'Birds are big business,' Joe says. 'One of the best crimes you can pull off.'

'Why?' Pam asks. 'I mean, I know about bird smuggling, but surely it's low-key.'

'No. Not now at least. Huge money for little risk. It's still not seen as serious crime.'

'What will happen to whoever it is? If they catch them, that is,' I ask.

'A fine perhaps. The most serious penalty so far is about eight months' jail.'

I take the electricity bill out of my bag, unthought of until now. 'I got this the other day. I thought it was a mistake. But perhaps, an incubator. Eggs as well as birds.'

Pam fingers the springy softness of the feather.

'What type of bird do you think?'

Joe looks at me.

'A Major Mitchell, according to the book.'

'But they're not from around here, are they?' she asks.

'No. Further west: western Victoria, South Australia, Western Australia.'

'Mitchells are where the money is.' Joe puts an arm around me in a sort of quiet elation. 'You've done it, Lyn. At last we know.'

'I'm the link,' I say. 'My shop. My house. The system works around me somehow.'

Joe nods agreement. 'Yes, but we're getting there now. At least now we know what the whole thing is about.'

An early morning conference at Joe's police station. I have showered away the dust and dirt from the shed and am dressed ready for work in an outfit from the wardrobe at the house. A red suit, with a slim skirt and tailored jacket. My reflection in the mirror is a surprise. I haven't worn red in years. I like it, though, its boldness is appealing.

Pam, crumpled from her night's sleep and the wrong size to borrow any of my old clothes, nods her approval.

'Good. A good time to make a statement.'

The feather is passed around. And like the laying on of hands, they all touch it, all run their fingers down the spine. Bruce Spence, Joe Mileto and members of the CID, Customs officers and officials from the Department of Conservation and Natural Resources.

The police machinery in full swing, the shed is under

inspection, fingerprints, photographers, casts of tyre tracks already taken. The dossier is growing, the case officially launched.

Pam is dubious at all the activity.

'Isn't this a bit excessive?' she asks. 'I mean, all this for some birds.'

A chief investigator from Customs answers, the hint of a Scottish accent in his voice. 'Fauna trafficking is second now only to drug running. It's big business, attracts big professionals, often the same ones that run the drugs.'

He outlines his department's work from the other end. The surveillance at Hattah National Park. The checks on cars going in and out. Someone they had their eye on who had disappeared. The surveillance of certain trees in the area. The old dead trees, hollow-centred, the breeding trees for native birds. A suspected link to a fauna smuggling ring operating out of Melbourne. So far conjecture, no real facts. And then, in dense scrubland, the discovery of a body. Cause of death, undetermined.

'Today is Friday,' I say into a pause in the discussion.

They look up at me surprised. Bruce Spence's fleshy face settles into easy, familiar patronisation.

'Yes, my dear.'

I return his gaze coolly. 'Today, after lunch, after Jordie leaves, Maggie should make her appearance in the shop, mark the book and the receiver will follow.'

'How do you know?'

'It's on record. I made a statement in hospital about some unexplained events in my shop. They follow a pattern. And you need to know.'

He consults quickly with Joe sitting at his side and turns back to face me. 'Yes, we do.' He nods briskly, the flesh on his cheeks quivering with the sudden movement.

'Whoever it is doesn't want me to be there. The phone calls did their trick of scaring me away. I guess they hoped I would get someone to fill in for me, Jordie or one of her staff.

Someone who doesn't know what's going on.'

'It could be dangerous. Especially now, if they are taking steps to get rid of you.' Bruce Spence looks at me. There is no concern in his tone or expression.

'Make whatever arrangements you want, but I have to be there,' I say, standing up. 'You need me to be there. To follow routine. I don't want Jordie to cover for me, I'm not putting her in danger. It's getting late and I need to go.'

There is a general stirring of movement in the room, undermining Spence's glare of disapproval at my taking over. Joe and Pam follow me outside.

'Do you want me to be with you?' Pam asks, her voice calm and composed.

'Best not,' I say. 'You've done enough. It's up to the police now.'

'I'll be there,' Joe says, turning from Pam to me, offering us joint reassurance. 'Someone will be there. I'll ring you, let you know what's happening.'

'Thanks Joe, I'll see you.'

He takes my hand and looks at me with concern in his eyes.

'Joe, I have to go.'

'I know. Just be careful, okay.'

'I'll be fine. You best get back in there. Promotion time, don't you think?'

'I doubt it. Not with Bruce in charge.' He grins suddenly, his face lighting up like a ten-year-old's. 'Did you see his face when you took over? All that cool matter-of-factness. He didn't know what hit him.'

Pam and I drive back to town, our thoughts preoccupied, conversation desultory.

'Sorry I was shitty last night,' I say at one point.

She shrugs. 'Forget it. Anyway, I hardly noticed.'

'Liar.'

'I don't blame you.' She pats my shoulder in small, quick movements. 'All this is enough to fray the toughest edges. And yours aren't as tough as you think.'

I make a face and she smiles.

'But we're getting there, Lyn. Getting closer to a resolution.'

A touch of eagerness in her tone that makes me smile. Conversation lags as I concentrate on changing lanes.

'Still think it's Smithy?' I ask some time later.

She shrugs beside me. 'I'm not so sure now. Funny what Barry said about a woman. It opens up the possibilities.'

'Only as far as Jordie.'

'Yes,' she agrees. 'Do you think it's possible?'

'I don't know.'

'Someone else with a secret in their life.' She shakes her head impatiently. 'I've had enough of it, Lyn. I know how you must feel. Anyway, today with luck it will all be over. We'll know beyond doubt. No more guesswork.'

I don't answer and she doesn't try and draw me out.

Outside her flat, she holds the car door open. Like Joe earlier, she is reluctant for me to go on alone.

'Are you sure about this, Lyn? Let me come with you.'

I shake my head. 'Routine, Pam. It'll be okay. The long arm of the law and all that.'

'Yes.' She bites her bottom lip. 'Ring me. Let me know what's happening.'

I nod and drive away. I can see her in the rear-view mirror, standing completely still, watching the car out of sight. I turn the corner and she is gone.

I am late. My first late day ever and Jordie is already hard at work. It is difficult in Jordie's familiar presence to give credence to my own suspicions of last night. In daylight the whole idea seems absurd. The morning slides past in a strange mix of normality and apprehension, broken up by phone calls and a steady flow of customers.

Just after midday I send Jordie off, asking her to call at the post office with some mail. She is willing enough as always, but looks at me curiously.

'Are you all right, Lyn? You seem a bit tense today.'

'Do I? Just tired, I guess. I could do with that extra time off.'
She nods. 'I'll get back to you about it. See you next week.'

Only an hour to go. The last hour. Once I am on my own, the fitful apprehension of the morning kicks in hard. The passage of time is patternless now, unfixed. The sweep of the clock erratic, sometimes fast, sometimes slow enough for me to think that time has stopped.

I take refuge in tracking down requested books. The elusive first edition of *Rebecca* comes to light in a nearby bookshop. I place it on hold. Joe rings with instructions from above.

'Lyn, Bruce says you're not to talk to the woman when she comes in. Not to interfere in any way, just let things run their course.'

I make no comment. 'What's happening out there?' I ask.

'Things are set up, the shop is being watched, both Maggie and the receiver will be followed.' He is precise and efficient. 'I'll be in later. Are you okay?'

'Never better.' I say, with a touch of irony in my tone.

I think of the process that I have set in motion, the shadowy business of surveillance. So many pairs of eyes at watch and Maggie as part of the prey.

Routine lurches on. The minutes grind past. At twelve-thirty, I hang a sign on the door, BACK IN FIVE MINUTES. I lock up and leave to buy food that I don't want, and won't eat. After the long dragging morning, it is good to get out. I walk around the block, trying not to stare into people's faces, but expecting to see Maggie at every breath. Expecting to see police in doorways. The watchers watching me. I see no one.

There is a cluster of pedestrians passing the shop door. I wait for them to clear the doorway and that's when I see him, mixed in with a group. I just catch the fall of light brown hair, the long jaw. In a flash he is gone. A man with his back to me, a man about his business, no haste, just fluent, efficient strides. Georgina's man. The man on the train. The watcher. He is here then, among the rest of them. Watching and waiting.

At five minutes to one a customer comes in. An unknown woman. She browses steadily, unhurriedly. The minutes fly

150

now, hands sweeping around the clock, faster than heartbeat. At ten past, I write a quick note on the back of one of my business cards and make my way to the classics shelves.

My heart is loud in my ears and my mouth is dry. Perhaps she will not come. Perhaps the watcher has warned her. Perhaps they have decided that the whole thing is too risky. The long morning of drawn-out tension has been in vain, but at least Maggie will be safe. The thought hits me like an answer to a prayer and I feel a flood of relief. The more I think about it, the more likely it seems and the more hopeful I become. At quarter past one, the doorbell clangs.

Again, without delay, without pause, she turns the last corner. She starts when she see me, hiding out of sight among the classics. She looks scared, but defiant, like a cornered dog, fight not far away. In her small square face, eyes like Adele's glower with resentment.

'You again. Can't you leave me alone?'

She is so close I can see the pores of her skin. She is paler then ever.

'Maggie, they're watching you. You have to get away.'

She gazes at me steadily and reaches up for the book. Her movements are deft, efficient, defiant. With the other hand she yanks out a hair, places it in the book. *The Mill on the Floss*. Pages 334 and 335.

'This is the last time. Don't give me away.' Her gaze is steady, her dark eyes burn.

'It's too late. They know about you, Maggie. They're watching you. I want to help you. Let me help you.' I press my card into her hand. 'Ring me. And whatever you do keep away from the man who scares you. Go somewhere – hide.'

The doorbell clangs and we spring instantly apart. The receiver has arrived. Maggie pushes past me and makes her way to the door. She passes him. He does not look at her or touch her.

The receiver is slower, takes his time, pretends at least to browse. I move out of his way. He takes no notice. Again it is someone new, someone I have never seen before. I hear the scrape of the book as he takes it down, the snapping shut. He pushes past me and he too is gone. The customer follows him out. The shop is suddenly empty. The action taking place elsewhere, out of sight, but not out of mind.

Minutes later Joe comes in. He is oddly elated.

'They want me to keep an eye on the shop. Just in case.'

'What do they think?'

'Too early yet.' He shrugs.

'What's happening outside?' I ask.

'As you said. The girl first, skin like chalk and eyes like possum's. I've never seen eyes so large. We had someone outside, set to follow her. And then, a few minutes after, the man came in. Everything happened exactly as you said it would. Someone was set to follow him. And someone else to watch the shop. For anything, or anyone, suspicious.'

'He was here. Outside the shop earlier. The watcher. The man from the train.'

He nods. 'There are people watching. Good people. They'll see him.'

I imagine the scene, up past Young and Jackson's. The footpaths busy with lunchtime shoppers. Would the receiver stop in the pub this time, eyes fixed casually to the intersection, waiting for the lights to change?

'Same page?' he asks.

I shake my head and show him. Pages 334 and 335. The hair is gone, lost somewhere in the process of checking for it.

'335 – the number I found in her things.'

Joe reads the close text and shrugs. Text and page number are meaningless.

My thoughts are with other things. Where Joe's are, I don't know. The action probably, wishing he was out there doing something. Mine are with Maggie. Where is she now?

This is the first time Joe has been in the shop for any length of time. True to form, he checks out the security system, the unobtrusive cameras.

'Whoever set this whole thing up must have known about the system. Known the classics section isn't covered,' Joe comments.

'Yes.'

I am noncommittal. It is something I realised at the start of all this. This is something Jordie had commented on.

'Oh, I almost forgot. I got someone on to finding out if the attack on you made the news.'

'Yes.'

'No, apparently not. He checked with all the radio stations. Not one of them carried it.'

'I see. Thanks Joe.'

I turn away so he cannot see my face. So Smithy lied. The enormity of this yawns before me, beats in my head like a hammer. Smithy lied. I had known it, though, had sensed it at some deep level of my own. Some instinct about body language had given him away, that last time, the early morning in the shop. But even now, with the knowledge of his lies drumming in my brain, I find the idea of his involvement difficult to believe. Even now, part of me wants to find some other explanation.

I cannot settle into work. I use the office phone to ring Pam. She answers on the second ring.

'Lyn?' Her tone is anxious.

'No news yet. Joe's here. The police are following the girl and the man who followed her in. We have to wait.'

'Not your strong point,' she comments.

'No,' I agree. 'It's shaping up, though. I'll let you know as soon as I hear anything.'

I put the phone down as Joe pops his head around the door and wanders off again. Someone else who is restless, who can't seem to settle. Still no news. The afternoon passes slowly, concentration impossible to find. Each time the phone rings my stomach knots with anticipation, hoping that it is Maggie, hoping that she has found the courage to call. Each time I am disappointed.

Joe spends the rest of the afternoon in the office, watching through the one-way glass. Every time the shop bell clangs, he takes notes of times, descriptions. To me, though, nothing seems noteworthy, nothing seems suspicious. And then, at last, release. A phone call for Joe. A message for me. Close up shop. It's all over.

# Chapter Twenty-two

*The roads come in, roads dark and long,*
*To the knock of hubs and a sleepy song.*
*Heidelberg, Point Nepean, White Horse,*
*Flemington, Keilor, Dandanong,*
*Into the centre from the source.*
'The Victoria Markets Recollected in Tranquillity', Furnley Maurice

Russell Street police station. A warren of corridors, a hum of activity. A duty officer takes us through its complex ways and opens an office door. A man rises to greet us. He is tall and slim, almost skinny. His face is pale, as though he spends too much time indoors. He shakes my hand and then Joe's, introduces himself to me as Inspector Paul Sweetman.

'Sit down.' He gestures towards two chairs on the visitor's side of his desk, and sits facing us across its cluttered surface.

'Exhibit one.'

He shows us a dead bird enclosed in a plastic bag. A pink cockatoo. *Cacatua leadbeateri.* A Major Mitchell. Even in death its colours are remarkable. That delicate blush of rose pink, the bright white feathers, the red and white crest. A crumpled, wasted life.

'A male, according to Customs. They can tell by the red in the crest. Didn't even make it to the airport.' His tone is thick with disgust. 'Customs have the rest. They have hopes for their survival, although one isn't looking too good.'

'Were there many?' I ask.

'Sixteen eggs, four birds. Three now.'

He outlines the combined efforts of police, Customs and the Department of Conservation. The police side dealt with following Maggie and the man from the shop. Maggie proved too elusive, her ease with public transport too great. She was lost early on, somewhere in the confusion that is Flinders Street station. I am not sure whether to be pleased or not. Not sure about her safety.

The receiver, Sweetman tells us, was an easier target. A straight route to Tullamarine, a ticket collected from the QANTAS desk. A flight to Christchurch. Flight number 335.'

'Page number,' I say. 'She marked the page to indicate the flight.'

Beside me Joe nods.

'And then back to the airport car park,' Sweetman continues. 'And at the back, a station wagon. The eggs already in the pouches of a special vest, warmed in an incubator. All he had to do was slip it on. He was arrested and charged. Name of Len Martin.'

'Who is he?' Joe asks.

Sweetman consults his notes.

'Male Caucasian, twenty-three years old, former student of Melbourne University, resident of Carnegie.'

'What sort of student?' I ask.

'Psych. Graduated last year. Up to now, unemployed. According to Martin, someone contacted him by phone. Said he was a friend of a friend. The offer of easy money. A down payment in the mail. We've pushed him on it, but that's all we can get out of him.'

'What was the page number last week?' Joe asks me.

'101.'

Inspector Sweetman looks between us and smiles knowledgeably.

'QANTAS flight 101. A Friday afternoon flight, bound for Auckland.'

Both flights out on Friday afternoon. The book marked Friday lunchtime. Flight numbers, page numbers. Simple.

'So just the page numbers were relevant. Nothing else?' Joe asks.

'Seems so,' Sweetman says. 'Did you have something else in mind?

Joe's gaze meets mine.

'No,' I say. 'At least, I had a theory about the books.'

'Only one of them, according to Martin. The page number was always marked in the first volume of *The Mill on the Floss* on the shelves. He said you always carried a few different editions of the same book.' He looks at me for confirmation.

'Yes.' I nod. 'It's popular enough. It's on a few different readings lists in schools.'

'Martin explained the whole thing. He said it was as good a scheme as any, considering his boss was paranoid about surveillance. She carried a wallet with her. He carried an identical one. She would buy a coffee at the kiosk at Flinders Street and he would swap wallets. It was payment. Nothing else. A stack of money.'

So it had nothing to do with trains after all. No bizarre romanticised meetings on trains, the train line established by Maggie's choice of reading material. Simpler than that. A set place and a set time. A kiosk at Flinders Street station. Monday morning. Some time before nine o'clock.

'The Auckland police have been told to look for station wagons in the airport car park, complete with incubators. And then there is this.'

He bends down behind his desk and lifts out a green bag, a hold-all. He puts it on his desk, removes the sleeping bag from the top, a familiar red sleeping bag. He takes out the other things and places them on his desk: the video tape filmed by Jordie, the photocopies of Maggie's notes.

'Where was it?' I ask numbly.

I see him look at Joe and know this is something they have discussed.

'Residence of Alexander Smith, Flinders Lane, Melbourne.'
His voice is even, noncommittal, but his eyes are on my face.

The sense of betrayal rises up fresh and bitter. All the time
it was what Pam had seen. Something I was blinded to because
of friendship. I think back to the night of the tunnel. Smithy
as rescuer, Smithy as confidant, Smithy as trusted friend. My
bag with its bits and pieces of information and all he had to do
was go into the tunnel and take it. Again simple. The evidence
concealed for as long as the game was to run. Evidence he
knew about only through me.

I think of the pantomime in the tunnel, his gestures of
reassurance. The warm squeezing of my hand. Our torches
shining in the filthy water, trying to see into its murky depths.
My feelings are mixed: a sense of shame at my gullibility, a
sense of outrage at his duplicity. And underneath all this, a hard
edge of anger.

Sweetman looks at me and organises tea.

'Friend of yours?'

'Yes. Hard for me to believe. He always loved wildlife.'

This is only a small part of what I am thinking.

'Loved money more,' Sweetman says bluntly.

'I told him everything,' I say. 'About the conversation with
Maggie. Everything.'

The tea arrives with sweet biscuits. Joe pours and hands me
a cup.

'Part of his plan, don't you think?' Sweetman asks. 'Part of
the conspiracy. Premises close by. A shop he knew well, down
to which areas weren't covered by security cameras. A business
run by a trusted friend, one whom he could rely on to tell him
if there was anything suspicious going on. And I bet he was
a frequent visitor, full of invitations. How's business going,
Lyn? – that sort of thing.'

'Well, yes, he was. Only I guess I misread his motive. I
thought he was being kind.'

Sweetman looks at me with sympathy. 'There's no doubt he
was behind it. And he's cleared out. All his papers, passport.

Everything. Just some clothes and a few paintings left. And the furniture, of course. Nothing left to incriminate him. But he did leave this.' He indicates my belongings, now part of the clutter on his desk. 'We'll need to keep these for the time being.'

'Yes, of course,' I say absent-mindedly, my thoughts elsewhere.

'So the recent attack on you, that was Smith?' Sweetman asks, picking up his pen, writing it down.

'Looks like it,' I answer, trying for a matter-of-fact tone that doesn't quite come off.

'Assault as well as smuggling,' Sweetman says, noting it down and looking pleased. 'And something else I'm not sure of yet. The men who followed the girl into your shop, "receivers" you called them. There were more than one?'

'Yes. The one today. And another on video.' I indicate the tape already on his desk, the film that Jordie took.

'Good-oh,' he says. 'Evidence courtesy of Alexander Smith.'

'Kind of him,' Joe says. 'Dobbing someone in. And Martin really didn't know about the boss?'

'Says he didn't. I'm inclined to believe him. Says his only contact was the shop, the woman and a few phone calls.'

'Anyway,' Joe says, looking at me, 'for you, Lyn, it's all over. Now you can relax while we tidy up the loose ends. The easy part.'

But not really so easy. The going through my story, confirming the evidence. A constable to take notes. Statements from Joe, the written work growing. I tell them about the watcher on the train. The unknown man, the outsider. They listen attentively, record the information. They aren't really interested in shadowy men on trains, who have done no more than stare at passengers. They have Smithy in their focus. A concrete villain, concrete motive, concrete evidence.

A constable enters with a stack of photos taken from today's surveillance. Sweetman looks at them and passes them over to me one at a time. I go through them, seeing again the main players. Maggie and the man who followed her into the shop, now known as Len Martin. There are photos of customers, photos of me leaving the shop to buy lunch, photos of me returning, photos of Joe. There are no photos of the watcher. Wherever he was, he stayed out of sight, unobserved and unnoticed. I am not surprised. Joe looks at me quizzically and I shake my head.

Sweetman puts it into words. 'So, Lyn, no sign of the fellow you suspect?'

I shake my head. 'No. He's probably too clever for that.'

'Best to make sure. Take a magnifying glass, study the people in the background. We can always enlarge them if you find anything.'

I work under bright lamps, taking my time, studying each face in the crowd. The photos are black and white and, under such close scrutiny, the faces are curiously grainy. When I have finished I stack them in a neat pile and hand them back to Sweetman, who, like Joe, looks at me quizzically. I shake my head.

Joe's part is over, he has work to do elsewhere. They take my statement and read it back to me, the story couched strangely in police jargon. They play the old video tape over and over. Freeze sections, collect photos of another man's face.

And soon I am free. I stand at the top of the steps and look up and down Russell Street. From here I can see the library dome. The same library that I worked in at the beginning of all this. It seems a life time ago, a different world, a safe world, where threats and fear and violence were unknown.

# Chapter Twenty-three

*From the corner of Swanston and Flinders Street*
*I had a vision today;*
*A Parrish castle was towering sweet*
*Over the crowded way.*
                    'Unconditioned Songs', Furnley Maurice

Joe appears at my side.

'Sorry, Lyn. I got caught up. They just told me you'd gone.'

'All my lovely theories,' I complain.

He smiles down at me.

'It's the literary mind that does it. All that delving into books, looking for significance.'

'Well, I didn't get the significance of the page numbers. I should have worked on that instead of running away on train lines.'

He laughs. 'Easy to be wise in hindsight isn't it?' Don't worry, Lyn. Everyone is delighted with you. There's a lot of political pressure to stamp out the trade, and conservation is over the moon. You'll probably get a medal.'

'Oh, sure,' I say, feeling strangely deflated. My mind preoccupied with the events of the day. Maggie. Smithy.

He tucks his hand under my arm. 'Come on. I'll buy you a coffee.'

We find a small coffee shop opposite the museum. I am

suddenly hungry, aware that I have hardly eaten all day. As well as coffee, we order egg and bacon sandwiches, a serving of chips. We eat our food perched on stools at the window and look out on to Swanston Street. A tram stops at the lights at La Trobe Street. People get off, spill out towards the library, RMIT, the station. I watch the changing procession without speaking.

'Gets you like that,' Joe says, watching me. 'It's the emotion. All that nervous energy. Worse somehow if you're the one waiting.'

So he felt it too, the long dragging day, wanting to be doing something, but forced to wait quietly inside.

'Yes,' I agree.

Outside, a woman is waiting for a tram. She is impatient, paces up and down, checks the line constantly. Someone else, I think, who can't bear waiting.

'I've enjoyed meeting up with you again,' Joe says quietly.

'Yes. Me too,' I say, rousing myself. 'I've never really thanked you for . . . well, for everything.'

His eyes are fixed on his coffee.

'Can I see you again?'

I study his face, catch a fleeting glimpse of the ten-year-old, incongruous above the official police uniform.

'We did mention dinner some time,' I remind him.

'I hadn't forgotten. I wondered if you had.'

I shake my head and he smiles. No trace of the ten-year-old now. An interesting face. An attractive mouth, a full lower lip. Policemen shouldn't look as good as this, nor childhood friends of the family.

'When?' he asks.

I touch his hand. 'Soon. Right now I need to go home and sleep for a week. Ring me.' A tram stops at the lights. The woman outside boards quickly, anxious to be away.

'What are you going to do now?' Joe asks.

'Go home, close up properly. Do the books,' I say.

He nods.

'Can I walk with you?'

'Glad of the company.'

We walk together to the shop, threading our way through the great flow of pedestrians making their way out of the city. Joe moves with a controlled grace, a loose-knitted easiness. Part of his training, I suspect, all that endless movement.

At the shop everything is quiet. There is no hint of the drama that unfolded earlier. The police and villains that sucked me into their world have spat me out again. I say goodnight at the shop door, but Joe hesitates.

'Are you sure, Lyn? We could make an occasion of it. After all it's not every night you crack a bird-smuggling ring single-handedly.'

'Hardly single-handedly,' I say, thinking of all the people involved. 'No, Joe. I have something I need to do. Another time.'

I am anxious about Maggie. The indicator on the answering machines tells me I have had no calls. No messages from Maggie. I ring Pam to tell her about Smithy. To tell her that it is all over. To tell her I'm staying the night in the shop, and that despite everything, I am okay.

'Even now I find it hard to believe,' I say.

'It's the childhood thing,' she says with her calm common sense. 'Impressions formed in childhood are the hardest to dislodge.'

'You're telling me,' I agree. 'Anyway, you were right and I was wrong. Next time I'll listen more carefully.'

'Oh yeah?' she says with enough scepticism in her voice to make me laugh. 'I'm glad it's over, Lyn. Sleep well. I know I will.'


On Saturday, Pam takes me out for dinner. Carlton again, but this time she insists we lash out. Steak and seafood, rich desserts, creamy cocktails.

Pam raises her glass. 'To safety. To life returning to some sort of normality.'

'I'll drink to that. And to you for, well, what can I say?'

She looks at me with amusement. 'Hard to sum up isn't it? Nurse, laundry, general saviour. I'll send you the bill.'

We drink our cocktails in celebration at the end of the danger, of simply being alive. For Pam it is all over and she is jubilant, but I am struck with more complex emotions. Guilt for keeping my knowledge of Jason to myself. Anguish at the fact that, through me, Pam too had been caught up in uncertainty and danger. Her face now is flushed with pleasure, lit with joy by the simple fact that I am safe. I make a firm decision. I will not involve her again.

The next day I move officially back to the office, despite Pam's protestations. I still harbour vague hopes that Maggie might ring, and there are things I have to arrange. I tell Pam about my plans for new accommodation. The shop as interim only.

'Stay until you find somewhere of your own,' she suggests.

'It's time to go,' I say, and she nods her understanding.

After Pam's spare room, the shop seems cramped and uncomfortable. I think with a pang of guilt about Jordie's reaction when she comes to work on Wednesday. But I have no choice. I need to be on my own.

On Sunday Joe and I make arrangements for dinner. I opt for a quiet pub meal at Young and Jackson's, the pub on the corner. The pub I followed the receiver into, at the start of all this. We eat in Chloe's bar, the upstairs dining room, and look out over the great intersection of Swanston Street and Flinders Street. Joe orders roast beef and Yorkshire pudding, a pot of draught beer. I have trevally and white wine.

'I forgot to tell you,' Joe says, cutting up his beef. 'Sweetman didn't know the other day, but apparently the Customs officials who checked Smith's flat found some more wildlife.'

'More birds?' I say, surprised.

'Not birds, Lyn, but lizards. In tubes, ready for posting. Addressed to Japan.'

'Lizards!'

I remember the postal tubes the night I went for a drink. The Japanese cities: Osaka, Tokyo, Kyoto. Lizards ready for the posting.

'Lizards are valuable too. A shingle back and two frill necks apparently. Conservatively worth about $6,000 each. Pocket money after a Major Mitchell, but useful. Your friend certainly knew his trade.'

'Were they okay? In the cylinders, I mean.'

'Customs think they were just out of the fridge. A nice dose of cold and they'd sleep all the way to Japan.'

After dinner we cross Princes Bridge and wind our way upriver, away from Southgate towards the distant bridges: Swan Bridge, Morrell Bridge. It is cold but windless. We sit on a bench looking out over the water, the lights of the surrounding city reflecting on its surface in long, still streaks of colour.

'What are you doing about a flat?' Joe asks me.

'I saw one today that I'm going to take. It's not much, but the rent is low, and the position's good. It'll do for a while at least.'

'I'll help you shift if you like.'

'There's not much to move,' I say. 'I seem to have lost some possessions along the way.'

'When's it happening?'

'Weekend after next.'

'Good. Done.' Determination in his voice.

I have a sudden memory of Joe as a ten-year-old. A bet he and Billy had made, a competition to see who could stay awake the longest. Billy had given in first, so tired he had fallen asleep simply by sitting down. Joe lasted twenty-four hours, was still awake when we got up in the morning, pleading the need for witnesses.

It is too cold to sit for long and we wander back though pools of street-lighting, patches of inky darkness. There is a small sound on the river behind us, like a bird landing, or a stone thrown from a distant bridge. I stop to listen.

'What is it?' Joe asks, his voice close in the darkness.

He is back-lit from a distant light that shines softly in his hair. I can't quite make him out but even in darkness he seems familiar, as though I have known him for ever.

'Nothing,' I say. 'Just a sound somewhere on the river.'

We walk briskly home and I kiss him goodnight at the shop door. A light kiss on the cheek, a gesture of friendship.

'Goodnight, Joe.'

He rings hours later, with news of a break-in at a small flat in Epping. The owner, a traveller, is often away, but his four-wheel drive is still in the garage. The police trace the owner through his registration. Alexander Norman Smith. Wanted for fauna smuggling and assault. Believed to have left the country.

This, then, is part of Smithy's other life. The elusiveness that Pam saw earlier on. The police match the tyres from his car to the cast of tracks in my driveway. Forensic confirmation of something that for us, at least, needs no confirmation.

# Chapter Twenty-four

I walk early on the river. The other way to last night with Joe. Princes Bridge, Queens Bridge, Kings Bridge. Mist obscures the city buildings, diminishes the view to a small arc around me. Apart from the muted rumble of city traffic, I could be anywhere. Above my head, through mist, a leaden sun, silver as the moon.

It's the noise I hear first, the rush of activity, of urgent shouts. A voice tight with panic. 'For Christ's sake, get her out.' And a splashing sound, eerie in the mist, punctuated by grunts and the sound of straining.

'Best stand back, miss.' A uniformed figure at my shoulder, startling me.

'What is it? What's happened?'

'Police Rescue, miss. Body in the water.'

My hair is damp with mist, the cold seeping into my bones. And then I see that they have a body up on the path. A limp body, boneless, muscleless. A thatch of blonde hair. I am drawn as though by magnet, without thought and without doubt.

Even in death, she looks like Adele. Her face is more bloodless than ever, her lips blue. The heart-shaped earring has gone, and her earlobe is torn and jagged. Her eyes are closed, no glint of accusing black.

Someone is saying, 'But she was moving. I saw her move.'

'It's the tide. She was moving with the tide.' The same voice turns to me, speaks softly.

'Better move on, miss.' A gloved hand touches my shoulder.

The mist has almost gone now, colour and shape returning to the land. There is no attempt to rekindle life, it is too obviously over. They cover her body, shut out the disturbance of death.

I remember Adele, after death, her body twisted and broken, damaged by impact. Only her face remained untouched, her beautiful face. I begin to cry, softly at first, tears escaping and then suddenly my whole body shakes, racked with sobs. The policeman is young, not yet hardened to death, unsure what to do. He places a blanket around my shoulders.

'I should have helped. I should have made her tell me. I should have saved her.'

But whether I am crying for Maggie or Adele I cannot tell. For some reason they have blurred into one, united in me, by the process of grief.

'Did you know her, miss?'

I nod. 'I knew her as Maggie.'

Joe stays the night. A shoulder to cry on becomes a body in my bed. The steps between, a blur of grief and need, the pleasure of being held, of skin on skin. The process of sex, sweet and loving, and then the holding on, the greedy clinging, waiting for his warmth to pass into my body. To melt that pit of coldness in my stomach that will not melt.

# Chapter Twenty-five

*Yet would I waken thee, O stream!*
*'To the River Yarra', Richard Howitt*

I dream of Maggie. She is swimming in water, running on land, always moving away. I call after her, but she doesn't stop. I try and catch her, but I don't try hard enough. Every now and then she pauses and looks back, puzzled at my slowness, beckons me. 'Come on, Lyn. Hurry up.' I need just to touch her to save her, but the effort is too great. I stop and she runs on, and somewhere close by is Adele. Her face emerges from shadows, clear and young and alive.

Joe is there in my dream, and in the middle of the night he holds me. In the early morning I am aware of his leaving, a cup of tea on the floor beside the mattress. A whispered farewell, his breath warm on my neck. I wake late, my head thick and muzzy, the tea stone cold.

Pam visits. A mix of sympathy and horror. The horror of murder, of being friends with a murderer. She has no doubt of Smithy's guilt. I am not so sure. Some part of me refuses to believe he is capable of murder. A criminal perhaps, now that the evidence is irrefutable. But not murder. And I alone have seen the watcher's face. The pale brown eyes, the long jaw. I alone have seen Maggie's fear.

I have not forgotten my appointment with Georgina and, this time, nothing will keep me away. The anger within me has solidified, set like stone, a hard, solid core. I shower and prepare, consult the street directory and take a tram to Fitzroy. From here I walk the quiet, inner streets. Georgina's house is set back from the footpath by the distance of three steps. In this gap, on either side of the steps, is a small garden, a cluster of lavender beneath a standard rose. Everything pleasant and well kept.

At twelve o'clock precisely I ring the door bell. She is expecting me and answers promptly. A tall, well-groomed woman wearing a knitted cream suit and high heels. At her throat and ears, a touch of fine gold. She looks more like a successful businesswoman than a writer.

When I introduce myself, she smiles and shakes my hand. We go through the preliminaries. I set the tape recorder up and also make notes, explaining that I want to go into more detail than is customary in a compilation of this sort. She is pleasant and agreeable to my request. I move through the basic questions and she answers patiently and thoughtfully. We move, by degrees, on to family, to influences on writing.

She is open and honest, expands on her early life, the Stavros family's dismissive attitude to literature, her older brother's inadvertent help. As a young girl she read the books he was set for school and understood them well enough to help him with his essays. At a young age, already delving deep into plots and characterisation. He just wasn't interested.

'Don't get me wrong, Ms Blessing. My brother is a clever man, runs his own business and does well, but, like the rest of the family, he's not interested in literature.' She smiles at me, a rueful smile. 'To tell you the truth, they don't quite know what to make of me. They are pleased for me, but think somehow that writing is not "real work", not like plumbing or running a shop. My success is good, but well . . . unexpected. A fluke.'

She stands up and reaches for a button on the wall, and soon a young woman opens the door and stands waiting for instructions.

'Ah, Mary. Can you get us tea and something to eat? Anything will do.'

Mary doesn't exactly bow, but she is deferential. It must be nice to be rich, to be able to afford someone to keep the demands of living at bay. The freedom to write, paid for.

I must look surprised and she laughs. 'Its not quite as bad as it seems. She only comes in two days a week. I must say, though, I wish it was more. I love it. I use her un-mercifully.'

After a while, Mary comes back, pushing a trolley. A tea tray is set up, a steaming teapot surrounded by the business of tea, cups and saucers, milk and sugar and, underneath, cake and sandwiches.

'Thanks, Mary. It looks lovely.'

We pause and drink. The room is like its owner, uncluttered and tasteful. There are small paintings on the wall, nothing else. No photos anywhere. No photos of young men with long jaws.

'I remember you from the book launch. You wore burgundy. The colour suited you.' She unbends a little, moves from formality to friendliness.

I smile. 'Yes, I remember you too. You were with someone.'

'A friend of my brother's,' she answers quickly, her tone evasive.

So, no, not a relative, as Peter Ireland had assumed.

'He looked really familiar. I wondered if I knew him.'

She pauses before answering 'His name is Jason. I don't know much about him – well, that's an understatement for you. I only met him that night, he dropped in unexpectedly. We got talking. You know how it is, and before I knew it, he was coming too. I liked him, you see. He was good company. I haven't seen him since.'

A painful topic, one she would prefer to close. I ignore the signs.

'Does he have a surname?'

She shrugs. 'He didn't say. I don't know who he is, or where he lives. To be honest, I phoned my brother, to find out about him, and he doesn't know him either. I can't understand it. I mean, why lie?'

She is genuinely puzzled, unable to find a likely explanation. A feeling that I have known too well lately.

'Can you remember anything that he said, or did? I mean, you must have got some idea of him.'

She looks at me intently.

'He had good manners. Table and otherwise. He was well dressed, and showed no sign of manual labour. Clean hands, a charming smile. But apart from that little list, there is nothing I can tell you.'

'A car perhaps?'

'No car. We went by taxi. You seem very interested in him. Overly interested, if I may say.'

I make a deprecating gesture. 'Only curiosity. Perhaps pride. Usually I am good with faces and I had the feeling that I've met him somewhere before.'

'Well, if you remember, let me know. I'd like to know about him too.'

'Would you mind if I asked your brother?'

'There's no point. I've already asked him and he was no help. He knows no one called Jason and no one that fits his description.'

'Perhaps the photographers at the party?' I suggest.

'I thought of that too. He was very keen to avoid the cameras. At first I thought it was politeness, his insistence on not getting in the way, in intruding on what he called "my night". I think now that perhaps he was a little too insistent.'

A small pause.

'It seems likely, though, that Jason must have known your brother. I mean even to know you had a brother shows some knowledge,' I say.

'Work from the other end, you mean. Who would know I had a brother?' she asks.

I nod.

'Everyone. I mentioned him in my last book. It's common knowledge.'

She looks pointedly at the clock. She has lost interest and I am becoming a nuisance. I thank her for the interview. She nods and smiles at me vaguely, her hand already moving towards the bell. Mary walks with me to the door and I step down into the quiet street. The door closes above me. At each end of the road, there is an endless flow of traffic, but here everything is peaceful, orderly, an oasis of calm. I have the unpleasant feeling that I pinned too many hopes on a non-starter. I am no further forward.

# Chapter Twenty-six

*Drenched with the colour of unexperienced days*
*We go our different ways,*
'The Agricultural Show, Flemington, Victoria', Furnley Maurice

A period of inactivity before the inquest. A day to get through. The long hours pass in a blur of grief and preoccupation, the requirements of work on automatic. The Coroner's Court. A subdued court, solemn with the business of investigating death. The players are all there – the early morning rower who first saw Maggie's body in the river, the young constable I met on the riverside. The medical experts: a forensic pathologist, a toxicologist.

The forensic pathologist outlines the extent of Maggie's injuries, lacerations to the head, a fractured skull. He cannot conclude definitely that her injuries were accidental, or if she was alive when she entered the water. He suspects, though, that she was. The injuries to her skull could have occurred through hitting rocks, or the stone river wall where she fell. But assault too is possible.

The toxicologist follows. He has tested Maggie's blood and urine for drugs and alcohol. Drugs were not detected, but alcohol was and measured .07. Enough to impair judgement.

Medical opinion places the time of death between the hours of midday and midnight on Sunday 13 September. Her body was immersed in water for a considerable period before being found, as much as twelve hours. My heart leaps at the news. Sunday. Smithy was long gone.

The time is certain, but the cause of injury is not. The Coroner, unable to ascertain the manner of death, adjourns the inquest to a later date. Maggie's death is inconclusive, the process of inquiry slow and uncertain. Real murders, definite murders are taken more seriously than a possible suicide.

'What about the earring?' I ask. 'Doesn't an earlobe ripped apart and a missing locket indicate murder?'

But the police are not convinced. Earlobes are fragile, bloodless things and can be explained away the same way as a fractured skull. If she was murdered, they already have their suspect, Alexander Smith, whereabouts unknown but wanted for smuggling and assault. Murder is just one more item on the list. With a suspect like Smithy, the police need look no further.

Fingerprints are taken to establish identity, but remain unmatched. Here the matter stays. Maggie is unknown and unclaimed. And then, two days later, when I am beginning to give up hope, she is at last identified. Her flatmate, a woman named Cynthia Oldroyd, had become concerned at the length of her absence and made inquiries with the police. I was right about the name, she identified her not as Maggie someone or other, but as Leonie Cope, resident of Burwood, lately of Hamilton, Victoria.

Joe passes on Cynthia's address noncommitally. He doesn't comment on my interest, doesn't question my motivation in asking. Whatever he thinks he's not saying.

On Sunday I visit Cynthia. She is a large woman, with dull eyes and lank, greasy hair, an infant son on her hip. The baby sucks at a bottle filled with milky-brown tea. She looks surprised when I introduce myself as a friend of Leonie's, but is keen to be important, to show me around. She invites me in.

Maggie's room is empty. A single bed in the corner, an orange chenille bedspread. The curtains are closed, the room dingy and bare, a faint musty smell.

'I packed up her things.' Cynthia explains. 'After the police came. I sent them on to her mother.'

'Was she all right, do you think?' I ask. 'Only the last few times I met her she seemed upset, like she was in some sort of trouble.'

'Tell me about it,' Cynthia says. 'Nerves shot to pieces, crying half the time. Wouldn't say why.'

'And you didn't guess?'

'Well, not really. She wouldn't talk about it, but if I had to guess I'd say she was scared.'

'What of?'

She shrugs and doesn't answer, doesn't know.

'Did she always drink?' I ask, remembering back to the train and the time in the shop, the pervasive smell of alcohol.

'Lately she did. Especially after the phone calls. She said it was the only thing that let her sleep.'

'Phone calls?'

'Mm. Late at night. They'd wake me and the baby.'

'Who was it? Do you know?'

Cynthia shrugs. 'She wouldn't say. The first time I got up to answer it, but she'd got there first. She was just standing there, not saying anything. She looked like she was going to faint. And then later, I heard her being sick in the bathroom.'

'When was this?'

'A couple of weeks ago. I'm not sure exactly.' She makes a rocking gesture with one hand.

'I see,' I say slowly, beginning to understand the tactics and results of fear.

'I've readvertised the room. I can't afford to live here on my own. Someone's coming this afternoon. I thought you were her.'

This is hint enough. It is time to go. There is nothing here of Maggie.

'What happened to her locket? Do you know?'

Cynthia looks surprised. 'Christ knows. Is it missing? I only saw her for a minute, just to make the identification. She always wore it, though. She said it was for luck. A present from her boyfriend.'

I remember the gesture in the shop, that automatic reaching up to touch it, the need for reassurance. Some luck.

'Who was he?'

She shrugs. 'I never met him. Jason someone.'

Jason someone. Georgina's Jason as Maggie's boyfriend. I try not to let the surprise show on my face. I had not thought of him as a boyfriend. But why would I? There was no sign of it that morning on the train. All I could see was Maggie's discomfort and his cold scrutiny, his unswerving stare. The same name though. The same man?

'Do you know his surname?'

She shrugs. The baby has finished the bottle, squirms in her arms.

'Do you know where they met?'

'Dunno. She talked about how he made her laugh. How charming he was, and such good company. No details, just mush.'

Cynthia is cynical and I think along similar lines. Maggie, how could you have been so blind? But Jason was charming, I think, when he wanted to be. Georgina certainly thought so. I remember his doting attention to her on the night of her book launch. His head thrown back in amusement at something she had said. The pleasure on Georgina's face. The heady feeling of flirtation.

'Do you have her mother's address?' I ask.

She passes me a grubby piece of paper from a box on the table. The child begins to cry.

'Keep it. I won't need it any more. I'd better go, sort him out.'

She closes the door. I can hear him wailing and her voice in the gaps between his cries. A tired voice, rising up.

I read the name and address: *Mrs Elaine Cope, 119 Thomson Street, Hamilton.*

There is a supermarket on the corner. I buy a bag of shopping: milk, bread, juice, butter, cheese, fruit, soap, shampoo, soap powder and a hot chicken. When I get back, the child is still crying. I have to knock loudly to be heard. Cynthia opens the door, her greasy hair pushed back behind her ears. She looks half dead. I hand her the food.

'For the baby.' A flicker of emotion crosses her face. Surprise, relief, hope. And then the dull eyes close down, stare at me impassively.

'Ring me if you think of anything.' I hand her my card.

She nods, takes it without seeing it, and closes the door.

Monday. Closing time, the work finished and put away. I pull down the blinds to Flinders Street. The door bell clangs and a man comes in. He is dressed solidly, a heavy winter coat, collar turned up against the cold, a hat pulled down hard. I cannot see his face. He shuts the door behind him, leans against it.

'Can I help you? I'm just about to close.'

I don't recognise him until he speaks. A familiar voice. A voice I have heard on and off, all of my life. Alexander Smith. My friend Smithy.

'How are you, Lyn?'

He pushes his hat back from his forehead and looks at me with steady eyes.

'I thought you'd left the country,' I say coldly.

'On my way.'

The shoulders of his coat are heavily padded, show no sign of distinctive, rounded shoulders. He looks quite different.

'Why are you here?'

'To say goodbye properly. And to tell you that I honestly never intended to hurt you. But when I saw the gleam of your jumper in the mirror ... well I panicked. But believe me, I didn't know it was you, not until after, not until I shone the light on your face – I couldn't believe it. I'd thought you'd left.

I thought you'd gone. No lights, no car. I thought you'd left. You should have left, Lyn.'

I'm not scared. Despite evidence to the contrary, I still find it hard to think of Smithy as an outright villain, but the thought comes crowding in, unwanted and unwelcome. If he is still here, he could have killed Maggie.

'There's someone crowding me, someone ruthless. You scared me that night, Lyn, the night in the alley. It showed me just how close he was. Getting closer, but still not sure.'

'Barry ...'

He almost laughs. 'Believe me, I was grateful for Barry. He clouded the picture. Confused him and you. Gave me more time.'

'Who is he?' I ask. 'The man in the alley.'

He looks at me closely. 'I don't know his name or even what he looks like. I only know he's there.'

'Tell me,' I say quietly, and he nods almost imperceptibly.

'Why not? The game's all over now. It began at the start of the year, last year really. December, the end of the breeding season. A shipment I expected never arrived, and the collector went missing. He was a friend of mine. I thought for a while that it was him, that he had organised things on his own behalf. And then – in the paper, a body found in dense bushland in the Hattah National Park. Found by bushwalkers, you know the sort of thing. Someone had got in somehow, was muscling in on me. Wanted what I had set up for himself. And whoever it was didn't stop at murder.'

'He murdered him, the man at Hattah?'

Smithy nods. His eyes are cold. He looks unfamiliar. 'If I'd known who he was, I could have done something about it. And believe me it would have been a pleasure. As it was I moved the operation. Got someone else in, and that's always a risk. One I don't like taking.'

I think of the man on the train. His eyes boring into Maggie, his intentness at the party with Georgina, his face in the street outside the shop. Smithy reads my thoughts.

'You know who it is, don't you?'

I shake my head. 'Not really.'

'But you know what he looks like.'

Why not? What harm can it do? I describe the watcher. The fall of light brown hair, the light hazel eyes, the long jaw. Smithy doesn't react. I wonder, for a moment, if he has heard.

'Where was he?'

'At Vanessa's party. On the train with Maggie. Once in the street, outside the shop.'

'Maggie?' he asks.

'I mean Leonie. The woman in the shop, the woman with the code. He was on the train with her.'

'So he'd got on to her, had he? I wondered.'

'The police think you killed her.'

'Killed her? Christ!'

'They fished her out of the Yarra, last Monday. Suicide. Murder. Take your pick.'

'And what do you think, Lyn?'

'I think it's murder.'

'And you think it's me?'

'No, I think it's him. But the police think it's you, and others.' I say, thinking of Pam. 'They think you killed her and left the country.'

'Christ,' he says feelingly. 'What a mess.'

'Tell me about her?' I ask.

'Leonie?' His tone softens. 'Silly sort of woman really. She had no idea of what she was involved in, at first anyway. I tried to separate things, that code business you got on to was all to eliminate any contact with me. No one working for me would ever see anyone else.'

'I guessed that part,' I say.

'Of course.' He nods. 'She placed the code and paid the courier. She was the only one he would see. No conversation. No contact. And it worked, after a fashion.'

'How do you know?'

'Because I watched.'

Another face in the crowd. Another watchful pair of eyes.

'You used me. You planned it around the shop, knowing that I'd tell you about it. You used me. And that night in the tunnel, you stole the bag.'

Strangely enough, this seems more of an outrage than the attack at the house.

'You gave me leeway. I just wanted one more season. A short season, Lyn, a few consistent weeks. And then ... when things began to fall apart, all I wanted was one more shipment. A big one. Some Major Mitchells, some Blacks.'

'I find that the hardest part. You always loved wildlife.'

He looks down at me with a faint smile. 'Well, yes, I do. But it was so easy. $6,000 for a galah. Pocket money, Lyn. A simple galah. There's millions of them.'

I think of the sweep of birds over my house that morning, the blush of pink and grey.

As if reading my thoughts, he says, 'That's where I started, Lyn. The bush behind your place. Just out of town. Collected them myself, way back then. They line up for them in Japan and America.'

'And the Mitchells? Are there millions of them too?'

He looks both scornful and amused.

'Always the do-gooder, aren't you, Lyn? The Mitchells are where the real money is. Up to $50,000 for a bird. Think about it.'

'I think about extinction more.'

'Well, pat yourself on the back, Lyn. You've got rid of one smuggler. But don't be too pleased, there'll be plenty more to take my place.'

I change my tone. He seems to need to talk, to tell me how clever he is. And I need to know.

'Where did you meet her?'

'The woman? In a café in Carlton. You know, one of these dreadful fast-food places, lots of attractive women on the staff, peanuts for long hours. I went in late at night, the graveyard shift. Hardly any customers. We got talking, she told me about herself, about how she hated the café. The long hours, the poor pay, the up- themselves middle management. She was lonely. She seemed to be what I was looking for.'

'And what were you looking for, Smithy?' My words burn with anger. I speak without consideration. 'I'll tell you exactly what you were after. In simple terms, vulnerability and poverty. A country girl, no circle of friends, no family to call on. I'll give you credit, you certainly picked the right target.'

He moves both hands downwards, a slight deprecating gesture, and smiles.

'Lyn, Lyn, you always did take things too seriously. A family failing. She was paid well. She knew the risks.'

'No, she didn't. She was literally terrified. A situation you put her into.'

'We had a working relationship. Nothing more, nothing less. An agreement on hours, duties. Nothing else.'

We look at each other with undisguised hostility. Smithy speaks first.

'Tell me something.'

'What?'

Anger is still churning. I take a deep breath, swallow it down like a lump in my throat. There are still things I want to know.

'How did you get on to it all? I thought I was so careful.'

I take pleasure in the answer.

'It was Maggie. Leonie. I noticed her because she looked like Adele.'

'Did she?' He looks at me blankly for a moment, working it through. 'I never realised. Funny, isn't it? It's always the little things that trip you up.'

'Like diaries, perhaps? Adele's diary.'

My tone is carefully neutral. We could be discussing the weather.

'Ah, the diary. I wondered when we would come to that.'

He looks unseeingly into the middle distance and I guess his thoughts are in the same place as mine. Adele's bedroom. The scene of the attack.

'Another mistake, Lyn. What can I say except try and explain? The night in my flat you mentioned your diary and I remembered that all you bloody Blessing women keep diaries. I also knew you were going back to the old place some time, you told me yourself. If Adele had written about what was going on . . . I couldn't risk you knowing that. It was just bad timing that you were there.'

'I nearly wasn't,' I say, remembering my decision to stay on that night.

'See. Bad timing.'

He seems pleased with the thought, as though timing alone absolves him of responsibility.

'You stole her diary. You rang the house late at night. You scared her,' I say coldly. My fists are clenched and my breath is running fast. Smithy doesn't seem to notice, continues almost conversationally.

'I had to pick up a shipment from the shed. It was a weekend. I usually steer clear of weekends, but this time I had no choice. Anyway, as luck would have it, Adele's car was in the driveway. I waited for a while, but she was there to stay. I couldn't risk it. I was sorry about it really, scaring her like that.'

He looks at me sharply, returning to the present, from the thoughts in his mind.

'The power of the phone, Lyn. Never underestimate it. The silent phone call trick. She left, and I was glad. An effective way to get rid of someone, especially someone on their own. She wasn't like you, Lyn. Two calls and she left. Why didn't you leave?'

'I thought about it, I almost did, but . . . I wanted to know.'

'You were always like that. Even as a kid. Scared of nothing.'

This defies comment. The sickening, debilitating feeling of fear has been my companion for too long. He looks at his watch.

'I must go, Lyn. I wanted to say goodbye and, well, to set the record straight. You see, Lyn, in my line of work, criminal work, if you like, it's easy to get sucked in, to go deeper, become greedier, more ruthless. The stakes are high. I had to draw a line, Lyn. And you were it. You were that line.'

I have not yet closed the blinds on the door. Behind us the street is dark and empty.

'I didn't mind anything else,' he continues. 'Tricking you, deceiving you, using you. In fact that whole episode in the tunnel filled me with delight. When I think of us solemnly shining our torches into that stinking water, looking for what I already had, I can't help laughing. But when I thought I'd killed you, I decided to get out – you've always been my friend.'

He bends his head down to mine, kisses me briefly on the cheek. A familiar gesture, old as childhood, but now almost a parody. A gesture that leaves me cold. He closes the door behind him. I turn the key in the lock and stand against the heavy door, breathing in deep gulps of air. I close the blinds on the door, shut out the darkness from the street. I ring the police and ask for Joe.

'I know who it is.'

'Who?'

'The real villain. The one who Smithy's scared of, the one who killed Maggie.'

'How do you know all of that suddenly?'

'Smithy told me.'

'Smithy!'

'He's just left.'

'Christ, Lyn. I'm too far away. I'll get someone. Someone will be with you soon. Are you all right?'

'I'm fine, Joe. Honestly.'

This time the police come to me. Sweetman and his offsider, a young senior constable. Again a long night. The passing on of Smithy's information. The detailed questioning. The dead body at Hattah. The conviction of his guilt clear in their eyes. Alexander Smith, wanted for murder.

'But he didn't do it,' I protest, dull with fatigue. 'You need to look further. The watcher. The man on the train. His name is Jason.'

They write the details but are unconvinced.

'Did Smith tell you where he was going?'

'No.'

'What did you talk about?'

'He apologised for attacking me that night.'

'Christ. A feeling crim. Do you have any photos of him?'

'No.' And remembering the photos at the house. 'Yes. But very old.'

'How old?'

'Years. He was a young man. Probably around sixteen.'

'And now?'

'Now, he'd be about forty-five.'

'And he has no family? No other friends?'

I can hear Pam's voice in my ear. *It's not natural, the way he lives. No friends, too much desire for privacy.*

'No. No family. I don't know of any friends.'

They ask for the family photo. Joe collects it and brings it to the city. From this they make up an identikit, cut and grey his hair, add lines and maturity to his face. He has not really changed that much. When they have finished, they show me the final result.

'Is this like him? Is it a good likeness?'

I nod. 'What's the charge?'

They look at me as though I am simple.

'Smuggling. Assault. Suspected murder. The body at Hattah, the girl in the river.'

'Not murder,' I remind them.

'Whether he did it or not, we need to question him,' Sweetman says. 'And take it from me, Lyn, there is no honour among thieves. Once in that criminal world, all crime is possible. Simply to keep going, to survive.'

I don't mention Smithy again. My opinion is markedly out of line with others, and I alone have seen Jason. The watcher, the man in the background, the interloper. Every time I open the shop door, I wonder if he is out there, his pale hazel eyes watching me.

# Chapter Twenty-seven

*O, Yarra! happy were those streams*
*Aye linked with love and sorrow –*
*      'To the River Yarra', Richard Howitt*

Life settles down for all of us. An interlude though, rather than a conclusion, for I know there is more to come. Joe helps me move into the new flat. I ring Barry and arrange a time to collect my possessions: a dinner service, an old chair, a coffee table, two paintings of the house at Yarra Falls. I introduce the two men, they shake hands with each other and busy themselves with moving and carrying.

At the flat we organise my possessions. I hang the paintings, glad above everything else to have them back. We stand back to admire them.

'Do you miss the old place?' Joe asks.

'Mm. Yes. But all this business has made me realise how stupid it is to let a perfectly good house stand empty.'

Joe, the police officer makes no comment. For him, this is too obvious.

'So what will you do?' he asks eventually.

'Sell up. Move back. I'm not sure.' I don't really want to decide. 'To sell up would be like cutting off a hand. All the years of growing up. To move back means committing myself to over two hours' travel a day.'

'Decisions, eh?' Joe says. 'Rather you than me.'

'It was different when Adele was alive. Two of us to share it. But now . . . It's just too far. That's always been the problem.'

'I've got something for you,' Joe tells me, hunting for his wallet in the pocket of his jeans. 'We found it in with Maggie's belongings.'

He hands me one of my cards. The dark green script bold against pale cream. The card is buckled and torn. On the back, the words I scribbled to Maggie are legible, but only just. The ink has run. *I want to help you. Believe me, I'm a friend. Ring me. Lyn Blessing.*

The card that I gave to her on the day of surveillance, the day I asked her to let me help. Joe watches me as I read it.

'It was in her wallet,' he says. 'In a plastic pocket with a stack of other cards. I guess that's why it's still readable.'

I nod.

'Did she ring?' he asks.

I shake my head.

'What did Bruce Spence say?'

'Something about orders, his express instructions.'

'Bugger his instructions,' I say. 'She needed help.'

I enjoy the process of organisation, of sorting things out, but mostly I enjoy setting things up. I take over the second bedroom, set up the desk, the computer, an old filing cabinet from the office. From this window there is an unexpected glimpse of the city, the Rialto Tower, the sweep of the Westgate Bridge behind. I find myself gazing out from time to time entranced by their height and shifting colour, the random glints of sunlight. I organise files for the new book, all the different poets stored away alphabetically. A file for each one.

Joe goes out while I am working and returns some time later. In one hand a standard lamp, in the other containers of take-away Chinese food.

'A house-warming present,' he says, handing over the lamp. 'For the study, so you won't go blind.'

'Joe, it's lovely. Thank you.'

He serves the food while I set the lamp up next to the desk. We eat the first meal in my new flat on the study floor, sitting in a circle of lamplight.


In the week I take up work on the book. It is easier now I am more organised and I spend long evenings this way. Joe gets involved in a case close to home and contact between us is less frequent. But on Sunday afternoon he rings and asks me out.

'What do you think, Lyn? Feel like going out? A walk maybe. Dinner at a pub somewhere. Movies, whatever you fancy.'

'Sounds great,' I answer. 'I need a break.'

'I'll be there in an hour.'

When he does come, he looks tired, restless with fatigue.

'Are you sure you want to walk? You look like you need to sleep.'

'Too many late nights. Too much surveillance. A walk is just what I need.'

We walk along the bike track as far as Fairfield. A brisk striding-out along the river. There is a cool wind, but the sun is out, shines warmly on our backs. At the boathouse, we buy ice cream and sit overlooking the Yarra, in a hollow in the hill, protected from the wind.

He finishes his ice cream and lies down next to me, stretching full-length on the grass. He closes his eyes and his breathing changes, settles into the even rhythm of sleep. The sunlight shows every line and plane of his face, every freckle and groove. A lovely-looking man, Pam had said. And yes, she's right. Not conventionally good-looking, but an interesting face. A definite sweep to the jawline, a full lower lip. A sensual mouth. I know from experience just how true this is.

I am tempted to trace its outline, to feel the warmth of his skin, but I hold back, not wanting to wake him. Not sure what

I want. The episode in my bed belongs to the past. Pleasure, yes, but mixed inextricably with the grief of Maggie's death. The need for comfort, for human warmth and contact. A time of need and dependence.

He opens one eye and sees me studying him. I look away towards the river at the family of ducks gliding close to the water's edge, the ripples of sunlight on the water.

'Interesting view?' he asks, propping himself up and following my gaze.

'Yes. Quite lovely.'

He moves closer and I lie down, my head in the hollow of his shoulder. Above us the sky is intensely blue. A few wispy clouds race across its surface.

'Nice, isn't it?' Joe asks.

I'm not sure whether he's talking about the sky or about us lying together in the warm sun. But I agree anyway. Both things are nice.

Pam comes to see me in the shop, announces a temporary departure for Sydney, a conference on Special Education combined with a well-earned holiday. We discuss, as we have discussed already, Smithy's late afternoon visit to the shop, his role in the sequence of events. Despite everything that has happened, I find myself defending him from Pam's hostility. Her unshakeable conviction of his guilt as murderer. I tell her once again about the line he had drawn between smuggling and murder, the line he wouldn't cross.

She looks at me as though I am a child, slow to understand.

'Lyn, the reason he got out is someone was forcing him out. If he stayed he'd be up on a murder charge. What did that policeman say? "There is no honour among thieves." Believe it, Lyn.'

I let it go. I am hardly in a position to prove her wrong.

Pam continues thoughtfully, 'It's not over, is it? You won't let it be over.'

Again I don't answer, but Pam is always quick on the uptake.

'It's him, isn't it? The man on the train. I thought when we went out for dinner, there was something . . . something you were holding back.'

'Pam, I need proof,' I say. 'Without proof, I have nothing.'

'So you're going to try to get it. You're mad, Lyn. You're getting in too deep. Leave it to the police.'

'The police are convinced it was Smithy. They're not going to do anything.'

'So you are!' Her voice flares in sudden anger. 'Why, Lyn? Why get so involved? Why do you care so much?'

A customer comes in, lingers in the children's book section. Pam lowers her voice but she is too angry to let the subject drop.

'I can't understand you, Lyn. I always thought you were such a sensible person. A good life, busy but safe. And here you are contemplating God knows what, like some lunatic on TV.'

She shakes her head in wonder.

'She was scared, Pam. Fear like I've never seen. No one should feel like that.'

'So because she was scared, you're deliberately going to put yourself in danger?'

'No. Not because she was scared. Because she was murdered.'

'It's Adele, isn't it?' she asks with a sudden flash of inspiration. 'You said she looked like her. That's why you care.'

I don't answer and she takes my silence as confirmation.

'Lyn, this is some unknown woman. Someone you don't know. Someone who didn't know you, someone who wouldn't give a toss for you. She is not Adele.'

Her face flushes with emotion.

'Pam, I know that. Believe me, I know that.'

Her green eyes search my face for understanding. In the soft shop light, they look slightly luminous. She follows it through.

'It was that night, wasn't it? Something about that night. The night you didn't go and meet her. You said then that you'd let her down.'

Her eyes flicker with comprehension, tying up strands of previous conversations.

'Adele was pregnant. She wanted to tell me about the baby.'

This gets her. She falters momentarily, her eyes on my face. 'Was she? How do you know?'

'It was in her diary.'

She shakes her head in frustration.

'Bloody diaries.' Her tone is savage. 'They've caused more trouble than enough.'

She puts an arm around me and pulls me into her body. I can feel the solid warmth of her flesh. The rush of her breath.

'Tell me straight, Lyn, is there guilt in any of this?'

Her voice is very calm. I step back to see her face. The flush has faded and her skin is pale.

'Only partly,' I say. 'At first, I guess helping Maggie was some sort of compensation for letting Adele down ...'

'Lyn, Lyn! You have nothing to feel guilty about, nothing more than in any other family.'

'I know.' I nod. 'It might have started that way, but it's gone way past it now. If you'd seen Maggie, if you'd seen her fear, you'd feel the same way.'

She grips my hand firmly in her own.

'Lyn ...'

'I won't change my mind. Maggie's fear was compelling. She was like an animal being hunted, like she was someone's prey. No one should be made to feel like that.'

So we have gone full circle. Pam takes a deep breath, the passion spent.

'Leave it to the police, Lyn. Go and see them again. Push them into doing something if you feel like that. But don't do any more. Leave it alone. Promise me.' Her voice is even.

I smile at her.

'Pam, thanks for caring. Perhaps you care too much about me.'

'Yes, but I wonder why sometimes.'

She bites her bottom lip and looks away.

I can't promise to do what Pam wants me to. He is out there somewhere, watching me. Somewhere close by. I remember him breathing down Maggie's neck as he followed her up the station ramp. At any moment it could be my turn, my neck he is breathing down. At any time, I could become his prey.

'I'll do what I can, Pam. I'll talk to them again. Honestly.'

She smiles, but dubiously, not really sure of my answer.

'Stubborn,' she says, bending to examine a rose in the vase on the coffee table. With a visible effort she changes the subject.

'How's Joe?'

She is not asking about his health, but if there is any sort of relationship between us. I think of our night together. That mix of complex emotions. Desire. Need. Grief.

'I'm not sure,' I say.

She looks at me for a long moment.

'Whew! Something else. I must say, Lyn, that life with you is never boring.'

'There is that,' I say drily. 'Hold that thought when I'm driving you mad. So ... what do you think?'

'Of Joe? He's a nice bloke. Genuine. A strong streak of honesty.'

'Yes.' I agree. 'I think so too.'

She smiles, her mouth turning up at the corners.

'Decisions, eh? Rather you than me,' she says, with an incongruous repetition of Joe's words in an earlier conversation. Even her inflection is the same.

She stands up and gives me a hug.

'Got to go, Lyn. The plane waits. And getting back to our earlier topic, what can I say? Just make sure you don't do anything stupid.'

Her tone is matter of fact. The emotions smoothed down. She kisses me goodbye and walks towards the door, her heels making little echoes on the wooden flooring. She waves from the doorway and I blow her a kiss goodbye.

I am on my own. Out of sight and on my own. Time to

make my plans. First things first. I ring Jordie. Make arrangements for her or an employee to cover me for the rest of the week. I have things to do.

'Good for you, Lyn,' Jordie answers. 'You need a break. Got anything special planned?'

'Just a trip to Hamilton.'

# Chapter Twenty-eight

*O the days, the cruel days creeping over Hamilton*
*Like a train of haggard ghosts, homeless and accursed*
*Moaning for a fleet o' dreams silver-sailed and wonderful,*
*Moaning for a sorrow's sake, the fairest and the first.*
                              'Hamilton', Marie E. J. Pitt

The Ballarat road, freeway into highway. The Western District unfolds, mile after mile of farmland, bushland and, at the roadside, a scatter of deep pink. The emblem of Victoria, the common erica, is in full bloom.

I pass through small country towns: Smythesdale, Skipton, Lake Bolac, Dunkeld. Sleet on the windscreen, brief patches of sun, a heavy coldness. As I drive, I consider the best approach towards a grieving mother, run different stories through my head, rehearse different conversations. And then out of a flat plain, the great bulk of sudden mountains rise up, ghost-like in the sleety mist. The Grampians. I am nearly there. Hamilton. Maggie's home town. This, then, was her last journey home. A blind journey, enclosed in a coffin.

Her mother's house is easily found, a small house in the town centre, opposite the gardens. An old house, bull-nosed, brick-fenced, run-down. Maggie's mother is a small woman and older than I expected. Grandmotherly rather than motherly. She is wearing a white lace collar over a black jumper. Her hair is iron grey, springing back from her forehead, softer both in colour and in texture around the ears.

'Mrs Cope?'

She nods uncertainly.

'My name's Lyn. Lyn Blessing. I knew Leonie in Melbourne.'

'Oh. Yes?'

'I hope you don't think I'm interfering. I just wanted to know about her.'

I hand her my card. She looks at the neat stylish words and then, unconvinced, looks into my face.

'Why? What's your interest?'

Her gaze is steady and courageous. All the different conversations I practised on the drive up seem inadequate or insulting. I settle on the truth.

'Mrs Cope, I was worried for her. I just wanted to be sure, just needed to ... well, find out for myself that her death was ...' I falter.

The sentence doesn't come out as I would have liked. It is a hard sentence to say. That her daughter could have been murdered – my main cause of suspicion, her fear and the flesh of her ear, torn and gaping.

She pauses before speaking. 'You must have some grounds for concern to come all this way. A strong commitment.'

'I was concerned about the man she was with,' I say with emphasis. 'I want to know where he was the night she died.'

'So *you* think ...'

Her pale eyes stare at me for a long moment.

'I don't know yet what to think. Let's just say there are a few things I'm not sure of. A few things I'd like to know.'

'I'm glad someone cares.' Her voice is suddenly strident, rings out unexpectedly. 'Perhaps if someone had cared earlier, things might have been different.'

'I'm sorry,' I say.

She nods blindly, the sudden rage swallowed down. 'Better come in, dear. We can talk more easily in comfort.' Her voice is smooth now, passionless.

The house is neat and tidy, almost austere, no clutter any-where. She leads me into the lounge. One bar of a gas heater reduces the outside chill, but only by degrees. There are photos on the mantelpiece of Leonie growing up. She indicates a chair for me closest to the heater. She takes the other one.

'Where do you want to start?' she asks.

'Well, if you could just fill me in. Tell me about Leonie.'

Again the pause, the consideration before speaking.

'I had Leonie later on in life, Ms Blessing.'

'Lyn. Please call me Lyn.'

'Lyn, then. I was in my late thirties when she was born. My first child, only child. At first she kept me young, but then things changed. She got older, and wanted more.'

She shrugs her shoulders, a large gesture in such a small person.

'She was such a lovely young girl, so open and trusting. Just the two of us. It was too lonely for her here. She kicked against the rails. I don't mind telling you, it was almost a relief when she left. I missed her of course, but the fights got too much. I think, though, that she was beginning to see things differently. Her letters changed, the tone less hostile, softer. But too late. Too late.'

'When did she go to Melbourne?' I ask.

'She left home in February last year.'

February, last year. The same month Adele died.

'She was eighteen when she left home. Nineteen when she died. Just a girl. All her life ahead of her. She was mad to get to Melbourne, to be away from here. I wanted her to go to Deakin University – they have a campus at Warrnambool, you know. She would have been closer, could have come home for weekends sometimes. But she couldn't wait to get away.' Her voice catches momentarily, but she swallows the emotion down.

'I'm sorry to make you go through it all,' I say.

'No, it's good to talk. To tell someone about her. Almost a relief.' She pauses for a long moment before continuing and I don't interrupt her thoughts. 'Anyway, where was I? Oh yes, Leonie had gone to Melbourne. It was hard for her living away, living on a study grant. She worked in one of those fast-food places in the city. Late-night shifts, poor pay. Treated like dirt. I couldn't help much. I barely have enough money for myself. Anyway, it seems as though she got mixed up with something in the city. The offer of easy money. Working as a courier, she said. I didn't like the sound of it much, but she was keen. Better money, less hours. It sounded too good to be true.' She gets up suddenly. 'Would you like a cup of tea?'

'Thank you. I'd love one.'

I examine the photos. All Leonie's years captured: toddler, schoolgirl, adolescent, young woman. The resemblance to Adele is less marked in childhood than in later years, as though the bones are still fluid, not yet set. A similarity, nothing more.

'Pretty girl, wasn't she?' Mrs Cope asks from the doorway.

In her hands a tray of tea and cake. Small blue and white cups. Tea in a silver teapot.

'Yes, very. She reminds me of my sister.'

I wonder what she would think if she had seen Leonie that last time. Skin as pale as chalk, eyes deep and black and frightened.

'I was so proud of her. English literature was her major. Whenever she came she would bring her books, spend hours on them. So many different ones. The Brontës, George Eliot, Dickens, Joyce. She read them all. She wanted to teach. She would have been a good teacher.'

So the books were simply Maggie's choice, part of her studies. Like everything else, simple. Not part of any code, as I had thought. She hands me my tea.

'Did you meet her boyfriend?' I ask.

She nods. 'He stayed here one weekend. Lee was so happy. The happiest I'd seen her for a long time.' She looks through the window, her thoughts distant ones.

'What was he like?' I ask.

She considers. 'Charming. Too charming. I might be cynical,

but I distrust charm. I sensed something ... I can't explain. Something shrewd, almost calculating. I didn't say anything to Leonie about it. Perhaps I should have, but we'd had so many fights in the past. To be honest, my dear, I chickened out.'

We smile at the phrase.

'I've got a photo of him, you know.'

The cup jumps in my hand.

'A photo?' My voice is strained, comes out more as a squeak. She bends over the teapot.

'He was camera-shy. I asked them to sit in the garden so I could take their photo. It was such a lovely day and Leonie looked so happy. They laughed and joked and got out of it. So I tricked them. I came with them to the bus depot to see them off and then just as they were getting on, I called out. They both turned to look. A good shot, face on. He wasn't too pleased. Would you like to see it?'

Would I? 'Yes. Thank you.'

She brings it from the dresser drawer and I take it from her hand with a sense of quiet elation. The photo shows Maggie and her friend, on the steps of the bus, but turned back to the doorway to say goodbye. Maggie is one step above him, and only the top of her face is visible. But Jason's face is clear, his expression registering both anger and surprise. The quarry getting closer. I am running him to ground.

I study the photo politely, relieved that it is him after all and not some insignificant boyfriend, as sometimes in the dead of night I had feared.

'There was nothing he could do, well nothing that wouldn't be rude and obvious. But it did make me wonder about him, even more, that is. Especially when Leonie asked me for the photo.'

'She did that?'

'The very next day. She rang me. And wrote soon after. I did send it on, but not before I got a copy made.'

'Did she ask you for the negative?' I ask, fascinated.

'Well, yes. I told her I'd lost it. It didn't surprise her. I'm hopeless with negatives.'

'Would you mind if I got one? I mean, take this and bring it back.'

She looks at me appraisingly. 'Yes. That's all right, dear. I pride myself on judging people. I didn't trust Jason. I know I can trust you.'

I hold the photo lightly, feel I should be clutching it like a life line.

Outside it is windy, the sky heavy with cloud and the smell of rain. I order two prints at The One Hour Photo Shop. Almost opposite are the offices of the Hamilton newspaper, *The Spectator*. On impulse I walk in and look through the recent editions. The report of Leonie's death, her death notice, and funeral notice are all in the same midweek edition.

> DEATH OF LOCAL GIRL. *The body of Leonie Cope was recovered from the Yarra River in Melbourne on Monday. The cause of her death has not yet been established. Leonie is the only daughter of Elaine Cope of Hamilton and we extend our sympathy on her sad loss. Leonie attended school in the district and was a champion athlete, representing Hamilton in track and field for a number of years. Leonie was a student at Melbourne University.*

Track and field. I wonder what it was that she did so well. I read on. The death notice next: *Cope, Leonie Jane. Dearly beloved daughter of Elaine Cope. Rest in peace, my darling.* I scan the page. There are no other notices. No other family. No friends. This, then, is her death. Such little fuss at the taking of young life. I feel suddenly bleak and dispirited. Leonie. Even the sound is lonely, like a small wind, shifting in the trees.

I collect the photos. The florist has large clumps of daffodils for sale, their golden yellow trumpets loud against the grey day. I buy two bunches.

It is almost dark when I get back. An early dusk under low cloud. A light rain begins to fall. Leonie's mother is waiting for me, opens the door promptly to my knock. I give her back the photo and the bright bunches of flowers.

'Thank you, my dear. They're lovely. I haven't had flowers for ... well, for much too long.'

'Mrs Cope, you mentioned her letters earlier. Is there anything in her letters that would tell me anything about him?'

She unlocks the drawer of her desk and takes out a small bundle.

'See for yourself. Take them with you. Then perhaps you can bring them back.'

'Are you sure? I promise to return them.'

'Of course.'

'Mrs Cope, what did Leonie do in track and field?'

She blinks at this sudden change of subject.

'She was a sprinter. Over 100 metres she could take on the best of them.'

I shake her hand.

'Thank you so much for all your help.'

'Good luck, my dear. And you are, you know.'

'Pardon?'

'You are a blessing. Like your name. An answer to a prayer.'

At the gate I turn to wave. She is still standing in the doorway, framed by a rectangle of light. A small, lonely figure. A courageous woman fighting her own demons of grief and loss. She waves back.

My bag is made heavier now by the small weight of two photos and ten letters. I carry it carefully, aware of it as precious cargo. The journey in reverse. The kilometres speed past, swallowed up in a buzz of quiet elation, a glow of success. The journey has been worthwhile, for locked in the boot is evidence at last.

At home I sort Maggie's letters into chronological order. Maggie was not a prolific writer, her letters short and spasmodic. At first they are just a precis of city life, a careful edit, suitable for a mother's eyes. The settling in at university, the workload, the part time work at a café. In August Maggie's letter writing becomes more frequent, as though she wants to re-establish the relationship with her mother. As though she is reaching out. In August too, the offer of a new job.

The letter reads:

*Dear Mum,*
*Good news. I've got a new job as a courier. A city courier for a bookie. It's not much, a few hours a week. But it's cash in hand and better money than I earn now. Just think, Mum. No more late nights, no more rude customers, no more middle management.*

Later, she meets Jason and writes about him in the first flush of love. He would have been nice to her then, when he needed to be. Turning the charm on like he had with Georgina, wanting his way, wanting her to lead him to Smithy.

*Dear Mum,*
*Everything is going well and I've met someone I like at uni. He's good fun, Mum, I'm sure you'll like him. He bought me this most fantastic locket. I'd like you to meet him. Can we come down on the weekend? Love Lee.*

At the end of August, she writes:

*Thanks for the weekend. I really enjoyed it. How did the photo turn out? Can you send it on. I'd love to see it. I'll bring it back next time I come. The courier job is not what I expected it to be. I'm thinking of quitting. Tell you about it soon.*
*Love Lee*

Doubt setting in. Beckoning questions that can no longer be ignored. No mention of Jason. Perhaps the relationship is already growing sour.

And then, in early September:

*Jason and I are finished, Mum. It was a mistake. Can I come down for a weekend soon? I'll tell you all about it then.*

And, of course, whatever it was she had to tell remains untold. Her voice silenced, nothing passed on. No facts gleaned, no surmises drawn. Who was it who said death is silence?

But this time an echo reaches out from the grave. Only a small echo, but there, in her mother's letters and in a photo. Jason someone. And she met him at university.

# Chapter Twenty-nine

*And weave them into your garment's shape.*
*O feverish finger loom!*
'On a Grey-haired Old Lady Knitting . . .', Furnley Maurice

I put one of the photos in an envelope and address it to myself
at work. The envelope I mark confidential. Jordie will either
follow procedure and lock it away in the safe, or she may post
it back. Both are okay. I cut the top of Maggie's head from the
other photo, so that only Jason's face remains, clear and sharp.
I enlarge his image by way of the library photocopier. I make
fifteen copies. The original I lock in the desk. I hide a copy in
the flat. The others I take with me. This is excessive, I know,
but I have learned the hard way about losing evidence.

Morning at the university. Past the old elms, shimmering with
new green and carpets of thick, lush grass. The buildings are a
mix of old and new. Turrets and spires among tin roofs and
concrete pillars. The sun is out and its light falls warmly on old
sandstone, on the clusters of students sitting out on the grass. I
walk through the tangled alleys and courtyards, past the old
crab apple tree in the Cussania Courtyard. Its pruned canopy
bare and stark, not yet touched by spring. The Old Arts

building. The ground-floor lecture theatre.

Ruth is already there, her lecture notes in front of her. Students file in. When they are seated and quiet, Ruth begins her introduction, paints in broad terms the milestones of Gordon's life. She introduces me as 'her invited speaker'. The expert to fill in the gaps. The students wait expectantly.

I present my lecture. Not as smoothly as last year, because I can't quite help looking at the faces. It strikes me that he could be here in this auditorium, watching me. A pair of eyes, blending in with the crowd. Out of the sea of people rising up before me, a face crystallises, sets into features that are almost but not quite his. Then another, and another.

I leave time for questions. This year's batch of students is equally reticent about speaking in front of a group as last year's and questions are few. The hour filled, the students leave, the noise level rising abruptly.

'Lyn, thank you so much.' Ruth is at my side. 'It's so nice to have someone to flesh out Gordon's bones as it were. To understand the person behind the text. Can I put you down for next year?'

'Yes, of course you can. Ruth, I need a favour.'

'What is it?'

Students are still filing out. Our voices are raised above the noise.

'In your office?' I say.

She blinks, but her expression doesn't change at my unexpected request.

'Yes, of course.'

We walk the brief distance, Ruth chatting intelligently about Gordon's life.

Up the stairs, grey linoleum on the floor, corridors wide enough for desks and seats. Student notice boards, heavy with information. A dingy, red brown carpet.

Ruth's door is the most colourful, stuck with brochures and pamphlets advertising literary festivals, here and overseas. She unlocks the door, indicates the visitor's chair at her desk.

'What is it, Lyn? What's the mystery?'

I sit down and spread the photos out. Fifteen photos. The same photo, fifteen times. She takes one up.

'Yes. An attractive man. A bit young for you perhaps.' She smiles.

'He's not mine, Ruth. I don't want him at any price. But I do want him found.'

She looks enquiringly at me. I tell her an abbreviated version of events and her face becomes grave.

'I had heard of her death. Such a tragedy that one so young ...' She falters and then goes on, 'And you think the man is a student here?'

'I hope so. It's the only lead I have.'

'But, Lyn, isn't this dangerous? You think he may have murdered already. I should leave it to the police if I were you.'

'The police think her death was suicide, and if murder, they have it down to someone else. They don't want to know.'

She pauses, makes a gesture with her hands.

'What do you want me to do?'

'Could we send this photo around the different faculties. Not for the students to see, of course – you've already pointed out the dangers of that – but for the staff. Someone on staff should know the face.'

'And what would we say? What reason could we give?'

I have thought this out.

'Explanations can be dangerous. I think the less said the better. Just bare bones. Couldn't we say it was an urgent matter and ask them to contact you? In confidence of course. No explanations.'

She is dubious but agrees to help. She goes out of the room for a short period seeking secretarial assistance, and comes back with a thick wad of paper.

'No good just sending them to the faculties. I've made enough for all the departments. That way we should be sure. They are all the same. The wonders of this modern age: word processing and photocopiers.'

She hands me the top one. It reads: *'If you know this student, could you please contact Ruth Stone on Extension 6178 or care of the English Department. The matter is urgent and confidential.'*

'How's that? Bare bones enough for you?'

'Perfect, Ruth. Thank you. It couldn't be better.'

'Don't thank me, Lyn. Just don't end up in the Yarra like your young friend.' She collects some internal-mail envelopes and we collate note to photo, address them and send them off. It is a long task, I had not reckoned on so many departments. Finally we are finished. There is a small hiatus. The wheels are in motion. The die is cast. I am suddenly in need of a drink.

'Have you time for a cup of something, Ruth? Tea, coffee, brandy?'

She shakes her head.

'Thank you, Lyn, but no. I have some work I must finish.'

I give her my card, with the flat phone number scribbled on the back. 'I'm having the week off, Ruth. Can you ring me on this number?'

'Of course. Soon as I hear.'

The rest of the day passes slowly. A parcel arrives for me, a small slim brown package that Jordie has forwarded on from the shop. The postmark, Ontario, Canada.

Inside is a purple diary, three keys and a note.

*Dear Lyn,*
*As you can see I made it okay. I thought you might like this back. I guess you will probably try and find the man we talked about. I told you recently that you were made of sterner stuff than your sister, believe me I am glad. But a word of warning. Be careful of him. He's a dangerous man. I'm sorry now to have involved you. Anyway, all my great plans and secrecy came to nothing. One key is to the studio. Take what you want, sell what you don't. The other key is to your house. Adele gave it to me the last time I saw her.*
*Alexander Smith*

Three keys. Two explained, the third one silent in my hand.

I flick through Adele's diary. Read her last message.

*8 February. A phoned to ask me for a drink in the week. Next time I come here I'll ask Lyn. We need to talk, to get things straight. I need to tell her about the baby. I need to tell her what's been happening. This house isn't safe any more. I'll give A a key to check the house, and then I won't need to come back. I don't feel like coming back.*

A for Alex. Alexander Smith. Smithy. Adele gave him the key. That night I locked the house against a man who had a key given to him by my own sister. The whole thing is so convoluted, so absurd, that I can only laugh.

I ring Ruth.

'Any news?' I ask.

'Nothing. Quiet as the grave.'

'I hoped ...'

'I know. I've asked around too, Lyn. Apart from being curious about why I'm asking, no one seems to know him. I checked with a few colleagues, but I feel I'm stirring the snake pit. Best, I think, to be patient.'

'Yes, of course.'

I am at a loss. Without the university connection I have nothing. No leads at all. I take out the folders on Melbourne poetry and begin work spasmodically, most of my attention on the phone. Despite this, the body of work grows. I spend time going through the photocopies I have gathered from the State Library. As well as this, I have brought home resources from work, old newspapers, poetry books and anthologies. Time passes. It is late afternoon the next day when the phone rings.

'Lyn, this is Ruth. I have news. Can you come?'

'On my way.'

It is almost evening when I arrive. The sun is going down behind the library. The mellow sandstone buildings are bathed in yellow light.

'Got him.'

Ruth passes me an envelope and waits expectantly, almost impatiently. I slide the photo out. There is a note attached marked for the attention of Ruth Stone. It reads:

*Dear Ruth,*
*This photo is of Jason Tucker, who completed his degree in psychology last year. He still visits campus from time to time and is often seen in the coffee shops and bars. No trouble, I hope. Regards, Alex Cruickshank, Psychology Department*

Psychology. The same department as the receiver, Len Martin. The connection firms and holds.

'And that's not all.' Ruth is bubbling, alight with success. 'I went to student records. As well as a name, we have an address and a phone number.' She produces it with a flourish from a pocket in her voluminous jacket.

'Jason Tucker, 15/27 Devon Street, Reservoir. 460 6538.'

'Well done, Ruth.'

I kiss her in delight and we both grin.

'Jason Tucker. Imagine! Such a young man to have so much on his conscience,' Ruth says, looking at his photo.

I don't need to imagine his crimes. I have a fair idea already. I know what she means, though. His face in the photo is unsmiling. Even taken by surprise, it is a good-looking face, young and innocent. Crime seems impossible, murder unthinkable.

'These are the photos that were returned.'

She passes me a thick envelope.

'You've done well. Thanks, Ruth.'

'I suppose now you'll have to find him.'

Ruth's grin fades, and then my own. I feel a sudden sense of dread. A hollow somewhere inside gnawing, growing. My mouth dries. I put my hand on Ruth's arm and smile at her.

'Piece of cake.'

I ring Inspector Paul Sweetman at Russell Street.

'I've got a photo of the man who murdered Leonie Cope. And a name and address.'

'Just a minute.'

A pause, the sound of flicking through a file.

'Leonie Cope. Suicide, possible murder. Suspect's name listed as Alexander Norman Smith, believed to have left the country.'

'No, Paul. Not Smith. This man's name is Jason Tucker.'

I explain my process of investigation.

'Lyn, we've got this file pretty well closed. I'm surprised to hear from you at this late stage.'

'Smith is the wrong man. I told you then and now I'm sure of it.'

'Have you anything on Tucker. Anything concrete?'

There is a hint of impatience in his tone.

'A name and a photo. The rest is for you to do.'

'Lyn, I can't stop now. I'm due at a meeting. Could you send me what you've got. I'll see it gets proper attention.'

He puts the phone down and I swallow hard, not really surprised by the brush-off. I had expected little else.

I ring Joe at home. His answering machine clicks on. His voice is friendly, but conveys the news that he is away for the time being and will contact the caller on his return.

'Joe. This is Lyn. I've found out about the man who murdered Maggie. His name is Jason Tucker. Ring me.'

Who else . . . ? Pam is still in Sydney. My support seems thin on the ground, but this is how I wanted it. This is something I have to do on my own.

I open Ruth's large envelope, containing the stack of photos of Jason, an unknown face to all the university departments, save psychology. I switch on the computer, add the recent information to the file I have created. The file on Maggie. I print out copies, add a photo to each. I post one to Sweetman, the other to Joe. One I keep. I take it with me.

I need make no other decisions. I have made them already.

# Chapter Thirty

*Know you what things your chains have noosed?*
*'On a Grey-haired Old Lady Knitting . . .', Furnley Maurice*

I take Pam's advice. The process of hiring a security guard is both easier and more expensive than I imagined. Requirements and fees are established. My requirements are pretty basic. A security guard in the office on dates to be confirmed. I explain that I need protection from some weird stalker whom I managed to photograph. But they are not overly interested in explanations.

On Sunday I hire a Ford Laser and drive past the block of units in Devon Street, Reservoir. A corner block, a quiet side street. The units stand alone, each with its own garden. A large block, fashionable, set well back from the road.

For once I am in luck. There is a For Sale sign out the front. Unit 19. An excuse to linger, an excuse for the returning of a car. I check the unit out, peer through cracks in the curtains, walk the side path.

'Can I help you?' A querulous voice from the unit next door.

I smile at her. 'Good morning. I'm interested in buying the

unit. Such a lovely setting. You must love living here.'

'Well, yes. We do like it. It's quiet, handy for everything, you know.'

'Its funny how things work out,' I say. 'I've been here once before, visiting a friend of mine. Jason Tucker. He lives in number 15. Do you know him?' I improvise, the story coming easily.

'You won't find him in, love. He's gone away.'

'What a shame,' I say, feeling a heady sense of relief. 'When will he be back?'

'Tomorrow or the day after, so I've heard. He doesn't talk to me much, bit surly for my blood, but he asked his neighbour to take in his mail.'

Perhaps this explains the period of calm, the interlude. But interludes end and he will be back.

'There's open house on the unit at half past two. You could see it then if you're interested.'

'Are they all the same? Same floor plan?'

'Yes. Some are reversed, of course.'

At half past two I return, wave at the neighbour and enter unit 19. A pleasant, conventional house done out in pastel shades; beiges and apricot, a frill of lace curtains. The estate agent greets me, hands me his card, tells me about the unit's features, invites me to look around. A young couple follow me in and he repeats his sales pitch. His attention taken, I am free to wander.

The floor plan is conventional: lounge, kitchen, dining room. Two bedrooms next to each other. Only two doors, front and back. A small laundry at the back door, a window next to the door. The back entrance leads to a small enclosed yard. I walk down three steps and onto the pathway. There is a clothes hoist and some established shrubs on the fence line, nothing else. The layout suits me fine. I say goodbye to the estate agent and he nods farewell, his attention still on the young couple, who, unlike me, are obviously shaping up as genuine buyers.

I walk slowly down the central driveway. Number 15 is off to the same side, two units away. It looks to have the same elevation at the back, a similar cluster of greenery in the backyard. It is obscured from the road by a peppercorn tree, but further along the footpath the angle is just right, the view unimpeded. I feel a lifting of the spirits, a surge of excitement. The way ahead is clear now and I enjoy the rush of thought, the moments of early planning. First things first. I confirm the dates with the security company. Tomorrow and the day after.

After dark, I drive past the units. Most of the lights are on now, but number 15 is still dark. No light, no movement, no sign of occupancy. At home I change into a dark track suit, put some house-breaking tools into a small bag and return. I park the car in front of the weatherboard, my view to Jason's flat unimpeded. It is still in darkness. I ring his number on the mobile phone. No lights go on. No one answers.

The night is cold and there is no one on the street. The planning is over, it is time for action. I sling the strap of the bag over my shoulder. The weight of the tools is both reassuring and unnerving. If I were stopped now … I feel a charge of adrenalin, all my senses alert, ready. I walk down the side street, my feet silent on the grassy verge. I keep close to the fence, as deep as possible in the shadows. I climb the fence into Jason's enclosed backyard.

I stand among the bushes, in the darkest corner of the yard. My pulse is fast, my breath unsteady. Televisions are on all around me, the discordant sound of different channels.

A blur of noise. Minutes pass. No sounds of alarm. And then, as I am about to move, a voice, sharp and loud. 'Marge. Marge. Where's the soap powder?'

A woman's voice in reply, a mumble, a door slams.

My heart rams in my chest. I breathe slowly, deeply, willing my heartbeat to quieten. I wipe the sudden sweat from my forehead and wait again, listening, waiting, and then I make my move.

The break-in is easier than I thought. The laundry window. A hammer in cloth. Not original, I know, but effective, and even to me the shatter of breaking glass doesn't sound too loud. My gloved hand reaches through the circle of jagged glass, turns the handle on the door. There are no bolts. The door swings open. I close it softly behind me. I place the hammer in my bag, exchange it for the torch.

I train the torch on the floor and begin to move through the silent house. Laundry. Kitchen. Lounge. In torchlight, the house is shadowy and uncertain. Odd shapes loom up unnervingly in the flickering darkness. A wall unit. A high bookcase. A pale, shimmering light. I stand stock still, my breath stopped, my blood racing. And then I understand. That unnerving light is simply torchlight reflected in a mirror. Light from my own torch. My breath escapes in a shuddering sigh of relief and I move on towards the bedrooms. Two bedrooms. A choice now. Which room is Jason's? Left or right. I choose right.

A scraping noise outside, like a footstep on concrete or a key turning in a lock. I snap the torch off and press myself against the wall and the darkness closes in. A thick, unbroken darkness. No light anywhere. For a moment I am back in the tunnel and terror overwhelms me. A moment of sheer, unadulterated fear. My blood pounds in my ears. I cannot hear. I cannot see.

Nothing for a long moment. But in that time, my eyes adjust to the darkness, take in some light, and the terror eases. I begin to count, to concentrate on breathing, on trying to keep calm. I strain to listen, to decipher sound around me. Voices now, loud voices on the central driveway. A man's voice followed by a woman's sudden ringing laughter. And then the sound of footsteps moving away and the voices fade. The house is silent once again.

I am anxious now for speed, risk a quick play of torchlight around the room. Bed. Desk. Dressing table. The bed made up. Papers on the desk. Clutter on the dressing table. A lived-in room. Jason's room. There is a small tin box on the dressing table. I want to pick it up, to look inside, to see if there is any trace of Maggie. But the voices have unnerved me. Too many voices. Too many people around. I do what I came to do. I pull back the covers from the bed and pin my business card onto one of Jason's pillows.

# Chapter Thirty-one

*My soul, methinks, would lose its fear, and*
*on this troubled heart and brain*
*Some light of knowledge would be shed,*
*and some few riddles would be read.*
                    *'By the Camp Fire,' Ada Cambridge*

The car is where I left it, starts up at the first turn of the key.
I am out and away. The challenge to Jason laid down. I am
elated, buoyed up by taking charge, the adrenalin still
pumping. I need to move, to put distance between the flat and
me. I drive to St Kilda and park on the seafront, waiting for the
tremor in my hands to settle down, for my heartbeat to slow.

In front of me is the stretch of water where Barry and I used
to come and watch the play of lights on the sea. Thick clusters
on the shoreline. Seagoing traffic in the deep-water channel to
the city. I sit for a long time and, in the stillness after fear, my
thoughts are reflective ones, a kind of taking stock. I think
about Barry. About how long ago the break-up seems and how
unimportant now. I think of Pam and her calm common sense,
her flush of joy at my safety. I think of Joe and that strange mix
of ease and desire. I think of Jason and his cold, staring eyes.

I grow cold sitting there, the heady mix of nerves and
excitement finally settled down. I book in at a motel nearby
and order food and coffee, surprised at how hungry I am. I

sleep fitfully, mind and body tossing uneasily. Before work I return the hired car.

A day at work, my outfit planned for the occasion, a deep-pocketed, lightweight jacket. A day of resolution mixed up with hefty periods of unease. Resolution undermined by the long day of waiting. But beneath it all a solid anger, deep and cold and still. My trump card is the security guard in the office. He is an older man, conscientious, patient and polite, content to stay out of sight, tucked away behind the office door.

The day passes in its usual blur of customers and phone calls. There is nothing untoward, nothing out of the ordinary. At five-thirty the security guard leaves by the back exit and I lock up. I walk slowly to Flinders Street station, stopping often to browse in windows, but seeing little of the displays. I am more interested in the reflections of people behind me.

Near the corner I stop in a coffee shop, sit at a table close to the window and watch the stream of people pass by. I see no one I know. I begin to feel ridiculous, like a character on TV, but for all that when I cross at Flinders Street, I dart across at the last possible moment.

I hail a taxi from the rank outside the station and give the driver the address of a different motel. When he pulls away from the station I look behind me. No taxi follows me, no cars pull away, no one seems interested. Once more I sleep uneasily, disturbed by the hiss of traffic in rain. My dreams are incoherent, mixed with disturbing images of eyes and rivers, a torn-out earring.

Today is worse than yesterday. Apprehension compounded by an ache of tiredness behind the eyes. Courage is harder to find, undermined by the long, unnerving wait. Each clang of the door bell a feeling of alarm. Each ring of the phone, loud and unsettling.

A new security guard today. This time, age is replaced with youth, and patience with surliness, an absence of manners. A smile plays around his mouth when I outline the possibility of attack, but his smile is contemptuous, eloquent of disbelief. He has labelled me as 'nervous', dismisses my story as some wild fantasy, some eccentricity that I am indulging in. But for all that, he studies the photo of Jason carefully. His attitude doesn't bother me unduly. He's right. I am nervous. But all he needs to do is be there. Today, with luck, it should all be over.

It is a quieter day than usual. There are few customers, few phone calls. Almost as though people know to keep away, as though the air in the shop is electric with tension. I stay out of the office most of the day, working as far as possible in the shop; shelving, dusting, sorting. It is hard to keep occupied, harder still to keep calm.

I go out at lunchtime to buy food that I eat because I need to eat, to keep alert. My mouth, though, is too dry to swallow and I eat the tasteless food in small portions, washing it down with water and half-drunk cups of tea. Time passes, but much too slowly, an unpleasant familiar blur of jangled nerves. No sign of Jason.

In the afternoon Peter Ireland rings, a courtesy call from a publisher. I take it in the office. The security guard is in his assigned position, the desk behind the door that looks into the shop through one-way glass. He is reading a car magazine and looks bored.

'How are you, Lyn?' Peter asks.

'Fine, thanks.'

'Did you manage to catch up with Georgina?'

'Yes, I did finally. But I've changed my mind for the time being about that piece of work. Two books at once really is too much.'

He answers noncommittally.

'I'm working well on the poetry, though. Making inroads at least.'

'Good. Vanessa sends her love.'

'Give her mine. Tell her I'll ring her soon, organise a day for the lunch she's got in mind. Listen, Peter, I must go, the shop's pretty busy.'

I hang up and look out at the empty shop. This is the second brush-off. He will not ring again.

Five o'clock and I begin to think that Jason will not come.

Perhaps he has not even been home. Perhaps the neighbour was wrong. Two days of anxiety all for nothing. I am no better off. Only half an hour to go now. I spend time preparing catalogue slips for a new consignment of books. I take both the slips and the books into the shop, and place them on the low table at the front. I begin the process of shelving, matching slip to book, filing them away.

Twenty past five. The phone rings. The bell is louder in the shop than in the office and my nerves are so stretched that I jump. I answer it at the front desk, looking out on to Flinders Street, my pulse racing. First the sound of the long-distance beeps and then a voice, thin and uncertain.

'Hello. Is that Lyn? Lyn Blessing?'

'Speaking.'

'Lyn, this is Elaine Cope. Leonie's mum.'

'Elaine,' I say, annoyed at my slowness. 'How nice to hear from you.'

'I told myself I wouldn't ring, but I couldn't help it. I keep wondering what you plan to do. I keep worrying that you could be in danger.'

Outside the pavement is busy with pedestrians. At this time of day the sun is low in the sky, casts an oblique light that glows in people's faces, shines in their hair. Turning brown hair to a golden chestnut, blonde to brilliant shades of silver and gold. I remember Maggie's hair that day in the city, the sun shining behind it, the day she looked so young and pretty. Maggie's mother on the phone, and Maggie's face in my mind, clear and alive. Resolution firms and holds, replaces fear.

'Elaine, I'm fine. Honestly. And don't worry, I have every-thing under control.'

Someone stops outside the window, someone with gleam-ing chestnut hair tied back in a ponytail. They walk on, and the momentary stillness outside is replaced by the usual steady procession.

'Just be careful, won't you? I couldn't bear it if anything happened.'

218

The ponytail returns, but this time from the other direction, and this time his hair is in shadow, not sun. No gleam of golden chestnut, but a light unremarkable brown. And side on, a glimpse of a long jaw. He is here.

I wonder what Elaine would say if I told her that her daughter's killer was outside and that this time he had come for me.

'I'll ring you, as soon as there's any news.' I say hurriedly. 'Don't worry. I'll be fine.'

I hang up and check the clock. Five-thirty. Closing time.

I follow routine. Turn the sign on the door to CLOSED, pull the blinds on the windows and then finally on the door. At this precise moment, the door is pushed open with such sudden force that I am knocked flying. I sprawl to the ground facing away from him, the breath knocked out of me. I realise then that this is the moment he must have been waiting for. He knows the routine, has probably seen it often, his pale hazel eyes watching from the street somewhere. Watching everything I do. Closing time. The shop empty, the blinds drawn. No witnesses. No one to see. He turns the key in the lock behind him, and stands unmoving, unspeaking, waiting for me to get up.

I take my time to recover, hold my stomach in distress and feel the welcome weight of the objects in my pocket. A small tape recorder and Jordie's can of hairspray. With my back still to him, I press record. This is something I have practised, a deft movement, the sure finding of a button. I turn to face him.

Jason. The photo come to life. The eyes that bored into Maggie now bore into me. A smile of pleasure at my disadvantage. I move back, move away from him, my breath ragged and laboured. Ruth commented on a certain innocence in his face, but in person he looks anything but innocent. There is something cold about his eyes, a downward twist to his mouth. We stand staring at each other, faces set like stone.

I move backwards again, closer to the office. This seems to please him. He has got me on the back foot. He smiles, but his smile is not pleasant.

'Lyn Blessing. You left your card. You invited me.'

'Yes,' I say. My voice surprises me with its firmness.

'A calling card. A mistake, though. I don't like visitors. I don't like snoops and I don't like damage to my flat.'

I am silent and he continues.

'It was you all the time, wasn't it?'

'What was?'

'You ran the show. You organised it. The code, the couriers, the lot.'

I say nothing.

'Leonie told me it wasn't you. I believed her. But now I'm not so sure.'

'You did well to believe her.'

He looks at me long and hard.

'How did you find me?'

'Through Leonie. I've been keeping a file on you. I know all about you now. Where you live. Where you go. What you do.'

'Leonie knew what I wanted her to know. Nothing else.'

'Then let's just say you left a trail. A trail that I followed.'

His expression tells me that he doesn't like this. He is the watcher, the gatherer of information, tracking people down. He obviously hadn't considered the possibility of someone returning the favour.

'Why did you invite me?' he asks. 'What do you want?'

'I want to know why you killed Leonie.'

He answers easily, almost contemptuously. I am no threat to him.

'Because she was in the way. I wanted to see what would happen after. I wanted to see which way they'd run.'

'So you killed her, just like that?'

He shrugs. 'She wasn't any use to me any more.'

The office door is still closed. I think of the security guard watching through the one-way glass, waiting for the right moment, biding his time. He follows my gaze, stares at me long and hard. Has he guessed the intention, seen the trap? He comes closer, stands over me, his body threatening. I feel the cool cylinder in my pocket. The present from Jordie.

'It was you, wasn't it? Someone as cool as you. You and the shop. I should have known. The track stopped here. I couldn't get past here. But Leonie insisted. Some fellah, she said, Andy. But there isn't any Andy. Only you.'

Maggie had talked about Andy. In the long nights I had worked it out. As kids we had known it. Sometimes we even called him it as a joke. Alexandy. A blend of names, a nickname. Alex. Andy. Smithy. Take your pick. Alexander Smith. A man of many names.

'You mentioned a file, Ms Blessing. Somewhere in your office, I assume?'

His eyes leave mine for the first time, look about the shop: the gleaming display cabinets, the leather-bound books, the vases of flowers on low tables.

'It would be a pity to destroy all these lovely things.'

'What did you do, Jason? Push her in the river?'

My words are clipped, the anger seething out. He regards me coldly, dispassionately.

'You scared her, following her about, turning up un-expectedly. Always in her path. At first she must have thought it was some weird stalking, but little by little she must have seen something planned, something calculating, something evil.'

He has had enough. He moves forward, uses his body as a battering ram, pushes me back against the door. I exaggerate the thrust, clatter against the wood, beat a warning knock with my heel.

'Where is it? This file of yours.'

He flings the door open behind me.

I step into the office, open the drawer of the filing cabinet. From here I can see behind the door, see the desk where the security guard is waiting. For a moment the world dissolves. I see nothing and no one. Not Jason, not the office, not the open drawer in front of me. Breath and pulse seem to have stopped. There is no security guard.

'Hand it over.' Jason says, his voice cold and threatening.

I pass him the envelope and the world re-forms. He is so close I can see the stubble on his chin, the light hazel of his eyes. He shakes the contents out onto the desk and the photo falls out uppermost. He stares at it as though mesmerised. I take the can out of my pocket, finger on the nozzle, waiting for the exact moment.

'An interesting photo. One I haven't seen before. Taken at Hamilton, I believe.'

He looks up for confirmation.

I spray long and hard into his eyes. He screams in blind, furious pain, lashes out with feet and hands. I dodge his groping hands, but his foot strikes my knee and I stumble forward. He has the range now and his reactions are fast. He grabs my arm, holds it in a savage grip, pulls me towards him. His eyes are streaming, sightless, his face a moving blur of rage. I swing the cylinder of hairspray above my head, strike it down into his face, hear the sickening crunch of metal against bone. He screams again, an unholy shriek of pain and fury. His grip loosens. I twist away. Dart through the open door. Slam it behind me.

The noise is the worst thing. The crashing fury against the door. The curdling mix of abuse and rage. I hold the door handle in one hand and fumble with the key, but the door shakes against the frame. I can feel the heavy thrust of his body against the solid timber. The assault of feet and fists and shoulders. A crescendo of noise and rattling timber. The key won't turn. A simple key. A key I have turned a million times before. A key that normally glides in the shaft. All trembling fingers and shaking wood, I can't engage the lock.

Silence now. An uncanny silence. Not sheer rage, but calculation. And then I understand. He has found the door handle. I feel it jerk under my hand. I wrench it back, make another desperate attempt with the key. This time it turns smoothly. The lock slides home.

I sprint to the front door, snatch the key from the door.

Behind me, the sound of crashing glass, a fresh volley of abuse. I throw the door open, lock it from the outside. Flinders Street. Pedestrians on the footpath. The normal flow of traffic. My abrupt appearance has aroused some natural curiousity. The terror must show in my face. Around me people stare.

'Quick . . .' I say to no one in particular. 'Get the police. He tried to kill me. I've locked him in.'

I race down the alley to the back door. It is still closed. Blinded as he is, he has not yet found the exit. I lock this door also. The office windows are sealed. Short of breaking them, he is trapped.

# Chapter Thirty-two

*I made a town of fantasies*
*Whereto I could retire*
*And leave a world of haste to be*
*With things of my desire.*

'Proem', Furnley Maurice

Among the cluster of people at the front door are two blue uniforms. I give one of them the keys.

'I've locked him in. But be careful. He's dangerous.'

I lean against the door and begin to shake.

Noise and confusion, thuds and grunts and cries of pain. And then, suddenly, silence. I stay where I am, surrounded by a group of inquisitive strangers. I hear them coming down the alley, the heavy thudding footsteps. He is between two police officers, yelling abuse and struggling. His eyes are red and streaming.

'It was her. She did it. She blinded me. The bitch. The bitch.'

He looks in my direction and struggles to get away, pulls against the police officers at his side. For a moment it looks as though he might succeed, might break away but then I realise his eyes are closed. He hasn't even seen me. He is pushed into the back of a police car and I see that he is handcuffed. The car moves off, another one takes its place.

Close by, a quiet voice. 'Better come with me, Lyn. They

want you at Russell Street.'

'Joe? I'd given up on you.'

I move towards him.

'I've been away. I came as soon as I got your message. Looks like I should have got here earlier.'

He puts his forehead against mine and rests it there. I lean against him, my knees still weak, and feel waves of emotion wash over me. Joe's body is tense, hard as steel. We don't say anything for a long time.

'So. He found you.' Joe says eventually.

'I invited him.'

I explain about leaving Jason a card.

'You planned to meet him on your own?' he says slowly, as if having trouble taking it in. His voice is tight.

'Yes. He was out there all the time. I had to force his hand.'

'Using yourself as bait. Christ, Lyn. I can't believe you'd do something so stupid.'

'I didn't feel I had much choice.'

This gets him. His head comes up with a jerk. His fists are clenched and his face is still with shock. His skin almost grey.

'Besides, I'm not as stupid as you think, Joe,' I say coldly. 'I employed a security guard. He should have been in the office. He was told where to wait.'

And at that moment we see him turning the corner, a bag of food in his hand. He looks startled at the activity.

'Where were you?' I ask, curiously emotionless, drained by excesses of fear and shock.

He looks at me and then at Joe, trying to work out the implications of the police uniform.

'I just took a minute to get some food. There was a queue, I was longer than I thought.'

The sneering curl to his mouth is gone, replaced by a tremulous uncertainty. He looks about sixteen. Joe stares at him with contempt. I am past caring.

I collect the security film from the camera and Joe organises a car to Russell Street. Sweetman's office again. Maggie's file resurrected, added to, amended. They talk around me, feed me with tea and sandwiches, tea and biscuits.

They examine the file I posted to Sweetman, referring to it offhandedly as the Blessing File. They play the security film from the shop, the film of Jason. I see it all again, but from a different perspective. The shop door ramming open, knocking me to the floor. Jason locking it calmly behind him, then standing there, watching me. They run the tape recorder that was in my pocket, synchronise it with the film. I watch the proceedings as though the main player is someone else. Someone remote.

The verdict is now official. Maggie's file updated and finalised. Leonie Cope, a victim of murder. Jason Tucker is formally arrested and charged. He confesses readily, easily, almost boastfully. I ring Maggie's mum from the police station. I want to tell her the news before she reads it in the paper. It is late, though, and she has been asleep. Her voice is groggy. I tell her the bare details, tell her I will see her soon, give her a full account. She is calm. Thankful he is locked up. Thankful it is over.

# Chapter Thirty-three

*O Melbourne Town's a lady*
*And her eyes are like the stars*
          *'The Old Love', Marie E. J. Pitt*

I wake to the alarm, feeling wonderful. It is over now, this time for good. The ghosts laid to rest. A sense of well-being washes over me, a bubbling elation, like fizziness in the blood. Outside, the day is warm and sunny. It is good to be alive.

Joe visits mid-morning, bringing with him a collection of photos that the police found in Jason's flat, locked away in a safe. A pile so deep he carries them in a box. There are endless photos of the shop, of Maggie, of the receivers, of customers, of friends, of Joe. There are photos of Joe and me together in gardens, pubs and restaurants, but most of all, there are photos of me. There are even photos of me at the new flat. I go through them, not really surprised at the volume, the extent of surveillance. I had known this, felt him watching me.

'I knew I was being watched.'

'He believed you could take him on to whoever it was. All these photos, the night in the alley, are part of that.'

'Yes,' I agree. 'And he nearly got there. I nearly took him to Smithy.'

'I wish you had. It would have saved you some pain at least.'

'If I hadn't used the tunnel that night, I would have led him to Smithy. And Leonie might still be alive.'

Joe shakes his head. 'I don't think anything could have saved Leonie. She was always Jason's victim.'

'The messenger,' I say, looking at a photo of her. She is half turned to the camera, as though checking behind her, as though there is someone on her heels, as though she is ready to run. She looks small and powerless, scared out of her wits. I sort the photos of Maggie into a pile of their own.

'I could have saved her, if she'd let me,' I say.

'But she didn't, Lyn. She didn't let you. There was nothing you could do.'

'No,' I agree.

Some of the photos of Maggie are good shots. The earlier ones, taken before she became quite so gaunt and hollow-eyed. She looks young and confident, strides out against a backdrop of the city as if it belonged to her. Which once, perhaps, it did.

'Can I take a couple of these? For Leonie's mother.'

'Of course.' Joe nods assent.

We are oddly formal, Joe taking refuge in officialdom.

We visit Smithy's studio, the collection of Smithy's keys in my hand. None of them fits the lock.

'Maybe the front entrance,' Joe suggests.

In all the years I have visited Smithy, the front door was unused, blocked off by a heavy table. But it is the only possible solution. We come out of the alleys and into Flinders Lane, enter the building by its main entrance. I don't need the key, though, because the door is already open. A man dressed in a business suit is standing in the lounge, scratching his chin. He smiles when he sees us, comes forward with his hand outstretched.

'You must be the owners. I was worried about your things.'

He shakes my hand and turns to Joe.

'No, I'm not the owner,' I say. 'But these things are mine.'

'Good.' He beams at me. 'The developers are coming in tomorrow. I was just trying to decide what to do.'

'So soon,' I say.

He nods. 'They're converting the entire building. Twelve units altogether. Have you seen the plans? We were sweating on this one, I don't mind telling you. The sale came through just in time.'

A touch of irony. Smithy's flat as part of the city conversion that he railed against. The decision to sell must have already been made the night I visited him in his flat.

Joe and I walk in. The paintings are still on display, the furniture in position. Nothing is different, save dust and dead flowers, the smell of neglect. The painting *Melbourne Moonrise* still dominates. Joe looks at it without enthusiasm.

I turn to the man at the door. 'I don't want anything save the paintings. Can you arrange for the rest to be sold? Give the money to charity.'

'No problems. Any preference?'

'A conservation group,' I say, pleased with the irony. 'Any one you choose.'

Joe walks about, idly touching things.

'What does he do for mail?' he asks. 'No deliveries here.'

And the thought strikes simultaneously. The unexplained key dangling with the others. A post-office box, somewhere.

'Give it to me,' Joe says bleakly. 'We're good at that sort of thing.'

I take the week's promised holiday. Jordie steps in, this time uninterrupted. I go to Hamilton. Joe goes to Queensland.

Again the long road west. I take with me Maggie's letters, some of Jason's photos and a bottle of brandy. Elaine is waiting for me, her face tense and pale. Over large brandies, I fill her in on the background to the arrest. Explain about the strength her phone call gave me, courage at the right moment.

'Thank you for everything. You've been so brave. My poor, poor Leonie.'

Brave to Elaine, insane to Joe. A matter of perspective. Elaine is resolute, dry-eyed, courageous. I find myself telling her about Adele. Maggie's similarity. That early blurring that Pam saw.

'It was her eyes as much as anything. Those lovely dark eyes.'

She pats my hand. 'I did wonder why. Why you were so involved. Thank you for telling me.'

She offers me a bed for the night. Her offer is sincere, but made hesitantly, as though unsure if it is appropriate.

'I only have the one spare room.'

'Leonie's,' I say, and she nods.

'If you don't mind,' I say.

She smiles and shakes her head. 'I'm pleased. It seems fitting somehow.'

A small room, a single bed, the things of Maggie's childhood around me. Elaine has not redecorated, has not changed anything. I know if I looked I would see her old clothes still in the drawers. I don't look.

I lie down in Maggie's bed. The night is light enough to make out the shapes of her possessions: books and running shoes, an old tennis racquet propped up in the corner. Maggie's presence is strong, but it seems an innocent presence, a presence from an earlier, happier time.

I look out of the window at the bright scatter of stars, as she must have done in the years she was happy here and in the years she planned her escape, her mind full of dreams. The stars are the same as she would see in Melbourne, but in darker skies they burn more brightly.

'Goodnight, Maggie,' I say into the darkness and fall asleep.

In the morning I leave for Melbourne.

The only thing of interest in the week is a letter addressed to me at the shop. A brief letter from the Society for Protection of Australian Wildlife, thanking me for my recent donation. They inform me it will be used as part of the funding for an educational programme for councils and ratepayers. A programme that stresses the importance of maintaining breeding trees for native birds, the old hollow trees that are too often cut down. Their philosophy is that with breeding trees protected, native bird populations will increase, vital now for certain species. I read the letter twice over and laugh in delight at the neat disposal of Smithy's assets.

Pam returns from Sydney, visits me on her way home.

She studies my new painting hanging on the lounge wall, reads the inscriptions, title and artist. '*Melbourne Moonrise. A. Smith.*'

She looks at it for a long time.

'Well, at least he could paint.'

I grin. 'Among other things.'

I tell her the official news. The basic facts of Jason's arrest, of how I acquired my new painting. I don't tell her about my part in things, but she guesses some of it, looks at me with a shrewd eye.

'Whatever you've done, Lyn, it's done you good. You're looking better than I've seen you for a long time. Danger must agree with you.'

She collects her bag and kisses me on the cheek.

'Got to go, love, I'm dropping with fatigue. What about dinner soon? You can tell me the uncut version.'

'If you like,' I say. 'If you promise not to lecture.'

'Bad as that, eh?' She waggles her fingers in a gesture of farewell. 'See you.'

She's wrong, though. It wasn't the danger. It was everything that went with it: the heady sense of excitement, the hours of planning, the buzz of energy, of taking charge.

Joe comes back mid-week and we spend a day together, tourists in our own city, our relationship unsure. Once more we cross the bridge, look down at the sprawling bulk of Southgate, the flat ribbon of river. I cannot bear to walk that way now, the memory of finding Maggie too pervasive. Instead we cross St Kilda Road, and walk again in the gardens. He takes my arm and I feel the familiar surge of electricity between us, but his mood is heavy.

At the edge of lake we stop to admire the swans, the small flotillas of cygnets. It has rained recently and the grass is wet.

'How's your mum?' I ask, sitting down on a bench near the water.

He looks at me, his face oddly still.

'She's in hospital, Lyn. A type of cancer.'

'I'm sorry, Joe. I didn't know.'

I have vague recollections of Joe's mother, dropping him off at the farm, taking Bill out for some expedition or other. A small woman, bringing up a son and daughter on her own, struggling.

'My sister's there with her. Goes to see her every day.'

'That's something,' I comment, aware of its inadequacy.

There is a pause. A black swan glides close, looking for food.

'Where did the real-estate people send the money from the sale of Smithy's flat?' I ask.

'A bank account in Switzerland. A well-used account, according to Sweetman. Deposits all the way. By the time we got there it was closed.'

So Smithy is home free. Safe, untouched, wealthy.

'We found the post-office box,' he tells me.

'Was there anything?'

'An envelope addressed to himself. Inside, photos of three men. The names and addresses. The receivers, you called them, the ones who came in the shop after Maggie. The ones who took the birds on. Len Martin was one of them. We ran your tapes, Lyn, matched some faces.'

'What will happen to them?' I say.

'They'll be charged and tried.'

'And Smithy escapes.'

'Mm. Justice for you.'

'Honour among thieves,' I murmur.

'What?' Joe asks, unhearing.

'Nothing. Just something a police officer said to me recently, about there being no honour among thieves.'

From where we sit in the green depths of parkland, the city

is unseen. Whichever way we turn, we see only sweeps of greenery, soft and cool and seemingly endless. There is no sound of traffic, only the quieter sound of birdsong. It feels like a sanctuary, far removed from the city, far removed from the topic of our conversation.

Joe continues. 'The funny thing is, though, we're almost sure that the death at Hattah was accidental.'

'Accidental! So there was no one trying to take over, as Smithy thought.'

'No. But that death had the effect of panicking him. The pressure was on. He took steps to protect himself, employed Leonie. Became increasingly paranoid about the whole thing. All that cloak and dagger stuff you got on to.'

'But he was right. Jason was out there,' I say.

'Yes. But later, and only as a result of the steps he took to cover himself, only after one of the couriers began flashing his money around a bit too obviously.'

'So if Smithy had left things alone . . .'

Joe nods. I consider the irony of the situation and find no comment.

'He nearly killed you,' Joe says, his voice tight. 'Let's not forget that.'

'He apologised. The night he came to the shop. He said he didn't know it was me.'

Joe snorts with contempt. 'Who else would it have been?'

And that is true. A moment of silence.

'Anyway, the courier led Jason to Leonie,' I say.

'Yes. He saw the wallet exchange, followed the girl.'

'As simple as that. Easy money. This whole business about easy money. Smithy. Even Leonie, but because of him, Leonie died.'

'Not because of Smith,' Joe says. 'She died because of Jason.'

'Yes.' I say, glad of the difference.

We find a pub and order food and drink. It is warm and cheerful after the long grey afternoon, a fire burns in the grate. An antidote to the gloomy weather and the sense of depression that holds Joe. A waiter brings our food, two steaming bowls of pasta that she places unceremoniously on the table in front of us. We eat without talking.

'I've got something for you,' Joe says when we have finished. 'A present for being alive.' He passes me an envelope. Inside is a single slip of paper, a voucher for a ride in a hot air balloon.

'Joe! Thank you,' I say, surprised. 'But just one ticket. You don't want to come too?'

'No. Not my idea of fun. I prefer both feet firmly on the ground.'

We sit close to the fire. The flame curls around a log of wood like a lover. Joe turns his beer glass in his hand.

'I've been doing a lot of thinking lately, Lyn. Not all of it good.'

'Yes, I know,' I say.

I understand his mood. That restless ghost of depression that clings and binds, and that was my companion for too long. I am free of it now, oddly released, a sensation like breaking through greyness into clean and sparkling air. The emergence of spring after winter. Of strength after weakness. Courage after fear.

'I keep thinking about Tucker. About how you could have been killed.'

'Joe, I know what you've been thinking. I took a risk, but I took it knowingly. What else could I do?'

'Nothing, probably, being you. You amaze me, Lyn, the way you persevered, the way you tracked him down. It was brave, Lyn. A genuinely brave thing to do.'

'I don't think of it as being brave,' I say. 'It was something I had to do, in terms of self-protection if nothing else.'

Joe continues unheedingly. 'I don't see much bravery in my trade. I see greed and jealousy and just plain evil.'

Evil. Almost a biblical term. Yet how else do you describe Jason? Killing Maggie to see the effect, to see "which way they'd run".

'But there's more to it, you see,' he continues determinedly.

'I never thought I'd find anyone like you. Anyone I'd feel so at ease with. Remember that day in the park, or even in the hospital with you, bashed and bandaged? I enjoyed being with you, Lyn, it was simple and easy. This business made me think about losing you, before we'd even had a chance.'

'Joe,' I say. 'I don't ...'

He holds his hand up. 'I know what you're going to say. That I never had you, that you came to me out of grief and need. I know all that. It doesn't matter. I know how I feel about you. I heard your message on the answering machine, the message about Jason. An old message, Lyn, because I'd been away. I knew then somehow that you were going to take him on. I couldn't get here quick enough, and all that time, all that long drive down ...'

He doesn't finish his sentence. Someone adds a new log to the fire, the flame leaps higher.

'Joe, listen to me,' I say. 'I'm okay now. I wasn't for a long time, but through all this I've come to terms with Adele.'

'A long process for you.'

'Too long,' I say. 'I was stuck in some sort of inertia. Perhaps I needed to take a few risks, to get things in perspective. Perhaps we all do.'

He shakes his head in disagreement. 'No. Not most of us. Most of us want to stay warm and indoors, curled up by the TV. A Stallone movie is as close as we want to come to danger.'

'Not you,' I say. 'Not someone in the police.'

'The police isn't what you think, Lyn. It's bound up in routine. Miles of paperwork.'

Through the window it is completely dark, a heavy darkness pierced with streetlights, the moving lights of cars.

'And that's the worst thing. You putting yourself in danger because the police didn't believe you.' A note of contempt in his tone.

'You did.'

'Yes. But what good did that do?'

'It's all Bruce Spence's fault,' I say, trying for lightness.

He is diverted momentarily and grins with sudden delight. 'I'll never forget the look on his face at the meeting you took charge of. You in your red suit, running rings around him.'

I grin back.

'You enjoyed it, didn't you?' Joe asks.

'The meeting?' I ask, surprised.

'No, not the meeting. Taking risks. All that.'

'At times,' I say. 'I enjoyed the planning, seeing it through, turning the situation around. Most of all, I enjoyed not being a victim any more, caught up in some situation I couldn't control.'

'Like Leonie,' he says.

'Exactly like Leonie.'

He nods in understanding.

The waiter clears our bowls, stacking them together, scraping the spoons and forks together. A young woman, white shirt, black trousers, her hair pulled back tightly from her face. Her expression is bored and set, she doesn't once look at us.

'The thought of you in danger overwhelmed me, Lyn, but it also taught me something. I learned about priorities. I learned how much it would hurt to lose someone I cared for.' His hands are firm around his glass, the liquid completely still. 'I've resigned, Lyn.'

'Resigned,' I repeat in surprise.

'Mm. They didn't do enough. You had to push them and still they let you down. I'm going away for a while. To Queensland.'

I turn towards him, surprised at this unexpected turn of events.

'It's time to be with my family. To help my sister out with Mum for a while.'

'I see,' I say slowly. 'Are you coming back?'

'Of course. It's a risk, I admit. Career-wise, as well as with you.'

'I can't promise anything, Joe. I need time. Time is something I didn't take after Adele died.'

'I can wait.' There is no doubt in his tone.

'What will you do when you come back?' I ask.

'I'm not sure yet. I have some options. I'll decide when I'm away.'

I take his hand, feel its warmth, the charge of electricity between us. A piece of wood snaps in the fire, the flame glows brightly for a moment, and settles.

'Here's to taking risks. May they always prove beneficial.'

I lift my glass and Joe follows the gesture. Someone puts some money in the juke box. A popular love song with banal lyrics plays out loud and strong. We grin at the unexpected irony.

Pam and I eat at Gertrude's in Collins Street. The same restaurant I ate at with Peter Ireland at the beginning of all this. We have a window seat, an uninterrupted view of the city. Outside dusk is turning to darkness and the lights of the city are coming on. I tell her my plans. My decision to sell the farm and buy one of the new flats in town, walking distance to the shop. The developers are outdoing themselves, offering communal swimming pools, spas, serviced apartments. I have a smorgasbord to choose from.

She lifts her champagne glass in a gesture of toasting.

'Well done, Lyn. So, decisions made, eh?' She looks at me with a raised eyebrow. 'All of them?' she asks meaningfully.

'Not quite all,' I say. 'There's one still on the back burner.'

'Ahh!' She smiles knowledgeably. 'Now before we get sidetracked, tell me the unofficial version of events.'

Over trout and champagne I tell her my story. Her eyes grow bigger, the glint of green more obvious. From time to time she shakes her head in a kind of baffled amazement.

'The quiet life of a city bookseller,' she says. 'And I always thought you were so sensible.'

I grin at her reaction and feel a sense of well-being, a quiet elation, like bubbles in the blood.

Far below, the Yarra River flows silently through the city, the dark ribbon of water defined by strings of burning lights. And all around us the lights of Melbourne shine out, brighter than the stars.

# Acknowledgements

The author would like to thank Peter Stewart, Senior Inspector, Investigative Branch, Australian Customs Service, Melbourne; Kay Craddock, Antiquarian Bookseller, Melbourne; and Lloyd Holyoak, Roycroft Books, East Kew. The author would also like to thank R A Simpson for permission to reproduce the first stanza of his poem 'The Tram Driver's Song'.

The epigraphs were taken from the following collections:

Cambridge, Ada, 'By the Camp Fire' in *The Poet's Discovery: Nineteenth Century Australia in Verse,* Richard D Jordan and Peter Pierce, eds, Melbourne University Press, Carlton, 1990

Howitt, Richard, 'To the River Yarra' in *The Poet's Discovery,* op cit

Kendall, Henry, 'The Melbourne International Exhibition' in *Leaves for Australian Forests,* George Robertson, Melbourne, 1870

Maurice, Furnley, 'Upon a Row of Old Boots and Shoes in a Pawnbroker's Window'; 'On a Grey-Haired Old Lady Knitting at an Orchestra Concert in the Melbourne Town Hall'; 'Memory'; 'The Agricultural Show; Flemington, Victoria'; 'The Gardens'; 'The Victoria Markets Recollected in Tranquillity'; and 'Proem' in *Poems by Furnley Maurice,* selected by Percival Serle, Lothian Publishing Co Pty Ltd, Melbourne, 1944

—*Unconditional Songs,* Sydney J Endacott, Melbourne, 1921

O'Hara, John Bernard, 'On Princes Bridge (at Dawn)' in *A Book of Sonnets,* Melville and Mullen, Melbourne, 1902

Pitt, Marie E J, 'The Old Love', in *The Poems of Marie E J Pitt,* Edward A Vidier, Melbourne, 1925

Simpson, R A, 'The Tram Driver's Song' in *Selected Poems*, University of Queensland Press, St Lucia, 1981

Wright, George, 'Adventures on a Winter's Night in Melbourne' in *The Poet's Discovery,* op cit

The Women's Press is Britain's leading women's publishing house. Established in 1978, we publish high-quality fiction and non-fiction from outstanding women writers worldwide. Our exciting and diverse list includes literary fiction, detective novels, biography and autobiography, health, women's studies, handbooks, literary criticism, psychology and self-help, the arts, our popular Livewire Books series for young women and the bestselling annual *Women Artists Diary* featuring beautiful colour and black-and-white illustrations from the best in contemporary women's art.

If you would like more information about our books or about our mail order book club, please send an A5 sae for our latest catalogue and complete list to:

The Sales Department
The Women's Press Ltd
34 Great Sutton Street
London EC1V 0DX
Tel: 0171 251 3007
Fax: 0171 608 1938

Ellen Hart
**Wicked Games**
A Jane Lawless crime thriller

When Jane Lawless takes a new tenant into her house, she has no idea what lies ahead. Shortly after Elliot Beauman moves in, Jane and her friend Cordelia find themselves drawn inexorably into the Beaumans' lives – and discover a trail of death and destruction in their wake ...

*Wicked Games* is a dark and compelling crime thriller by one of the most acclaimed, up-and-coming writers in the field.

**Praise for Ellen Hart:**

'**The psychological maze of a Barbara Vine mystery.**'
*Publishers Weekly*

'**The mysteries pile up so relentlessly that you'll just have to wait and see who gets caught without a seat in the game of murderous chairs.**' *Kirkus Reviews*

'**Her style is tight and hypnotic. Her action brisk and riveting.**' *Washington Blade*

Crime Fiction  £6.99
ISBN 0 7043 4590 0

Val McDermid
**Booked for Murder**
The fifth Lindsay Gordon crime thriller

The freak 'accident' that killed bestselling author Penny Varnavides
takes on a more sinister aspect when police discover that her latest
unpublished novel featured murder by the same means. Of the
handful of people who knew the plot, the prime suspect is wise
enough to call in her old friend, journalist Lindsay Gordon, to
uncover the truth that lies behind the seething rivalries and
desperate power games that infect the publishing world ...

**'Has the reader gripped from the first page ... both moody
and hilarious and thoroughly unpredictable.'** *Tribune*

**'The writing is tough and colourful, the scene setting
excellent.'** *Times Literary Supplement*

Crime Fiction £5.99
ISBN 0 7043 4595 1

Alma Fritchley
**Chicken Run**
The first Letty Campbell mystery

'Julia was watching me carefully. "Well?" I said, "What gives?" Before she could answer, the inner sanctum of Steigel Senior's office was revealed and Steigel Senior herself appeared in the doorway. Julia leapt to her feet and in that sudden movement all was revealed. Julia was wonderfully, newly, ecstatically in love, probably truly for the first time in her life, and who could blame her? Steigel Senior was a cool-eyed, blond-haired Lauren Bacall, complete with Dietrich's mystery and Garbo's gorgeous accent . . .'

When Letty Campbell warily agrees to let her land be used for a classic car auction, she has no idea what lies ahead. Why is her gorgeous ex, Julia, really so desperate for the auction to happen? Is the new love of Julia's life as suspicious as she seems? And why does Letty have a horrible feeling that she should never have got involved?

'Hilarious.' *Evening Standard*

'Irrepressibly bouncy.' *Pink Paper*

'A breath of fresh air . . . Alma Fritchley is a talent to watch.' *Crime Time*

Crime Fiction £6.99
ISBN 0 7043 4515 3

Manda Scott
**Hen's Teeth**
A Kellen Stewart crime thriller

Shortlisted for the Orange Prize for Fiction and the First Blood Award

Midnight in Glasgow. A bad time to be faced with a dead body. Especially if the body in question is your ex-lover and the woman grieving at her bedside used to be your friend. Add a corpse packed with Temazepam, a genetic engineer with a strange interest in chickens and a killer on the loose with a knife, and you have all the reason you need to walk away and never come back.

Except that it's Bridget who's dead and she has always deserved better than that. For Dr Kellen Stewart, ex-medic, ex-lover and ex-friend, a simple call for help rapidly twists into a tangled web of death and deceit ...

*Hen's Teeth* is an extraordinary, powerful, tough crime thriller which marks the arrival of a superb new writer.

**'Eloquent, excellent ... A new voice for a new world and it's thrilling.' Fay Weldon**

Crime Fiction £6.99
ISBN 0 7043 4496 3

Marcia Muller
**Wolf in the Shadows**
A Sharon McCone crime thriller

Sharon McCone's employers have issued her with an ultimatum. They want her to take a promotion – a desk job designed to curb her often unorthodox behaviour – or leave. Just when her new lover, the enigmatic Hy Ripinsky, has gone missing.

At first, tracking him down seems an adventure. But soon McCone is caught up in a deadly game of kidnapping, played out in the badlands of the American-Mexican border. Here decisions won't wait, and McCone is confronted with some tough choices that put her life, her future and everything she holds dear at risk . . .

**'Marcia Muller has received a good deal of attention for her McCone novels and she deserves all of it.'**
*New York Times Book Review*

**'Muller produces the sort of thrillers that enthusiasts always hope for but rarely get.'** *The Sunday Times*

Crime Fiction   £5.99
ISBN 0 7043 4389 4

Penny Sumner, editor
**Brought to Book**
Murderous Stories from the Literary World

With Mary Wings, Barbara Wilson, Stella Duffy and many more.

Authors wreaking revenge on editors, perfidious plots at award
dinners, murders at sales conferences and in writers' groups – in
*Brought to Book* top women crime writers expose the lethal
reality of the literary world . . .

**'Sharply written stories that shift the emphasis away
from the macho gun-toting and car chases that plague the
genre.'** *Gay Scotland*

Crime Fiction £6.99
0 7043 4578 1